I0611417

Trevor Kip And The Cosmic Blender

Book One

Russell Douglas Crumley

Trevor Kip and The Cosmic Blender:

Book One

Copyright © 2006 by Russell Douglas Crumley

All rights reserved under International and
Pan-American Copyright Conventions.

Published in the United States by PLG Press,
a division of Performance Learning Group.

ISBN 978-0-6152-1327-9

Thank You

Jesse, Zoe, Emmie, Ginger and Debi

Adrift

"Within an infinite universe, time is relative.
The stars may sputter and die, but our quest for
truth and meaning will never end."

Maximillian Augustus Gladwell
Cosmic Enterprises dedication ceremony,
August 24, 1868

The Day Before Yesterday

Trevor Kip found himself standing in a sea of bored students, drifting in and out of the school cafeteria. A skinny kid with long oily hair, pale skin and a faded black t-shirt approached Trevor as he tried to choose between cold pizza and a soggy hamburger. He glanced casually at the wrinkled shirt as its glassy-eyed occupant approached.

"Life sucks," it proclaimed. Trevor wondered if the shirt reflected a permanent attitude or just a bad choice in clothing. He grabbed two slices of pizza and dropped them onto his plate. He snuck another look as the boy walked past.

"Trevor: today you die" was written in an old-fashioned white script across the back of the shirt. Trevor's heart skipped a beat and he quickly looked down at his tray, trying to swallow as he felt his throat tighten. What the—how could the shirt say that?

Every kid in the town goes to the same school, he thought. The old brick building housed every grade through high school, including three floors of classrooms and fewer than three hundred students. He had only managed to make a few friends since moving here, and certainly no enemies. There was no way he could have overlooked someone this… unique.

Was it some kind of practical joke?

Trevor realized he was staring absentmindedly at his tray. He whipped his head back to the spot where he had last seen the boy, and barely glimpsed the stringy black hair as it melted into a crowd of more familiar faces. He couldn't just let this go. He had to find out how the other kid knew him and if it was all just a big mistake.

Trevor dropped his tray and dashed after, forcing everyone out of his way as he dodged a tangle of chairs, backpacks, and uneaten school lunches.

He pushed hard to separate two tall boys with long gray faces and dark green eyes. He realized they were wearing black shirts identical to the one he was chasing. Was the entire school in on the gag? He forced his way between them and...

Trevor found himself standing in the middle of New York City. But it wasn't any street he had ever walked. This one was completely empty. No people, cars, or buildings. Instead, a forest of trees the size of skyscrapers lined each side of the street, their branches too high and far away for him to see. Orderly rows of smooth, black rectangles punctuated the trees' rough bark.

The dark windows began to open. *Snick. Snick. Snick.* He watched as one after another, each rectangle revealed a domain of dark, dreary spaces. Within each of them, he could clearly see the frozen silhouette of a person staring down at him. He looked up as far as he could, and an army of shadows stared silently back. Row by row. Floor after floor.

With an especially loud *Snap*, an enormous tree to his right gave birth to a double set of glass doors. The boy in the black t-shirt disappeared quickly inside.

Trevor sprinted toward the doorway, which was odd, because he had not commanded his legs to move one single inch. They propelled him faster and faster toward the entrance, with a will of their own. As he approached the glass doors, he could see a vast lobby inside the tree. His feet skidded to a stop, just inches from the threshold. Above the door, a gnarled wooden gargoyle peered down at him. It opened one eye as Trevor hesitated.

"Defeat the black shirt… if you want to live." the creature screeched. Trevor paused for only a moment, and then pushed the doors open and entered the lobby.

What an ornate lobby for a tree, he marveled. He noted the polished green and black marble floors, the gilded chandelier hung from an impossibly high ceiling, and a massive curving staircase set against the far wall. Across the lobby his nemesis darted up the stairs and out of sight.

Trevor's shoes squeaked as he sprinted across the marble and hit the stairs running. He grabbed the wooden handrail and pulled his body upward, taking two steps at a time.

He rested at the top of the landing. There were no doors, only more stairs. He held tight to the railing and leaned out into the empty space, looking up. An endless loop of stairs spiraled up to infinity. And the other boy was now several flights ahead of him.

Trevor would need to hurry if he wanted to catch him. He raced up the stairs, turning at each landing faster and faster, until each floor seemed a mere three or four steps. He counted his progress as he passed each landing. Thirty-three. Thirty-four. Thirty-five. His head began to spin as the floors flew beneath his feet. Fifty-nine. Sixty, sixty-one . . . He began to wheeze as he counted.

The first sixty floors somehow passed with a magical ease but now each step seemed impossible to take. His legs weighed a hundred pounds each. He raised his right foot and planted it deliberately on the next step. Sixty-two. He lifted his left foot with Herculean effort, and then dropped it on the landing above. Soon, he was using his arms to lift his legs and move them up each step.

Sixty-three. Trevor could barely walk, but he had to catch the boy in the black shirt. Come on!, he commanded his legs. Just one more step . . . He fell to his knees, and shakily pushed himself up with both arms. Trevor looked up the flight of stairs to the next landing. An exit waited just beyond. Only one more flight of stairs remained.

He pulled his legs up each step; the very weight of his body threatened to drag him down. Sixty-four. He crumpled onto the bare concrete landing. Trevor looked up, and to his surprise, found that he was lying in front of a gray metallic door. Sweat stung his eyes, but he was too tired to wipe them. The word "Exit" was scrawled in mud across the metal.

He ignored the pain in his legs and reached toward the silver doorknob. He clung to it with his right hand, and with a loud grunt, threw his left hand over it and pulled himself up. With his remaining strength, he twisted the heavy knob with both hands. The door opened more easily than he had anticipated.

Trevor fell unceremoniously through the exit and landed hard, pain shooting through his side. He took a deep breath, and then opened his eyes.

No marble floors or golden chandeliers. Trevor was on an ordinary roof of an ordinary building. The space wasn't big. In fact, he realized with horror that he was standing on a precarious perch, what seemed to be a thin beam or girder. His breathing quickened as he tried to maintain his balance.

A voice suddenly boomed out, sounding as if it were everywhere at once. "How do you like things now, Trevor?" It was so loud it almost knocked him from his perch. The blue sky echoed with thunder, and the building trembled and swayed.

Crack.

Trevor swung his arms, frantic to keep his balance, as he shot a quick look skyward. A small rip had appeared in the sky directly over his head, exposing only darkness beyond.

Crack.

Green dust rippled about the hole as it continued to widen. White clouds swirled briefly around the opening, before disappearing into the black space beyond. A dark, jagged scar soon covered the sky above him. "What will you do now, you insignificant speck of humanity?" the thunderous voice demanded.

Trevor twitched as a giant, wrinkled face with a swirling orb of an eye peered down at him through the opening. Cables of thick black hair fell through the hole and whipped about the sky like giant serpents in search of prey.

Insignificant?

Without thinking, Trevor moved his legs apart to balance himself. He thrust his hands left and right, as if to clasp some unseen object, to wield the weapon he needed to fight this teenage mutant with a God complex. He looked at his outstretched arms and found . . . nothing. His hands were empty.

The hideous face cackled with delight as it watched Trevor struggle to stay upright on the slender beam.

"I know what happens next, Trevor. You *die*."

The force of its decree rocked the entire building. The walls tilted violently from side to side, as Trevor was thrown onto the roof once more. He rolled onto his back and watched in horror as a giant hand forced the crack wider and emerged through the opening. The leathery fingers seemed far too old for any student. Misshapen brown spots formed a patchwork of decay between countless tiny wrinkles. The hand searched for him.

"No!" Trevor ducked as fingers clawed the air above him.

The building swayed violently and the ledge shook with a spastic cough, as the entire building began to disintegrate from below. Trevor felt the floor shift under him. He scrambled to keep his place on the roof as the building collapsed and... started to transform back into a tree.

Without warning, the tree shrank rapidly, growing younger and smaller, becoming the tender sapling it had once been. Trevor fell freely, the tree shrinking below him, as his body raced toward Earth. The giant hand was reaching for him, and five yellowed and cracked fingernails swiped the air within inches of his shirt as Trevor plummeted to the ground.

He sucked in one last breath and closed his eyes, bracing for impact. He held his breath, but didn't feel the sharp smack of concrete or the slice of rotten nails. Instead, his body landed softly, as if landing on a pillow. He slowly opened his eyes and found himself staring at a ceiling. He turned his head and looked cautiously out the window beside him. Home.

Breathe, he commanded himself. It was just a bad dream— not the worst nightmare I've ever had. But at least it's over. He released the breath he'd been holding, and he lay still as his thumping heart returned to a more normal rhythm.

"This is my bedroom," he said out loud.

He finished the rest in his mind. This is my bedroom, on the second floor of a house at 314 Vivada Street, near the edge of a small town called Silver Lake. I moved here a few months ago with my Mom, my Dad and my dog, Moke. It's all good.

He lay for a while, perfectly still, and he watched the leaves on the tree outside his window dance to the rhythm of a gentle breeze.

It's Just a Monday

Trevor was exhausted and covered in sweat from his most recent adventure. His feet hurt and his arms felt weak. These were no mere dreams. They were different and real, and...

He didn't want to get out of bed, but he kicked at the sheets to get them off his legs. He rubbed his face and looked at the clock on the dresser against the opposite wall. 8:12 a.m. Two sleepy blue eyes, with their peculiar gold flecks, stared back at him from the mirror above the dresser. Everything seemed to be in order.

He was lean - some kids called him skinny - and he was slightly taller than most other 10-year-olds. A wrinkled nightshirt hung loosely around his shoulders like a grocery sack. His wavy hair, more blonde than brown, had been cut short in anticipation of summer break. He placed his hands on his head and vigorously rubbed his scalp, staring at the pillow creases on his cheek. He frowned at the dark circles that had begun forming under his eyes.

Trevor rolled to the edge of his bed and shivered. He had forgotten to shut the windows. Again.

As he reached over to close them he saw the trunks of the towering pine trees that covered the short hill above their house. The pink-and-white blossoms of mountain laurel brightened the landscape and were drawing the attention of some honeybees. Tender green shoots were beginning to push up through the cool ground below. Finally. Spring was creeping into the higher reaches of Maine's hilltops and mountains, and not a moment too soon. His friends in New York told him it was practically summer back there. He closed the windows, rubbed his arms together and stood up uncertainly.

He leaned forward, stumbling down the hallway, and tried not to wake his parents. He caught himself against the wall to avoid going headfirst into the bathroom, which he wound up doing anyway. He fumbled for the light switch as he tumbled inside.

Ouch

He stubbed his big toe on the cabinet by the sink. Trevor rubbed the toe with one hand, as he reached for the partially hidden shower handle with the other. Nothing in this house seemed to be where it should have been. The house was interesting, but, like the bathroom cabinet and the faucet handles, countless things always seemed slightly out of place.

Who built this mess, he wondered, as the water finally began streaming out of the faucet, a family of beavers? The inside walls and ceilings were covered in raw cedar, while the exterior of the house sported the same wood and windows framed by green shutters. A crooked stone chimney towered precariously above the roof. Perched on a bluff high above town, the house was surrounded by a narrow yard bordered by a crooked cedar fence. In front, a tangle of wisteria completely covered the two gateposts on either side of the front walk.

A nest of drunken beavers, he concluded.

Trevor stepped into the shower without thinking and yelped. He fumbled desperately for the handle, turning it in search of warmer water. Stupid solar water heater, he fumed, the thing took forever to warm up. He was already having a rough time, and his day had not yet started.

The water finally warmed and he stepped back into it, leaning his head wearily against the tile, letting the water cascade down his back. He relaxed as he thought of the day ahead. Even though school had just ended for summer break, he had a long list of plans. It wasn't like him to have any plans, but keeping busy was the only thing keeping him from going crazy.

The first day of another week… it was… Monday! He was supposed to meet Jay at the library - at 8:30. It had to be later than that by now, he realized. Trevor rubbed on some soap and washed it off just as quickly, dried off, and tiptoed down the hall to his room. The clock on his dresser displayed 8:48 in giant red numbers.

He threw open all the drawers in his dresser and tore through them, trying to find something clean to wear. Well, at least clean enough. His jeans, a shirt—and then he remembered soccer practice – that was another set of clothes he needed to take… and his lunch with Julie. He would take it all with him. He stuffed his soccer cleats, his team jersey, and some extra clothes into his gym bag and ran down the hall.

He skidded to a stop just before the front door and u-turned into the kitchen, peering around the countertop piled deep with articles, printouts, and scraps of pottery. Two sleepy-eyed adults in terry cloth robes stared back, each holding a cup of coffee in their hands. His father Gavin Kip, the writer. And his mother Annie Kip, the artist. He glanced over at what had once been a kitchen table. Lumpy pieces of damp pottery and newspaper from his mother's latest project formed a small mountain and practically covered the kitchen.

He stared at his loony, artistic parents and tried to remember when this disaster had begun.

The Artist's Code

His parents had visited Silver Lake the year before for vacation and, as his father had said, some fresh mountain air. Upon returning, they had breathlessly told him how they felt 'drawn' to the town. The Kip's always lived by the artist's code of conduct: Follow Your Heart. They came back long enough to retrieve their son, pack everything into a van, and rent out their apartment in Brooklyn to another artist.

Almost overnight, Trevor found himself living in the middle of Maine, surrounded by a seemingly endless forest, a few nearby towns and loads of "rustic charm", as his mother breathlessly phrased it. The most exciting things in town were the gigantic lake (he had yet to visit), the almost endless forest (he felt no desire to hike), and the out-of-date stores along Main Street. In general, the shops sold things he either did not want or did not need: flannel shirts, hunting gear, carved wooden bears or paintings of Silver Lake. Trevor sighed. It was rustic all right, like a musty old pipe organ.

Despite this, he was trying, really trying to fit in. He had made a few friends and had tried to get involved. First school, then soccer, and soon after, longer and longer bike trips around town.

He was curious and thoughtful, a borderline bookworm with a love for reading, a trait he had picked up from his father. He wasn't sure what he got from his mother… He wasn't good at painting or pottery. He could barely make an ashtray out of clay.

But he was good at one thing: maps. It was a strange and peculiar secret he shared only with his family. Not only did he enjoy looking at them, but he also made maps. Lots of them. He could spend hours imagining what other kids in other places were doing in their houses and backyards. He would map out new, imaginary places he could explore and invent creatures to live there. He liked the feeling it gave him when he was able to assemble all the places into some kind of order. In fact, he had just begun to make a map of the town…

His recollections were interrupted by a small cough.

"Hold up Trev." His mother pointed her mug at him while his father slowly sipped his coffee and stared sleepily past him at a random spot on the wall. "Where are you going at…" she paused, consulting the large kitchen clock, "8:53 in the morning? You don't have school."

Ignoring her for the moment, Trevor pushed aside one of the lumps of clay. He spied his prize: an energy bar hidden between a printer cartridge and a stack of typed pages. "I'm supposed to meet Jay at the library." He forced a smile at her as he snagged the snack with his right hand. Then he gave his mother a quick hug and turned to leave. "Oh yeah, and I have soccer practice and Julie and I are going to meet later…" his voice trailed off as he headed out of the kitchen, toward the garage. He could imagine his mother rolling her eyes behind him.

"I don't know what's gotten into you lately… I'll let Moke out now, but don't forget to walk your dog sometime today," she called to his back; her emphasis on the words "your dog" was not lost on him. His chocolate Labrador retriever sat patiently near the door, watching him approach and wagging her tail hopefully. Trevor leaned down, stared into her brown eyes, and scratched under her chin.

"Count on it, Moke." He patted her head and turned. "Later, Mom."

Trevor peeled off the wrapper and bit off a chunk of sweet banana-y granola as he hurried into the garage. He strapped his gym bag onto the rear of his bike and hit a button on the wall that opened the garage door.

Leaning low, bike and all, he squeezed through the opening before the door had finished going up. In a minute, he was peddling down his driveway and onto the brick street below. Trevor looked back, just long enough to see his mother shaking her head as she pressed the button to close the large door behind him.

A Town Called Silver Lake

A raven cruised the air currents high above Trevor's house. Her silky black feathers fluttered in the wind.

Springtime in Tri-Valley meant new places for her to hunt and new meals to eat after a long, cold winter in the mountains. The bird flew higher, and then, caught by a strong gust rolling over the hills north of the town, she nearly flipped over. She righted herself with strong wings and caught the current once again as she scanned the landscape below.

The town appeared to cling to a cliff on the edge of a large lake. She knew the water was full of minnows and woods full of creatures she liked to eat. She was lucky to have nested in a town surrounded by so many forests. Hunting was relatively easy, between the scraps of food to be found in the town's garbage cans and the small woodland animals that scurried below. Even high up, any sharp-eyed bird could usually spy an interesting clearing that might provide a tasty morsel or two.

She turned her wings slightly west, toward the White Mountains, as she considered her options.

It was still too cold in the higher hills to offer any decent hunting. For now, she would forage closer to the lake. Banking to the east, she passed over Silver Lake, high above the broad park that ended in a steep, jagged bluff. She rose briefly in the air, almost pausing, and then raced down the rocky canyon toward the lake below, skimming just above the surface of the clear water, toward the Wilding Forest that lined the shore opposite town.

Approaching the distant shoreline, the raven spied something completely different, but potentially more interesting than a dead mouse or gooey slug. She drew in her wings and banked neatly into the trees as Trevor rode out of his driveway.

Wake-Up Call

Measured in city blocks, Trevor lived about four from downtown, six from the library, and fifteen from the lake for which the town was named.

However, measuring distance by city blocks was almost useless up here. Trevor had discovered that mountain towns and their roads wandered about the terrain at odd angles. There was no easy way to measure a bike ride other than by the time it took to get somewhere. Silver Lake was no exception.

Ignoring the blocks and miles, Trevor knew he could easily get anywhere within minutes. 12 minutes to the grocery store. 8 minutes to the park. 18 minutes to school... assuming he wanted to get there quickly. He could walk out his back door and reach the shores of Silver Lake in about twenty minutes, assuming he ever wanted to go there at all, and so far, he had not. This morning, he was not going to either the lake or to the school. He was coasting easily downhill on his way to the large public library near the center of town. The bricks on Vivada Street made his bike bounce up and down as the tires drummed out a steady rhythm.

There wasn't another kid or even a stray dog to be seen. Of course not, Trevor thought. School is out for summer. I am probably the only kid awake this early. But of course, a few grownups were already up and beginning their day. He noticed a few cars on the road and some neighbors off in the distance.

Mr. Hopkins was tilling the soil in his garden, and Ms. Evers had begun her usual morning run. Trevor waved to them both as he turned off Vivada Street onto Park Lane. He soon settled into a steady pace, peddling as he watched the green lawn of Town Park approaching through the oak trees on his right.

Town Park was one of the highlights of downtown and the place where he usually walked Moke. Tourists never failed to stop and meander through its large open spaces, admiring the flowers and the canopy of trees that lined its perimeter. The real attraction was at the north end of the park, where the meadow ended in a low stone wall. Below the wall, the ground split into a canyon, like two rocky arms embracing the lake far below. Trevor had to admit it was a spectacular sight.

A bronze statue stood near the center of the wall, of some hero or founder. The man gazed eternally over the lake, with his arm outstretched, as if pointing to tourists that had slipped over the wall. And in fact, Trevor realized a man and a woman were already standing below the statue this morning, taking pictures. They were pointing over the canyon wall and talking as they held up their cameras.

Trevor looked down at the road and kept pedaling. This is such a boring place, he thought, as the red bricks passed under his wheels. Right now, he missed the excitement of living in a big city. The friends he had there, the places they would go... but there was also more noise, more pollution, and more traffic...

"Wake up!" The other side of his brain - the side that had been peddling the bike and watching the road - screamed at him.

A black van pulled out of the alley directly in front of him. Trevor pulled hard on the brakes and skidded up to the side door. The driver stopped the vehicle, and then glared at Trevor and drove quickly away. Trevor stared back, wide awake now. Bad attitudes were one of the things about the city he didn't miss. The folks in Silver Lake were always friendly.

He didn't recognize the man in the car. Just another stupid tourist, Trevor concluded. He readjusted his helmet and pushed his bike forward. He turned down the same brick alley the van had exited, leaving the tree-lined bricks of Park Lane behind. Trevor weaved between trashcans and a few scraps of paper before exiting onto the smooth paved asphalt of Main Street.

He could see the top of the library peeking above several large trees, just beyond the old fashioned shops that lined Main Street. Like something out of a painting, he thought. His mood was improving block by block, and he was humming to himself as he rode up to the front steps of the granite and brick library.

Silver Lake's only library was an old stone fortress of a building, its massive columns lined up like soldiers guarding the front. Two stone lions looked down at Trevor from perches on either side of the steps. These weren't ordinary statues, however. The lion on the left was sitting on his back legs with his head held high, alert to the slightest noise or danger. The lion on the right was lying down and appeared to be sound asleep, his head and mane resting on his front paws. However, if someone looked closely, they could see he was secretly spying on people as they walked by.

"Hello Gus." Trevor waved to the lion on the left. "Hello Goober." he called to the sleepy lion to the right. He had given them names on the spot. He pushed his bike into the rack and grabbed his gym bag.

Trevor knew the front doors were locked. The library cut back its hours when school was out for summer. However, Ms. Perkins, the town's librarian, always kept a side door unlocked for students and her small, but dedicated fans of literature. Anyone could check out a book simply by leaving her a note with a promise to return it in one or two weeks. Only locals knew that at least one door was always open for them. Quirky, but useful, he thought.

Trevor followed the columns to the south side of the library. Turning the corner he walked along a gravel path adjacent the side wall until reaching an old wooden door with faded white paint set deep into a metal frame. Trevor paused and then turned the knob. The rusted hinges creaked as he pushed the door open. Light streamed in behind him and he could see several doors lining a dusty hallway. A set of stairs waited at the far end of the tunnel.

Trevor squared his shoulders and tiptoed inside. Little flecks of dust danced above the black and white tiles on the floor. He was three steps inside when the door closed behind with a loud thunk. Trevor sucked in his breath, crouching in the dim hallway. No one called out, no one replied. Determined to maintain his composure, he shook his head and hustled through the darkened tunnel, running up the stairs as fast as he could.

Reaching the top of the staircase, he could see the entire library in front of him, as well as stacks and stacks of dimly lit books. He wound his way through the tall metal shelves, keeping an eye out behind, just in case. Still spooked by the tunnel, Trevor collided with something hard and landed on the floor with a thump. On the way down, he managed to knock over an entire row of books, and the last one to drop landed squarely on his head.

"*Dude . . .*" Trevor heard a familiar voice complain.

Trevor realized he had tripped over the very person he was there to meet. He took the book off his head and dropped it in his lap, leaning against the shelf as he regarded his friend.

Jay Fox was probably the most creative person in Silver Lake. He played the piano, drew cartoons – the most recent had featured a particularly boring teacher – and he was the town's youngest science wiz. He even turned some of his sketches into 3D animations for Dimension 64, the latest online game, and he hosted a popular D-64 player forum. And, as Trevor examined his friend more closely, Jay even made his own clothes.

Jay was wearing one of his colorful tie-dye shirts, along with a pair of baggy old jeans held together with hundreds of small patches. In a small town like Silver Lake, Jay's clothes made certain he would stand out. He was also well known for his backpack. The famous backpack. The giant canvas backpack lay crumpled in a pile around his feet. He carried it with him everywhere, always delighting people with the endless variety of items inside. One day it might be an old scientific device, a book of sketches, a shirt, or some sort of tool. Last month, he shocked everyone by pulling out a baby squirrel he found on the way to school.

Although he was only two years older than Trevor, somehow Jay seemed much, much older this morning. His light brown face was almost hidden by tangled ringlets of brown hair, his glasses were crooked, and the floor around him was littered with stuff from his backpack as well as the library books he'd been carrying. It looked as if he had spent the entire night inside the library.

Jay shook his head, laughing. "Trevor-man, who needs earthquakes when we have you?"

"Sorry Jay", Trevor offered. "I'm running late. I hope I still have time to help with your project." He started picking up the books he had knocked off the shelf.

"No worries." Jay flashed a peace sign as he lay there on the floor. Then his smile faded. He moaned and held his left elbow as if he was wounded.

"At least, I don't think I need a lawyer—*yet.*"

Both boys laughed out loud. They always made fun of those advertisements that invited people to call a lawyer if their daughter sneezed or a strange dog barked. They enjoyed seeing who could find the worst commercial and then share it over the Internet.

Trevor looked at one of the books he had picked up off the floor, the one that had fallen off the shelf and hit him in the head. "Madame Butterfly?" he asked, and raised a curious eyebrow at Jay. "What's that?"

"Who knows? Maybe it's about the queen of the butterflies."

Trevor turned the book over and examined the pictures on the back cover.

"Okay, let's see… Japan. Samurai soldiers. Warships. Geishas. Oh, I remember seeing a billboard for this one time in New York. It's the usual love / hate thing." He flipped through the book and read the captions below some of the photos. It was an opera about a Japanese woman, Madame Butterfly – and her marriage to an American soldier. Together, they stared at the photos of ancient Japan: fierce Samurai warriors in battle armor, massively fortified castles, and delicate bridges that arched gracefully over water gardens.

"Hmm," Jay said. "I wonder if she gets married to Mr. Toad?"

"Who?"

"Get it? Butterfly? Toad?"

Trevor finally figured out the lame joke. He groaned and threw a book at Jay, then collected the others scattered about the floor.

"Dude, I'm just tryin' to open up the old playground." Jay pleaded his case as he tapped Trevor gently on the head. "Especially if you're going to help me come up with a most outrageous idea for this competition."

Jay reached into his backpack and pulled out a crumpled advertisement announcing the science competition he was going to enter. Trevor took the flyer and glanced at the heading. "Isn't Cosmic Studios the company that makes that game you like so much?"

"Yeah, Dimension 64, it's theirs. That's how I found out about the contest. They're part of some foundation that does research into scientific stuff, I think."

"Zzzzzz. Sounds boring."

"Well, maybe. But I'm only entering for the grand prize. It's a scholarship for their summer camp. Gamers on the web say it's going to be awesome." Trevor looked again at the advertisement:

Hey Students!

The Cosmic Studios Summer Science Competition includes a $5,000.00 award, along with an engraved glass trophy. The winner will also receive an all-expense paid trip to our summer camp in Switzerland.

This Year's Theme:

"Buildings that help mankind"

Criteria for Judging:

Three (3) students will be chosen based on their written entry. Each entry should describe your idea for a radically new building. The judges will evaluate the entries using the rules below to determine a winner. Our distinguished panel of judges includes educators, scientists, and industry leaders.

Points will be awarded for the following:

Design Effort: How innovative is your design? (70 points)

Research: Is your design based on proven science? (15 points)

Concept: Provide an illustration of your design (15 points)

Scale Model: Provide a scale model (10 bonus points)

Trevor noticed the first deadline was only two days away. He passed the flyer back to Jay. "Nothing like 'opening the playground' at the last minute," he grumbled.

"Okay, so I don't have much time." Jay grinned, defending his last minute decision. "Besides, I work better under pressure." He picked up some of the stack of books. "Let's grab a table and see what we can make out of this."

Trevor carried the collection to a big round table in the back of the room and let it fall unceremoniously from his arms. The books landed onto the wood table with a loud *smack*, and then slid across each other, settling into various positions. The two boys looked around to see if anyone else had heard. That was not a single cough, mumble or whisper. There was nothing around them but silent rows of metal bookshelves filled with dusty old volumes of books that that very few people would ever read. It was most likely they were still the only two people in the building. Trevor sat down to survey the collection.

The table was covered in books. He counted three books on architecture, another two about bridges, one leather-bound ledger highlighting every invention from the 20th century, a few science journals, and a very large picture book of "futuristic" vehicles that had flown only in the imaginations of their designers. And, of course, the book about Madame Butterfly.

He leaned back in his chair and watched his friend, waiting for him to speak first. Jay simply stared off into space. It reminded Trevor of his dad standing in the kitchen, earlier this morning. After eight very long minutes, Trevor prompted, "Well? Why all the books?"

Jay came back from wherever his mind had wandered. "I was going to design a normal building like an office or a bridge," he said. "But since you got here, we've been talking about all kinds of things, like castles and butterflies." Jay shrugged. "So I thought, why don't I use some of this stuff for my project?"

Trevor considered the idea. Part of him wanted to say it sounded like a stupid idea, but his mother had taught him to count to five before ever giving an important answer. That way, he could consider the other person's feelings before adding his opinion. Trevor counted, tossing the idea around in his mind. He really couldn't see where Jay was headed. How could an opera, oversized butterflies, or Japanese samurai warriors help Jay win a science project about buildings?

"How can you turn all this into something for the contest?" he finally asked, dumbfounded.

"It has everything to do with science, at least . . . sort of." Jay shook his head slightly, as if trying to clear it. "Look, I'm not interested in the opera, just the ideas I can take from it. I know the play isn't really about a butterfly, but singing is made by vibrations, and when butterflies flap their wings they vibrate the air around them, and..." He voice trailed off as he stared blankly at the space behind Trevor.

Uh oh. Trevor was afraid he would lose Jay to another daydream. He quickly counted out 5 seconds. "Okay. And...?"

"So even if we start with something that sounds crazy, I can take all this and twist it into something that's really cool."

Trevor slowly nodded, beginning to understand what he was talking about. Jay pushed his point. "Every great idea begins with a wild dream. Know what I mean?"

Trevor felt a shiver run up his back. Dreams... like the ones he had been having recently?

"What if," Jay continued, closing his eyes, "what if I could design a building that withstood vibration or impact of any kind? I could call it The Fortress of the Floating Warrior . . ."

Trevor stared at the table, imagining he could see the tall, graceful building taking shape in front of his eyes exactly as Jay described.

"It'll be as strong as it is beautiful, with enormous panels of flexible, shockproof glass that will shimmer like the wings of a butterfly. Behind the glass, its beams will have joints that can bend and twist like the arms and legs of a samurai warrior. Each leg will create an interlocking structural support. This kind of building will be able to absorb amazing amounts of impact."

Jay stopped speaking and the vision in front of Trevor evaporated. He wondered if he had imagined the whole thing, or if a miniature version of Jay's building had actually materialized on the tabletop. Trevor rubbed his eyes and tried to re-focus his attention on what Jay was now doing.

Jay began to draw his ideas on a sheet of paper. With a pencil, he sketched a rough version of the building. Trevor watched as Jay drew the exact building he had just seen on the table… or in his own imagination. He exhaled quietly through his lips.

"Now," Jay proclaimed, setting the pencil down, "all I need is someone to help me make a scale model of my building. That's a key part of the contest. Although I only have two days…or less." He looked at Trevor doubtfully.

He arched both brows as he reached for the stack of books. Unexpectedly, Jay froze in mid-reach and clapped his hands over his ears. "Ouch. What the—"

"Sorry." Trevor fumbled in his pocket for his cell phone. "That's my new ring tone, it's called "dog whistle." He checked the screen, where a familiar face appeared. "Hey Sam, what's up?" Samantha Hudson the best player on the school's soccer team.

Jay returned to his books as Trevor listened.

"Coach is looking for you, Trevor. Everybody's here, and practice begins in… five minutes. Where are you?"

Trevor jerked the phone from his ear and checked the time. He was shocked to see it was almost 10 o'clock. He had become so involved in Jay's project that he had completely forgotten about soccer practice.

"I'm at the library," he explained. "I'll be there as fast as I can." He ended the call and looked at Jay. "I've got to run to practice."

"No worries, go ahead." Jay replied, waving a hand over his sketches. "I think I have a really cool design."

Trevor picked up his bag and looked around for a restroom. He noticed a sign on the back wall. He hurried over to it, went inside, and changed into his soccer uniform as fast as he could.

When he came back out, Jay was leaning back in his chair, feet on the table with his eyes closed, earphones on, and a big smile on his face. He opened one eye and pulled an earbud out, giving Trevor a thumbs-up.

"I'm going online to register for the contest today. Go on soccer star, don't worry about me," he said. "Then, I'll clean up my sketches for the fortress and upload them to the contest site later today."

The shiver returned and traced a cold, thin finger up and down Trevor's spine as he thought about Jay's dark tower. Something about last night's dream... something about a tall building. He could only remember bits and fragments. Trying to see it again was like chasing a wisp of fog. He shook his head and then hurried down the stairs and through the tunnel beyond.

The Athlete

"Go. Go. Go." Coach McCorkle yelled as seventeen pairs of legs turned and sprinted back down the field.

Trevor had raced all the way from the library to the soccer field. Now, he was running with the Silver Lake Sharks as they practiced wind sprints. Blue jerseys emblazoned with the image of a toothy shark with a friendly smile bounced down the field. Up and back they ran, in stops and starts, until the entire team was almost ready to collapse.

"Coach – help," one of the players sputtered. "We can't take much more." Everyone kept running, but they all looked over at their coach with hopeful faces.

"Anyone else need a break?" he asked the team.

"Yes." the entire team yelled back.

"Okay," he said, looking at his watch. "Ten minutes, and make sure you get plenty of water." He gave a nod of his head toward a cooler full of water bottles, and continued writing notes in his clipboard. Trevor grabbed one and dropped onto the grass.

Samantha Hudson, or 'Sam' to her friends, jogged over to where Trevor had collapsed and sat on the ground next to him. She had been the first addition to his small circle of friends and, like

Trevor, was also new to town. Sam twisted off the cap to her bottle and Trevor watched her chug the cool water until the plastic container was dry.

Sam was the same age as Trevor, and her long blonde hair was now gathered into a ponytail with an elastic tie. A few loose strands fluttered about her perfectly tanned face and strikingly blue eyes as she casually flipped the water bottle in her hands.

He knew her first weeks in school had been even more awkward than his. She did not fit neatly into the small town's assumptions about girls. She didn't waste time on gossip, frequent shopping trips, or fancy clothes. The clique of pretty girls quickly decided they didn't like her, which seemed okay with Sam because she didn't particularly like them, either.

She mainly preferred doing anything outdoors. That long list of activities included riding her horse, Major, that she kept stabled at Jansen Farms on the outside of town. It had not been long until the entire school discovered how much she enjoyed sports. The guys on his team quickly, and painfully, learned just how good she was on the soccer field.

On the field, Trevor secretly hoped Sam could teach him to become a great player, or at least good enough to make it through an entire game. It was odd, he realized suddenly, in Brooklyn he never played sports. He would not have even considered it. But here, where the school was so small, anybody that could move was invited to play on a team. He had picked soccer, with Sam's encouragement.

At first, his quiet demeanor fooled some players into believing he was the silent but deadly type, but after a few minutes on the field, his gentle manner gave him away. Trevor didn't exactly strike fear into the hearts of his opponents, and other players soon realized they could easily take the ball from him. Sam had agreed she would improve that situation by giving him a few tips and some friendly support.

Trevor struggled upright and looked over at his friend with a tired expression. He stuck out his tongue like a dog panting in the heat. "I've been running all morning. So far, today feels like one long fire drill. Why," he asked, between big gulps of water, "…are we doing… all these sprints?" He huffed. "This is going to kill me." Sam looked over at Trevor with an amused smile.

"Only if we're really, really lucky." Her blue eyes seemed to sparkle in the sunlight as she relished her own joke. Trevor laughed so hard, water shot through his nose and he lost his balance. He tipped over and landed on his side next to her, causing Sam to burst out laughing as well.

It took Trevor a minute to regain his composure before he could say, "No, I'm serious. You know exactly what I mean. Why practice? Why can't we just go out and play?"

Sam rolled her eyes. "Maybe Coach misses being a kid and wants to take it out on us." Even Trevor grinned at the thought of their coach ever being the same size they were now.

Trevor glanced to the bleachers where their coach was intently studying a clipboard held between two thick hands. Coach McCorkle was built like a life-sized action figure, one that had been inflated with a bicycle pump. Oversized arms with bulging biceps bracketed a massive chest. Legs the size of small oak trees seemed to grow up from the ground.

His tan face was partially shielded by a crown of wavy red hair and a pair of dark sunglasses. There weren't many redheaded men in Silver Lake. However, his muscular frame was even more noticeable than his hair. Despite his fierce appearance, his Coach was one of the nicest people Trevor knew. Even though soccer practice could be tough, he never imagined his Coach scolding them, much less using his strength to bully them.

Trevor gazed back at Sam. Her eyebrows were pinched together and she had a thoughtful look in her eyes.

"Well Kipper," Sam had made it a habit of creating nicknames for him by using variations on his last name, "I think Coach wants us to be in shape so we can play a decent game, no matter how good the other team might be."

"Well, whatever." Trevor didn't buy her argument. "I already know how to run. How about teaching us something cool like some passing tricks or neat shots?" He searched her face for a tiny bit of agreement. Sam shook her head, and gestured with her hands for emphasis.

"Anybody can learn a cool trick, Kip-mo. That's not the point. Soccer takes more than a few moves. It takes endurance. Besides," she added teasingly, rolling the practice ball at him, "I want to run faster than anybody out here so I can steal the ball from slowpokes like you".

Trevor realized those were fighting words. He tried to jump up and chase her, but to no avail. Sam was too fast. She was already on her feet and pushed him playfully back onto the grass. He was left staring at the sky as Sam strolled away to the benches. Coach McCorkle was gesturing to some of the other players who had gathered around him.

Sam takes this game pretty seriously, Trevor observed with a sense of pride. Even though she is fairly intense about the game, she keeps a good attitude. He knew her joke about running faster than him was only meant as a friendly challenge.

"Maybe one day I'll take this game seriously too," he stated out loud, speaking to the empty space where Sam had just stood. Trevor stood up and dusted himself off, brushing stray pieces of grass from the front of his jersey. Then he called after her, "But today I'll be happy if I can just kick the ball without falling down," he added hopefully. Trevor kicked the ball once and then dribbled it all the way back to the bench where the rest of the team had now gathered.

During the second half of practice, he felt he did a decent job of keeping control of the ball and was able to steer his around some of the defenders. True to her promise, Sam tore the field up with her amazing bursts of speed. After they finished their drills, the team gathered on the sidelines for their usual wrap-up meeting. There, the coach handed everyone another bottle of water . . . and a big surprise.

"The Edgewood Wolves are coming over for a practice scrimmage" he looked at his watch, "in less than an hour." The team was shocked. Edgewood was by far the best team in the Tri-Valley area. Silver Lake was a much smaller school and always lost to Edgewood during the regular school season.

"Listen everyone, this is just a practice game before the summer season begins." Coach McCorkle looked at each young player gathered around him in a circle. "Don't worry about how good they are, just concentrate on your game. Keep thinking about the running, passing and defensive moves we just practiced, and you'll do fine."

Then, as the coach opened his playbook for a quick review, the small huddle of nervous players looked at Sam, as if trying to reassure themselves they possessed at least one player with the skills necessary to beat the Wolves.

***

The bus from Edgewood arrived around 11:00 and the Sharks watched nervously as the Wolves unloaded their equipment. Every kid tired to measure the competition as the other players walked toward the visitor bench at the opposite side of the field.

The other team's red and gold uniforms were boldly emblazoned with a snarling Edgewood Wolf across the front. Their team was known as the Wolf Pack for obvious reasons, and it seemed as if each player lived up to the name. Not only did they win more games, but also each player seemed bigger than any of the Sharks. Among the giants, two players stood out immediately. Trevor stared in disbelief at two identical twins that appeared old enough to be in college.

Gary and Larry Moss were not known for any particular soccer skills, but were known throughout the valley for their cruel and illegal plays, both on and off the field. Last year, one of the boys had hit a Highland Hills player so hard the referee had stopped the game. And now, Silver Lake was going to play its first scrimmage of the year against this team—and the Moss twins. Trevor let out a small groan.

The Edgewood players reluctantly began warming up near their side of the field. Eventually, the referee's whistle blew and they shuffled back to the bench. Trevor tightened the laces on his cleats and slid shin guards underneath his socks. He glanced at the sea of blue uniforms around him. He wished their mascot did not look so friendly, and maybe a little more menacing. He stared at Sam with a long face.

Sam pointedly stared back at him. Then she growled like a snarling wolf and snapped her teeth at him.

"Okay, okay. I get it." he laughed and sighed. "Let's go kick some Edgewood butt."

"Or some ankles, if we can't reach any higher." Sam added playfully.

Both teams took their positions. Trevor would play right defender. Sam assumed her usual role as the team's forward striker. There was no fear on her face. In fact, she seemed to be excited by the challenge.

The referee dropped the ball and Sam quickly took possession. Led by Sam and two other teammates, the Sharks made a bold opening dash up the middle of the field. Sam passed the ball to a player who made a shot straight at the net . . . and into the waiting arms of the Wolves' goalkeeper. It was the last time the Sharks would be near the opposing goal posts during the first half of the game. The Wolves were good—very good. They ran circles around the Sharks, repeatedly stealing the ball from their best strikers.

With only 10 minutes left in the game, the Wolves had scored a total of four goals and the Sharks had scored zero. Silver Lake's players were growing tired and frustrated. Trevor watched dejectedly as an Edgewood player easily intercepted another Silver Lake pass and forwarded the ball to his teammate.

It took Trevor a second to realize the player that had just stolen the ball was Larry, one of the Moss twins. Gary received the pass from his brother, and Trevor turned in pursuit, when without warning, Larry barreled into him from the side.

The impact sent Trevor flying. He landed behind Gary, who just laughed as he continued charging toward the Silver Lake goal. He wasn't really hurt, but the foul had gone unnoticed and unchallenged by the referee. The fact that one of the Moss twins had gotten away with a foul made him angry. He sat up to catch his breath as Sam ran over to check on him.

"Are you okay?"

Trevor nodded, too out of breath to speak. Sam had a look of determination on her face that he had never seen during practice. She made a final check on him and then took off after the twins. Trevor got up and signaled toward the bench to let Coach know he was okay. Coach McCorkle wasn't watching him. He was tracking Sam with both eyes as she sprinted down the field. Trevor turned his head in the same direction.

She was moving incredibly fast. In fact, Coach McCorkle was slowly waving his clipboard downward as if he could somehow lower her speed by remote control.

Trevor could barely keep up with her progress as she zigzagged down the field and closed in on the twins. Gary had possession of the ball and Larry was running next to him in a defensive posture. Despite their size, Sam did not hesitate as she approached from behind. With only a few feet separating them, Sam sprinted hard until she was directly beside Gary.

Suddenly, she threw her left leg out and trapped the ball.

She moved so fast the twins could hardly follow her maneuver. Larry, who had been moving closer to defend his brother, missed Sam, and instead collided with his brother. The twins collapsed over her and onto the field in a heap.

Sam scrambled back to her feet and pulled the ball from Gary's left foot. She turned, heading back toward the Edgewood goal. The oafish twins were too slow and too tangled up to respond. As the boys lay there, the surprised Sharks and the stunned Wolves tried to quickly take on new roles: Silver Lake on offense and Edgewood on defense, minus their two largest players. The tables had finally been turned.

But one Edgewood defender adjusted quickly enough to get a foot on the ball before Sam reached the goal. His play sent the ball spiraling out of bounds on the Edgewood side. As Trevor hustled over to throw in the ball, Sam ran over and grabbed his sleeve.

"Stay on the right and pass me the ball as soon as you can." She spoke rapidly. "I'm going to break through on their left." Sam turned and sprinted away from him.

The twins were limping back downfield, and Silver Lake had mere seconds before they could attack and recapture the ball. Trevor stood on the sideline holding the ball behind his head, looking for the best opening as Sam ran into a clearing and motioned. He released the ball over his head, it bounced behind Sam's feet and she took off running after it.

What a stupid mistake! Trevor scolded himself, surprised by his sloppy throw. Sam would lose her momentum and valuable seconds trying to chase down the ball. He was supposed to put the ball in front of her, not behind her.

Sam didn't seem to care. Without breaking her stride, she turned around and recaptured the ball before Gary or Larry could reach her. Then she took off running and dribbled right past another surprised Edgewood defender. It was like watching a streak of blue lightning shoot down the field.

Sam lined up her shot with her left foot but then kicked the ball to the right side of the net. The Edgewood goalkeeper, who had been expecting a shot to the left, tried to correct his position, but he was too late and too far away. The ball sailed past his arms into the back of the net. The Silver Lake Sharks had finally scored one point against a formidable foe. Smiles and cheers broke out across the field. Sam jumped up and threw her arm into the air as she let out a whoop of victory.

The team had to refocus as the game resumed with a kick-off, but within a few minutes the referee blew his whistle and signaled the end of the game.

The Wolves had been too distracted to mount any kind of last minute drive, and the Sharks were too energized to let them. From the level of noise and their exuberant cheering, any neighbors who happened to walk by would have safely assumed the Sharks had won the game. The teams formed two moving lines to congratulate each other, with opposing players offering each other the customary good-game salute as they passed by. The twins were still visibly angry. A pair of vicious sneers greeted each Shark.

Trevor watched cautiously as the twins approached Sam. Gary kicked at the ground as he passed in front of her. She was unable to dodge the scrap of mud that landed on the center of her jersey. Meanwhile, Larry pretended to miss her upraised hand and instead slapped the side of her head. Sam and Trevor stopped as the twins continued walking down the line. Sam's hands curled into hard fists. Just as quickly however, she shook her head, took a deep breath and simply brushed the mud from her jersey. Then she finished congratulating the rest of the Edgewood players.

On the way back to the bench, several of the Silver Lake players were still complaining about the twins' bad behavior, and three of them wanted to start a fight. Trevor glanced over at the other team. The twins were staring back, taunting them. He could tell by their faces that they would welcome a new round of competition—off the field.

Coach McCorkle stepped into the middle of the group and broke up the discussion. He shot a disapproving look at the twins as he circled his team in front of their bench.

"Awesome game, everyone." He stuck his arm into the center of the group and the kids threw their arms on top, shouting "On three: 1, 2, 3..." The team shouted back in unison, "Go Sharks!" He was truly excited and proud of them, as if they had actually won the game.

"You played great against a very tough team, and some very—" he paused, glaring back at the twins—"challenging players." Then he looked around the circle of faces. "I'm proud of everyone

here for keeping their sense of fair play." Coach smiled, turned and
pointed his clipboard at Sam.

"Great play Sam" he said. "And," he said, pointing at Trevor,
"nice assist. Sam couldn't have made that shot without everyone's
help." Trevor felt himself blush as his coach briefly scanned the
clipboard.

"Remember, be here Wednesday by 10:00 a.m. to warm up.
We'll be playing our first real game of the summer against the Sky
Park Eagles at 11:00."

As everyone walked off the field, Sam jogged over to her
father, the only parent who had watched the practice and who was
now standing beside the short row of bleachers. Unknown to Sam
and the rest of the players, at least one person had watched the
entire game. Mike Hudson rubbed his daughter's hair and gave her
a quick kiss on the forehead. Sam turned around and motioned for
Trevor to join her. After a brief introduction, she reached out and
raised her hand in the air for a high-five. Trevor reached up and she
smacked her hand against his.

"We showed them," she shouted, jumping up and down and
pumping a fist into the air. "Didn't that feel great?"

Trevor nodded, and looked in the direction of the other team
that was loading up for the return trip home. The twins were arguing
about something, and one of them shoved a smaller player out of
the way as they stepped onto the bus.

"I just had to score at least one goal against those horrible
brothers," she flapped a hand dismissively at them.

He had to admire her spirit. She had been so focused and serious during the game, he hadn't realized how excited she was.

"Yeah, good game, Sam. You played great," he offered sincerely and returned her smile. Sam's father put an arm around his daughter's shoulders and gave her a hug. Trevor could tell he was very proud of her, even though their team had lost. Then father and daughter turned and began walking back up the hill toward Main Street.

Trevor stayed for a minute longer. He couldn't stop thinking about the game, and Sam's goal in particular. By now, Sam and her father were almost at the edge of the parking lot, but he wanted to ask her one last question.

"Hey Sam," he called out. Sam looked back over her shoulder.

"How did you know you could get past the twins?"

"Oh, that was easy." She stopped walking. "Their 'keeper favored his right side over the left side of the goal. So, I figured if I sprinted fast enough I'd lose the twins and have a clear shot to the left." He suddenly realized Sam had been analyzing the other players to see how she could beat them. As they turned to leave, he heard Sam's father speaking proudly to his daughter.

"You're going to be a great soccer player, Sam. How about a World Cup trophy for my shelf?" Sam laughed out loud.

"Sure! I'll get two for you, Dad."

Trevor knew she probably meant it. Sam could do anything she set her mind to. He was both proud and little bit envious of Sam's confidence. Winning seemed to come easily for her. Maybe a little of her ability would rub off on him. As he crossed the field, he dribbled one of the team's practice balls, and dreamed about championship games played inside enormous stadiums. He imagined the crowd cheering so loud he could barely hear the announcer call his name.

"Now taking the field . . . three time world champion…Trevor Kip!" he yelled the mock announcement to an empty field. He kicked the ball and watched it roll into the net.

Something suddenly interrupted his daydream. His stomach had growled. What time was it, anyway?

He pulled his cell phone out of the gym bag. Lunchtime. He was supposed to eat with Julie Meriwether, and not a moment too soon. Julie had kept their plans a secret, but now he was so hungry he didn't care what she served. Trevor set off across the soccer field toward Julie's house and a much-anticipated lunch.

The Chef

Trevor dropped his bike on the yard and took two steps onto the front porch of the big colonial house. Strangely, the front door was slightly ajar. He pushed it open a little farther - just enough to stick his head inside - and looked around.

"Hello?" he called out to an apparently empty house. No one answered, except for the echo of his own voice.

He pushed the door open all the way and took two steps inside, hoping to find someone home. The front hall was empty. An old school clock tick-tocked loudly from its spot on the wall to his left. It was perched a safe distance above a narrow hall table which was piled dangerously high with newspapers, business binders and cooking magazines. Two comfortable-looking chairs stood in the larger room to his right, on a rug that almost covered the entire floor. A massive stone fireplace dominated the far wall.

"Hello, anybody home?" he called out again, a little louder this time. Maybe he had misunderstood, and Julie wanted to meet him somewhere downtown. But he couldn't remember her mentioning another location.

Trevor had just started to back out of the house when a heavy-set man in jeans and a brightly patterned shirt strolled into the foyer from behind a swinging door. He was smiling, but the smile quickly turned into a scowl as he examined Trevor. At first, Trevor thought he was mad at him for walking in without permission. Then he pointed an accusing finger at Trevor's feet.

"Trevor Kip, you come into my clean house with those dirty shoes and Mrs. Meriwether will have you walking on your hands for the rest of your life." Trevor almost giggled – there was not another family in Maine with an accent like the Meriwethers – and then he looked down at the floor. His cleats were caked with mud.

He backed sheepishly out of the house and removed the offending shoes. He reached into his gym bag and pulled out a pair of old, but clean sneakers. Then he stepped back into the foyer.

"Despite what my daughter says, I still think you are a good egg, Mr. Kip," Mr. Meriwether announced, as he picked at Trevor's blue jersey and examined it closely with a frown. "Even if you are dressed up like a man-eating shark." He finished his examination of Trevor with a little rub on his head. Then Mr. Meriwether stood back and beamed proudly, as if Trevor had just won first place at the county fair.

"Now, if you're looking for my little girl, I believe you will find her hidin' behind that door." He gestured behind his back to a white swinging door. Then he placed his hands on his knees and bent lower as if sharing a secret.

"To tell you the God's honest truth," he whispered, "I believe she's in there tryin' to juggle peas between her toes." Mr. Meriwether stood up and laughed at his own joke. Trevor didn't know how to respond. Yuck . . . green peas between her toes?

"Really?"

Mr. Meriwether sighed. "Sorry, son. That's just a southern expression that means she's in there trying to do the impossible." Trevor tried to imagine Julie performing that particular act. She'd once told him she'd been helping around the kitchen since she was six, and that the first Christmas present she ever wished for had been an E-Z Bake Oven. Come to think of it, it wouldn't surprise Trevor at all if she *could* juggle vegetables using her toes.

"Now, wander on back." Mr. Meriwether pointed to the kitchen door as he scurried past. "I've got a farm and forest report to finish before Mrs. Meriwether gets back from the store." Trevor watched as the roly-poly man disappeared quietly up the stairs. As the area's chief farm and wildlife inspector, Trevor imagined Julie's good-natured dad spending more time eating off the land than studying it.

He proceeded into the kitchen through the swinging door at the end of the foyer. His friend looked up from her place behind the kitchen counter.

"Hey Trevor, watch out." Julie playfully waved a gigantic wooden spoon with one hand as she balanced a tattered green book in the other. True to her calling, she was wearing a puffy white chef's hat from which wisps of curly brown hair shot out in all directions. The matching chef's jacket and pants were decorated with bright red flowers that seemed to highlight her round cheeks. "I'm whirlin' and twirlin' in the kitchen, shortcake."

The kitchen itself wasn't very big, sort of the perfect size for two people—or one very busy chef. The walls were painted tomato red and there were pots and pans hanging from the hooks in the ceiling. On the wall behind Julie was an entire cabinet stuffed full of cookbooks and recipes. There were big books, skinny books, and books that had been written by schools, churches, and local clubs. One shelf was so crowded it seemed ready to drop several of the books onto a stack of bowls on the counter below.

He could tell she was busy at something, perhaps even more than one thing, from the looks of the kitchen. All three counters were now covered in a variety of pots, pans and metal cooking sheets. A bag of flour had spilled and a thin layer of flour covered most of the counter in front of Trevor. On another counter, several stacked trays were covered in sheets of wax paper. Julie was standing in front of the stove examining a sauce that bubbled slowly over one of the gas burners.

Trevor spied two stools hidden under the island counter and sat down on one of them. He followed Julie's non-stop activity while nibbling on small pieces of orphaned dough. She had carefully removed another large cookbook from the tipsy shelf and now examined it on the counter in front of her. Without looking away she removed a small jar from her spice rack and sprinkled a small amount into the simmering pot. Then she snapped the book closed and set it on a short bookstand. The entire scene reminded Trevor of childhood fairy tales where witches stirred their cauldrons while consulting an old tattered book of spells.

"Hey, Kitchen Witch. Who you got cooking inside your pot?" he said to her back. Julie turned, paused, and then laughed at her new nickname. She waved the spoon high above her head with a dramatic flair and answered him, a hint of mystery in her voice.

"I wanted you to come over and help me with a very top-secret project." Julie studied her visitor and could tell he was falling quickly under her spell. She continued weaving her magic on Trevor. "I've been asked to create a very special dessert for Silver Lake's anniversary celebration on Monday. It's also going to be a surprise birthday party for Mayor Jansen." She spun around and stabbed a slice of raw meat with a fork. The long red slice jiggled like a worm as she waved it in front of his face.

"Ugh…" Trevor groaned. The spell was broken. "You're making a dessert out of meat?"

Surprised, she looked at the meat in her hands and then at Trevor, quickly realizing the source of his concern. Julie laughed as she dropped the meat into a pan, then leaned over and whispered to Trevor.

"Yes, of course. The mayor of our town is a vampire like the rest of us. You are a vampire, aren't you?" She poked Trevor's bony arm with her fork and inspected him closely. Trevor laughed and looked back at her.

"Not today." he replied earnestly. "Today I'm Caveman Trevor. I'm so hungry I might go hunting for wild pigs in the woods if I don't eat soon." Trevor dropped his head onto the counter, pretending to faint from hunger.

She shrugged. "Well, I guess I'll just have to cook this up for your lunch then." Trevor quickly raised his head and smiled.

Julie laughed as she wiped a bit of dough off his face, and then dropped another slice of meat into the hot pan. The meat instantly began to sizzle. Trevor was glad she was preparing a real meal for lunch, but then he realized she still had not let him in on her secret. "Seriously, what are you making for the big party?" he asked.

He resumed picking at the scraps of dough and placed them neatly in a row. He curved the row slightly and arranged them as Julie returned from the stove. Two more for eyes... one for the nose... and a doughy face smiled up at him from the counter.

"Ahhhh. Where to begin was the easy part. The party committee told me to make something suitable for a Canivale in Venice." Julie twirled once before the kitchen island, then leaned over the counter and rested her chin in her hands as she raised one slightly pudgy white leg somewhat gracefully into the air.

"It's a theme party. The real challenge was deciding what I could make that would fit into the theme. How can I set the moood with the fooood...?"

Trevor was clueless. "Is it a circus theme?" he asked.

Julie turned and walked over to the stove to turn the sizzling meat. She returned and placed the fork down while retrieving a sheet of oil-stained paper that had been tucked inside one of the books.

"Well, Carnivale is not a circus. Just so you know. I had to learn that for myself." She shuffled in a few more sheets of paper.

Trevor could see that they were copies of web pages, and they were marked up with red pen and highlighter. Julie explained the concept of Carnivale to him and turned several pages around as she described the event. She held up a page that showed people in elaborate costumes staring at the camera. Their faces were covered in masks of all types: funny faces, animals, and some masks that covered only the eyes.

"It's a time in Italy when cities hold big festivals and parades. Everyone wears masks, goes to parties, dances, and eats a lot of delicious food. And," she said, pointing to the computer tucked in next to the wall, "I had to learn more about Venice, too." Trevor was certain that Julie was the only person he knew who had a computer in her kitchen.

"Did you know," Julie said, and she held up her hand and began counting off on her fingers, "first, Venice is in the north of Italy and they have recipes that are different from anywhere else." She put down one finger. "Second, Venice is surrounded by water and is near the sea. Three, they cook the kinds of things that are grown or caught in the area, like fish, pine nuts, onions, and even… liver."

With the last fact, she turned and pointed to the stove.

"Oh no," Trevor suddenly grabbed his stomach and made a sour face. "Please don't tell me you're cooking liver for lunch." He had played right into her joke. Julie clapped her hands.

"No, that's beef," she smiled and pointed at him. " But I almost had you there."

Trevor thought about the dessert as Julie moved the meat from the burner to plates next to the stove. She fussed for a minute and then set one plate in front of each stool. Their lunches included thin strips of grilled beef placed into a puff pastry, asparagus in a cream sauce, and potatoes on the on side. It smelled wonderful, and it tasted even better. Trevor was so hungry he had finished before Julie had even started her own meal.

"Sorry." He apologized, realizing how fast he had wolfed down his lunch. He sat back and rested his hands on his stomach. "That's just what I needed Julie. Thanks."

After Julie finished eating, Trevor grabbed both plates and took them to the sink. He scrubbed the dirty plates and utensils. "At least I can clean up while you tell me more about this party," he said over his shoulder.

Julie pointed to a small slip of paper with a recipe on it. "I am making a fabulous Italian dessert that I will call the Dessert of Sighs."

"It's going to be really big?" Trevor looked at her doubtfully from the sink. Julie replied with one of her famously loud laughs.

"No silly, s-i-g-h-s," she spelled, "in honor of the most famous bridge in Venice, the Bridge of Sighs." She moved off her stool to the counter where something had been covered in with wax paper. She pulled the wax paper off one of the trays with a flourish, and stood back so he could see. Trevor wiped off his hands and moved closer to examine the flat, brown squares.

"This is a dessert?" he asked doubtfully. Julie smirked and put both hands on her hips.

"Come on Trevor, it's chocolate. You've got to use a little imagination." She began to lift up the pieces of chocolate and Trevor could now see the outline of an arch. He finally understood.

"Oh I get it... you're making a bridge out of chocolate," he said, finally solving the mystery.

"Yep," she said, putting one finger on her nose. "Bulls eye. But that's not all."

She reached under the counter and handed Trevor a sketch showing a canal with buildings on either side. The bridge connected both buildings as a boat passed underneath it. Julie pointed to the boat in the drawing.

"That's a gondola."

That name sounded familiar, but he had never seen one before. Julie moved her hand across the photo.

"They travel up and down the canals of Venice. I've cut out the chocolate so we can make the walls, the bridge and a gondola. Now all we have to do is create the water." he looked at the ingredients she had assembled to the right side of the sink.

"For water, we're going to make a pudding the Italians call budino di riso. In the south, we'd just call it plain old rice pudding."

For the next hour, she guided Trevor as they followed the directions on the recipe, combined all the ingredients into heated the milk, and then poured the finished mixture into the pudding molds she had selected.

Julie popped the molds into the stove and they turned their attention to the chocolate. They assembled the chocolate buildings, the chocolate bridge, and chocolate gondola while the pudding baked in the oven. Julie then brought out a giant blue platter and they erected the walls using toothpicks. She had already cut out and painted cardboard roofs and they now used those to hold the walls of chocolate in place. The oven buzzed loudly and Julie hurried over and removed the warm pudding.

Once it cooled, Julie turned the molds upside down and they spread the rice pudding between the small brown buildings. Julie let

Trevor place the little boat on the canal as she tried to connect the two buildings using her miniature bridge. The dessert looked incredible. Trevor could envision their little boat sailing along the water…

He stared at the platter. Something seemed wrong.

The pudding was swirling on top of the dish. He bent over and examined it more closely. The pudding was actually moving. It slowly began to rise. A small strand flowed over the edge of the platter onto the counter. Trevor realized Julie didn't seem to notice. She was too focused on her bridge and its delicate pieces of ornamental icing.

"Umm…" Trevor paused. The little boat had just sailed off the platter and onto the floor.

"Julie?" Trevor nudged his partner.

She looked up at him distractedly, as if there were no reason for him to interrupt her bridge-building efforts. Trevor pointed to the soupy puddle of pudding as it flowed with greater speed and volume from the platter onto the countertop and below. Streams of pudding were now cascading onto the kitchen floor.

"Holy Mother of Pearl." Julie exclaimed. "I wanted it to look like water, not actually become water."

She grabbed a handful of towels and threw them over the little cream-colored lake that had formed in the middle of her kitchen. Julie thrust another handful at Trevor and he quickly joined in to help. Within twenty minutes, they had filled four large buckets and two-dozen towels with rice pudding. They dumped the buckets and towels into the kitchen sink and washed everything down.

Finally, everything appeared normal once again.

Julie set aside a small amount of pudding that had not left the platter. Trevor was astounded. Had there even been this much pudding on the platter?

She wiped her brow and looked at her friend. He was spattered from head to toe with rice pudding. She started laughing as Trevor tried, unsuccessfully, to wipe pudding off his clothes.

"Next time," Trevor advised her, "why don't you imagine trying to make a frozen lake and not a raging river."

Something about what had just happened nagged at Trevor, but he could not put a finger on it. He was no cook, but he didn't think pudding should act quite like that.

"Well." She surveyed the remaining dessert "It's not a complete disaster. I'll just add something to make up for the pudding we lost." She turned and began looking through her collection of recipes.

Trevor slipped quietly out of the kitchen, retrieved his spare clothes and cleaned up in the hallway bathroom while she studied her books. When he returned, Julie was staring at the counter top. "I swear, I can't figure out what caused the pudding to overflow like that. It's such a simple recipe."

"Yeah. That was kind of . . . strange," His mind was still a tangle of thoughts. At least he looked better, without pudding clinging to his clothes and hair.

"But do you want to see something really wonderful?" Julie asked, and held up two fingers as a solemn oath. "No monster puddles of pudding. I promise."

Trevor hesitated. What could be more interesting than a river of pudding? An avalanche of vanilla icing? A hailstorm of chocolate chips? Julie opened the swinging kitchen door and bowed regally.

"If you will do me the honor, Mr. Kip," she said, pointing to the miniature reproduction of Venice.

Trevor carefully picked up the large platter and followed her as she guided him down the hallway and out her front door. Julie retrieved Trevor's bike from her front yard and proceeded to lead him up Laurel Canyon Road, around the soccer field, past several stores, and through the short alley that led onto Main Street.

Transformation

Trevor almost dropped the platter as they emerged from the alley. He and Julie were standing directly across from the Community Hall – the same one he had passed on his bike only a couple hours earlier - but now it looked completely different.

Silver Lake's Community Hall was unlike any of the grand brick and stone buildings in town. Its plain block walls formed a perfect rectangle, with a stone roof on top. It did not sport any turrets or gargoyles—in fact, it lacked any trim or decoration of any kind. In short, it was rather frumpy and plain by comparison to the other buildings in town. Although it was a very efficient and useful space, it would never win any beauty contests.

That's how it normally appeared.

But now, scaffolding and ladders covered the entire building as workmen crawled over it. Several trucks and two white vans were parked beside it, and several more were parked in the street nearby. "Cosmic Enterprises" was stenciled neatly across the side of each vehicle. Trevor and Julie both stood in amazement as they watched the blur of activity. They listened to the shouts of the workers as they called to each other for tools or assistance.

Most significantly, the plain exterior walls of the hall were now almost completely covered in fake bricks, vines and turrets. The drab building was beginning to resemble an ancient castle. Several theater sets crafted to look like walls and doors from old buildings were stacked against the hall, awaiting installation inside.

Julie pointed to the bridge now rising to its place on top of the building. A small crane was lifting an ornate metal arch that would be installed between the community center and the bank next door. It appeared to be a larger version of Julie's chocolate Bridge of Sighs.

"They're even constructing a real bridge to connect the two buildings, Julie said. "Just like our dessert..." Julie looked down at the platter, suddenly remembering their original mission. "Great gizzards! We need to get this into a refrigerator right away."

She described another detail about the event as she rolled Trevor's bike into a nearby rack. The space between the bank and the Community Hall would be filled with water so people could ride in a real gondola. Trevor could now see the gondola parked on a trailer behind the bank. Julie opened the front door to let them both inside.

Within the hall, the normally bland interior was rapidly being transformed from an empty shell into an Old Italian village. Strings of lights now crisscrossed the ceiling. Round tables with checkered cloths were scattered about. Workmen in white coveralls were busy putting some of the theater sets against the walls.

Trevor and Julie watched as a group of workers raised a tower against the far wall. A small stage was being pushed into place on the opposite side, near a pair of doors that led to the large commercial kitchen. Soon, the entire building, inside and out, would resemble the courtyard of an Italian plaza, surrounded by old buildings.

"Wow," Trevor said, his eyes wide at the scene around them. He followed Julie around the stage and into the kitchen. She opened the door to an oversized refrigerator and Trevor gently lowered the platter onto one of the shelves. He closed the door and turned back to the hall. Julie stood near one of the kitchen doors and let out a long, happy sigh.

"Oh Trevor. Just think how magical it will look once everything is in place and all the lights are on."

A siren broke the silence, and Julie gave a start. Trevor dug his cell phone out of his pocket, and shrugged at Julie apologetically.

It was his mother sending him a text message. He had promised to walk Moke this afternoon. He looked up at the clock on the wall. It was almost 3 o'clock. He quickly tapped out a reply. "Sorry, Mom. Helping Julie with big project. Be there in 10." Trevor slipped the phone inside his pocket.

By this time, Julie had gone to the back of the meeting hall to look at the stage sets and explore the decorations. Trevor called out to her, thanked her for lunch, and waved goodbye. He would have to catch up with her later. He took one last look at the hall and whistled.

This was going to be one amazing party.

Trevor weaved through the jumble of tables, out the front doors and backed his bike out of the rack. He put his helmet on and peddled up Main Street toward the north side of town. He had almost reached Vivada Street when a very strange noise made him come to a complete and unexpected stop.

Ready. Fire!

Boom! Trevor clearly heard a loud bang, followed by a muffled yell. No – it was more like a scream. Trevor stopped pedaling and looked around. He couldn't see anyone else nearby. He stepped back on his bike and pedaled slowly up Vivada Street, keeping his ears open for more sounds in between breaths. Turning the last corner, he rolled his bike through the gate and dropped it onto the front yard.

He stood still for a few seconds, trying to catch his breath, and stole a glance inside his house. No signs of life. The noise had not come from his house. He figured Moke could certainly wait a few more minutes, and his mom didn't need to know he was back... He hurried toward the largest tree near the side of their property.

Midway up, on a very large limb, a wooden platform nestled between two branches of a massive oak tree. It wasn't elaborate, but his dad helped him make it large enough to hold all his things. It was the perfect spot to watch the world below without being seen. Trevor reached up to the crooked ladder that served as his only way up to the platform. The boards were barely visible through the dense thicket of bushes and vines that surrounded the tree.

Climbing to the top, Trevor set his pack down onto the deck and unfolded a small piece of paper. The seams were taped and it was ragged from constant use. The map he now spread out on the wood deck was small enough to carry in a pocket. However, this map wasn't like any of the maps tourists could buy in Tefton's Drugstore downtown. Of course, it included the usual roads and buildings, but in addition to the traditional markings, he had also added notes showing some of the people he had met and any of the buildings he had visited.

Trevor carefully noted a few locations marked for further exploration. His index finger rested on one particularly well-worn spot. Trevor drew a '?' on the location using a ballpoint pen. He wondered if this place was the source of the noise he had heard.

"Something about this house seems… wrong." He murmured quietly to himself. Trevor was looking at the map when another loud bang echoed over the hill. He stood on his toes and stared into the distance. He looked down at his own house and listened. Nothing. No movement. His parents were either in town or so absorbed in their work they didn't hear a thing.

He peered back in the direction of the noise; toward the roof of the very house he had marked on his map, and then climbed down from his observation deck. Something strange was definitely happening at that house. Trevor hesitated as his feet touched the ground.

At least check it out, part of him reasoned. You can go and get back before your mother even notices or Moke gets desperate…

He hopped over the low wooden fence that surrounded the yard, ducking and pushing his way through the thick shrubs that surround the house. Once over the hill, he stumbled onto the narrow dirt road that ran behind his house.

Trevor followed the path before arriving in front of a decrepit and seemingly abandoned house. He had never seen it this close before. There were weeds instead of flowers in the garden. Faded green paint was peeling from the walls as if from a bad sunburn. Large sections of paint lay scattered about the front porch. A portion of a once-white fence was leaning against a wheelbarrow where someone had left it long ago. He tried hard to imagine who could live in this house.

He stood at the edge of the yard, peering intently at the door, trying to see inside the old house without getting closer. Trevor jumped slightly when a loud crash and a series of thumps came from inside. He was even more startled when he realized he was actually running up to the front door. This was definitely not like him, but he was certain something was wrong inside. Trevor leaned his head against the door, but could hear nothing inside. He pounded both fists against his head.

If you knock on the wrong door you'll get your butt kicked Trevor, the worrier inside him scolded. What are you doing here, asked the small panicked voice. He looked around the yard. Who would live in this mess, and what if all of these strange noises are not human...?

Soon, Trevor found himself having a spirited debate inside his head. You know you heard something fall, the adventurer, the one who had led him here so far, firmly insisted. You should investigate.

The other more cautious side that knew how to survive big city's streets disagreed quite adamantly. Whatever is in there must be really large to make that much noise. I vote no.

"Shut up!" Trevor shouted to both the voices. He thrust both his hands outward, as if he could physically dispel his inner circle of friends. This wasn't a big city. It's a small town. People look out for each other here. There is no harm in looking around. If I don't see anything, he informed them, then maybe I can leave a note for the owner and head back home… and then he remembered leaving his backpack in the tree. No note.

Trevor walked through the remains of an old gate and up a cracked walkway to the nearest window. He wiped a thick layer of dust to clear his view and leaned in closer. Through the front window he could clearly see tomatoes, a carton of eggs, a magazine, several cans, and a grocery bag scattered about the floor. It looked like a recent accident – that would explain the noise - and that meant someone would be walking in to clean it up. And then he spotted the edge of a woman's arm.

The pattern of doubt he had constructed quickly unraveled. Trevor pushed on the window and tried to open it, but it was locked and remained in place. Moving to the front door, he twisted the handle. Locked, just like the windows.

Trevor stepped back and looked to the left and right. Maybe the owner had come in through the back door. He raced around the corner to the back of the house. A screened porch ran the entire length and a screen door, hanging by a single rusted hinge, grated noisily in the gentle breeze. He jumped up two short steps, pushed open the broken screen door, and raced to the door. He reached out and twisted the knob. It was also locked. He quickly scouted the porch for a hidden key or another way inside. Nothing.

He ran into the back yard, just off the porch, and stared up at the top of the house. A trail of grey smoke was quietly snaking through a hole in the second-story window. Trevor grabbed his cell phone and began dialing.

"911, what's your emergency?" a man's voice crackled on his phone. He could barely hear the operator.

He looked at the display - the signal was weak. He looked back up the hill. The fire would be an inferno by the time he made it home. He stared at the phone. He didn't even know the name of the dirt road, or if it even had one. Trevor suddenly felt very silly.

"There's a woman," he stammered. "She's lying on the floor, and there's a fire in her house. I have to get her out right now."

"Hello?" The dispatcher's voice cracked through the static. He could not hear any response. "I'm on a dirt road behind 314 Vivada Street…there's a fire, mister!" He waited a few seconds and listened. He heard nothing but static and garbled noise.

Trevor switched off the phone and slipped it back into his pocket. He took a deep breath and took off running toward the front door, hoping the dispatcher had sent help anyway.

An Unexpected Hero

Trevor reached the front door and threw his entire body at it. His shoulder screamed with pain. It always seemed to work in the movies, but now he realized it didn't work that way in reality. The door remained firmly shut. He rubbed his shoulder as he looked around for another option.

He spied one on the front lawn.

Trevor grabbed a brick from beside the sidewalk and ran back to the window. He hesitated for a moment, and then tapped the glass with it. The pane shattered instantly, raining shards of glass on the floor inside. He dropped the brick and reached inside, flipping the window latch and trying not to cut himself in the process. Once unlocked, the window slid up easily, and he climbed cautiously inside.

The woman lay motionless at the foot of the stairs in a jumble of spilled groceries. He watched as smoke from the second floor crawled across the first floor ceiling like fog turned upside down. The slithering carpet of gray was hypnotizing and Trevor found it impossible to move. A small voice jolted him back into action.

"Stay low and get out fast. Get out. Get out. Get out," his internal protector shouted.

As if to emphasize the point, Trevor's lungs began to fill with smoke and he started to cough uncontrollably. He ducked low and crawled to where the woman lay.

"Hello?" he yelled at her still body. Oh… please don't let her be dead. Trevor cringed. He had never seen a dead body… He tentatively reached out his hand and gently shook her. The woman didn't respond. He shook harder. After a few more tries the woman's eyes fluttered opened and her head turned slightly as she tried to focus on her visitor.

"Who…" she coughed, "… get away." She demanded angrily. Trevor shook his head.

"We've got to get out." He insisted. Trevor crawled over to the front door flipped the lock and opened the door. Then he crawled back to his neighbor.

"Can I move you?" He reached around her, sensing that she was not entirely happy to see him. In fact, she looked angry instead of relieved. He tried to ignore the strange reaction. After all, she had fallen down the stairs and her house was on fire. What type of reaction did he expect?

He glanced back up the carpeted stairs.

Trevor realized they did not have much time, judging by the thick clouds of smoke curling about the ceiling. The fire was getting closer every second, and he could now feel heat from upstairs. Somehow he knew the second floor of the house could explode into flames at any moment. He tightened his grip under two thick shoulders and began to pull. He only managed to move her a short distance.

Although she was not exceptionally large, Trevor was smaller, and the woman was more muscular than he had guessed. He knew he couldn't give up - not yet - he had to get her out of the house first. He squeezed his eyes shut tight and gripped his neighbor's shoulders once again. This time, he bent both knees and arched his back as he pulled on her with all the strength he could muster.

Her body had begun to slide across the floor when Trevor suddenly felt a pair of strong arms lock onto his shoulders. Before he could understand what was happening, he felt himself spinning through the air in a wide arc. In a blur of images, he saw the overgrown yard, flashing lights, and a crowd of faces. Sirens, smoke, and voices filled the air. When the motion stopped, he was lying on his back in front of the house. He sat up and looked directly into masked face of a fireman.

"That lady . . . needs help," he managed to get out between a spasm of loud and painful coughs. He aimed a finger in the direction of where two medics were carrying the woman's limp body toward an ambulance. Trevor noticed army fatigues peeking from under the medics' lab coats. That was odd... maybe it was the smoke, or perhaps some kind of police or hazard team had responded. Regardless, he thought it was curious that the ambulance now pulling away looked more like a van than a rescue vehicle.

He turned to share his thoughts, but was forced back down by a gentle hand. The fireman quickly checked his pulse, pulling off his mask at the same time. Trevor blinked in surprise. The fireman that had rescued him was a woman, and not just any woman. It was Susan Pierce, Chief of Fire and Rescue for Silver Lake.

"Breathe," she commanded, and glanced at his wrist as she took his pulse. Her face was drawn up in a scowl, and Trevor wasn't certain if she was going to lecture him or help him. But then her face softened and she smiled.

"You're lucky to be alive, but you do understand that was a dangerous thing you did by going in there?"

Trevor tried to respond but all he could manage was a small cough. Chief Pierce placed a hand on his chest to silence any protest. His entire body felt weak. She placed a hand on his back and guided him onto the grass. The Chief finished her rapid examination, making certain he was not seriously injured. He watched as a second ambulance pulled into the yard close behind the Chief's car.

"You're okay, but I want them to take you to the hospital for a routine checkup." With that, she smiled briefly at him before placing the mask back over her face.

He watched as she jogged over to where another firefighter was preparing to flood the burning house with a torrent of water. Trevor wanted to thank her, but all he could manage was a loud, hacking cough. Before he could get her attention, a pair of emergency workers had placed him on a stretcher and loaded him inside the back of the ambulance. A few minutes later, he was on his way to Tri-Valley Hospital in Edgewood.

All Clear?

Trevor looked at his cell phone as the ambulance pulled away from the burning house. No signal. He wondered how he could ever explain this to his parents. He dropped his head down on the stretcher as the ambulance winded its way along the narrow roads and between the hills that led to Edgewood.

Once there, the nurses bustled around him and then handed him his phone back with the instructions to phone his Mom. Her scolding quickly turned into concern as he explained his situation. A half an hour later, both of his parents walked anxiously into the emergency room and stepped inside a small curtained area. Behind it they found their son and a nurse laughing as he tried unsuccessfully to juggle three large balls of paper.

"Mom. Dad." Trevor dropped the paper and ran to his parents. After the medical staff had made certain there were no major burns, bumps or bruises, Trevor and his parents left the hospital, and within another hour he was back safely in his own room. Several minutes passed before he reached into his pocket to retrieve his map. He dropped it onto his dresser and then stared at the wall behind him.

The small map was just a portable version of a much larger one that had slowly engulfed one entire wall in his room. He had been working on it almost since he moved into town. Unlike the smaller map, the section on the right-hand side of the large one also included newspaper clippings from the local newspaper, the *Silver Lake Current*. News articles about the opening of a new store, some local history of Silver Lake, and articles about locals and neighbors were attached at various locations.

The center and left side of the wall was dedicated entirely to a map of the Tri-Valley area. Using several travel maps, online maps, as well as his own notes and observations, he had filled in the entire valley from Sky Park in the south, all the way north to Edgewood. Of course, the very center of the map, the section containing Silver Lake, was the most complete. Trevor walked closer to the wall and touched his finger to the center of town.

Trevor had identified almost every building, and was in the process of trying to identify the name of each store and office, as well as the people who belonged there. Colorful little pads of sticky paper were placed next each location. On them, he had written notes about the people and activities he had observed from his platform.

He ran his finger along Park Lane and up to Vivada Street. He easily spotted the roof of his house and then looked to the right. He walked closer to the map and placed a blue sticky note labeled "Mystery" near the house that had just burned.

"What were you doing in there?" he wondered out loud as he sat down heavily on the side of his bed.

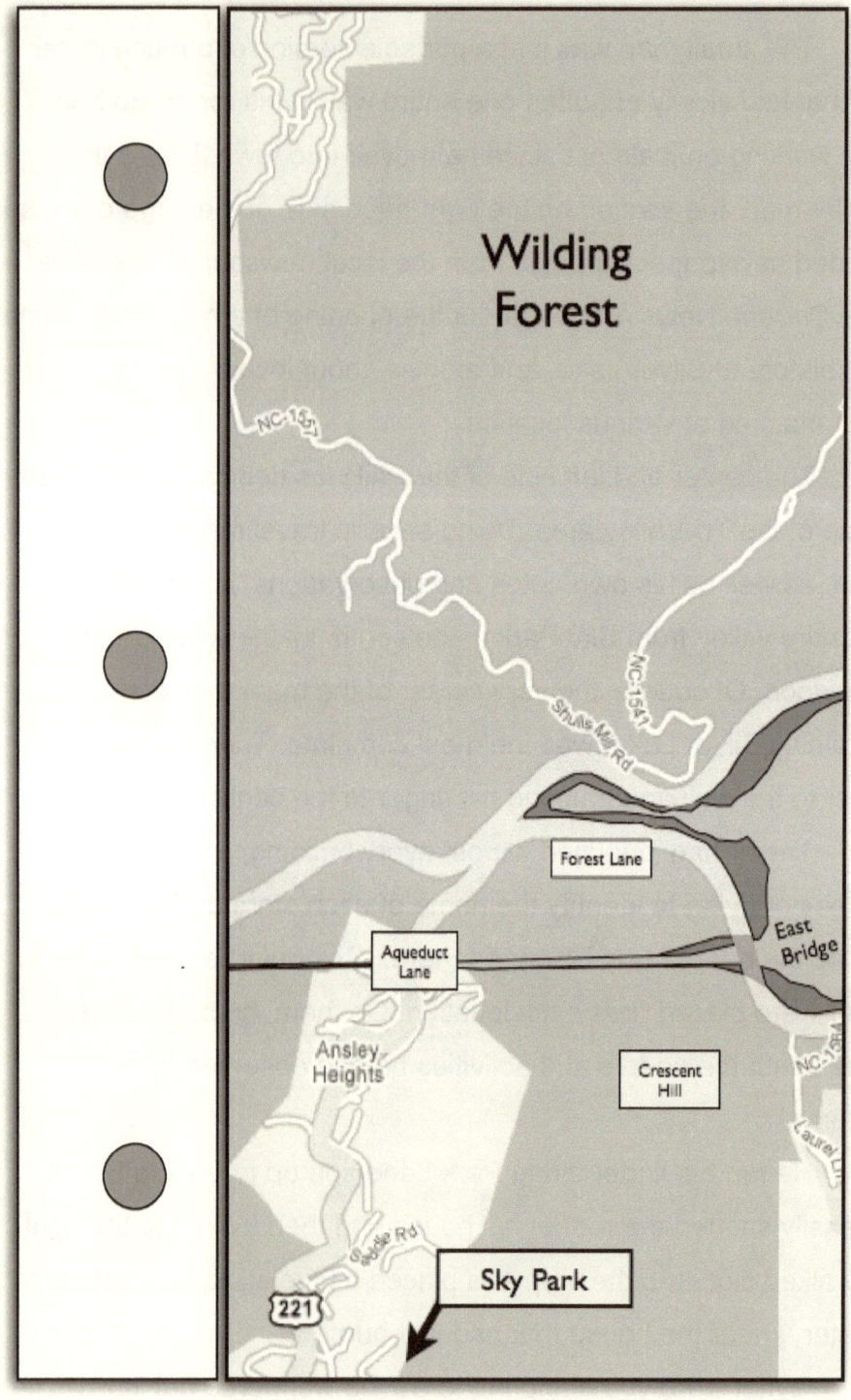

Trevor looked up suddenly as he heard a soft tap on the door. His mother appeared around the corner of the doorway and smiled at him.

"Feel like getting something to eat?"

With all the excitement of the day, he had almost forgotten about dinner. He jumped up and followed her back into the kitchen. After a brief huddle to discuss options, his folks agreed on the Big Valley Diner, one of his favorite places to eat. Trevor could smell fresh baked apple pie even before they left the house.

On his way to the car, he noticed several neighbors standing in their yards. People were still talking about the fire—it wasn't every day a house caught fire in Silver Lake—and several of them paused to wave. Gavin Kip waved back and reached down to hug his son.

He was gone. Trevor had slipped into the car without anyone noticing.

Deep Sleep

Trevor lumbered up the stairs, his stomach full of meatloaf, mashed potatoes and two slices of apple pie. He dropped his clothes and took a hot shower, stumbled back down the hall, and fell into bed.

Alone in the still and darkened room, he played back events from the day. Jay, Sam, Julie...and of course, the fire. When he first arrived, he thought he would never make friends or have fun in such a backwoods town. Today he realized how differently his new friends acted. More... active? Intense?

He turned his face toward the wall and picked at a spot on the rough cedar paneling. He pulled out a long splinter and turned it between his fingers. Back in Brooklyn, hopping from one activity to another was his talent. It seemed like that was all he did again today – hop from one thing to another. His friends had things they were good at, but what could he do? He let his arm drop onto the bed. The answer seemed hidden by a swampy mental sludge.

He yawned and nestled inside the comforter. It had been a long day. He could think about it all again tomorrow. He might even take a walk around the lake...he thought dreamily. The shy kid scared of the outdoors, out for a hike. That would certainly impress his new friends.

Soon, his smile faded and his eyes closed, his chest rising and falling with every sleepy breath. He knew the dreams would come, just like they had every night since he moved here. But for now, for the first time in the entire day, his little corner of the world was dark and quiet.

However, not everyone, or every thing, slept at night. Had Trevor known about one particular individual awake on this particular night, he might not have ever slept again.

"Stasys Never Sleeps"

The motto had been etched into the stone above the glass doors. Beyond the hills surrounding Silver Lake and far beyond its lakes and rivers, thousands of lights burned brightly inside a tall dark building as people continued working.

The researchers and scientists of the Stasys Global Corporation worked night and day to make products people could not imagine living without: clothing, food, cars, communication devices, and even some products they could not imagine at all. In this building, these particular workers were paid handsomely to create very unpleasant weapons for one unquestionably unpleasant man: Julian Hartch.

Julian Hartch was not like other people. He knew things other men did not. For instance, he knew the human race was on the brink of tremendous discoveries. Had he not been on Earth, humans might have cured cancer, discovered interspatial travel, or even ended all human suffering.

But Julian Hartch would have none of that. If he did his job very well, every person on Earth would one day end up living in Stasys buildings, eating Stasys meals and working in Stasys factories. They would need Julian Hartch to fulfill their every need.

Only he would decide what they ate, where they worked, and what they needed. And, if all went according to plan, the world would soon be his to rule. Until then, he would have to deal with far less important matters, such as trying to comprehend the report now spread across his desk.

"I'm surrounded by incompetent fools," Julian Hartch mumbled, as he thumbed through several pages of a report. Do I have to do everything myself?

Despite the late hour, all of his employees were expected to put in long hours, especially when he wanted results. Especially during report week. He threw the collection of papers boldly marked "HARTCH ONLY. MASTER COPY – NO REPRINTS" onto the massive mahogany desk in front of him. Papers scattered everywhere and slid onto the floor in a jumble.

"Mister Willington!" he bellowed. The veins in his temples were now visibly throbbing, and his flushed skin practically glowed in contrast to his white hair.

The white hair topped a red face, which topped an enormous blob of a body. He had no neck—at least, no neck that anyone could see. One of the largest business suits ever constructed tried to contain Julian Hartch's massive body like some gigantic sausage. He awkwardly navigated his massive frame into the oversized black leather chair located behind the desk.

Julian Hartch's second in command, a skinny, simpering worm of a man cautiously crept into the office as his back was turned. Nigel Willington's face revealed a look of disgust as he observed the man's grotesque posterior sliding into the chair. He spun the large chair around to face his employee. Fortunately, Nigel Willington was able to regain a look of utter subservience and forced charm before Hartch's beady eyes could focus clearly on his face.

"It's about time. Where have you been hiding?"

Nigel Willington's only response was an involuntary twitch in his right eye.

"I want results from you. Not hints and hopes. Not this pile of rubbish . . . "

Hartch gestured to the papers littering one corner of his desk and most of the floor as if they were the rotted remains of his last meal. He flicked the largest pile remaining on the desk. The papers fluttered and joined the rest of the report at Willington's feet. Aside from the small tremble in his hands, he remained perfectly still, frozen to the spot like a rabbit caught in a pair of headlights. Julian Hartch caught his breath and continued.

"I will not dignify this useless collection of trivia by reading another word." he finished with a roar and a thump of his fist upon the desk.

The Slimy Worm

Nigel Willington stood up and waited for a chance to speak. He knew Julian Hartch never wanted workers to defend their failures. He simply wanted them to take their verbal beatings and then deliver more solutions. Willington was frantically searching his mind for a new approach. His team had worked for months to create this report.

Their research had cost millions of dollars and taken an unusual amount of planning and effort. Several teams had breakthroughs using technology they had stolen - or borrowed permanently - from other labs.

However, their primary source of inspiration had been discovered by accident, deep beneath the Sahara Desert. While secretly drilling for oil near Libya, the Stasys Global Energy Group had stumbled upon a large cavern, almost 1,000 feet below the vast desert sands. Although the chamber at first appeared abandoned, his team of researchers had uncovered three small pieces of machinery. Each piece bore a small brass label with the inscription 'Cosmic Enterprises'.

Since the discovery, his team had not been able to determine how such ancient, yet sophisticated equipment had found its way deep inside the Earth, or even how to even operate any of it. Although the equipment looked old, the source of their power, the way in which they operated, and even their primary purpose remained a mystery to his team. The mere fact that they had been able to guess what tasks the machines might perform was seen as a tremendous victory.

And now, his boss had discarded all of their hard work with a flick of his wrist, without even bothering to read the documents. Willington fumed as he tried to think of a way to turn this into something he could use to his advantage. If he was only a little bigger than Hartch, more powerful, he would have strangled him there on the spot. Why, he would have…

"You imbecile! What do you have to say about all this?" Hartch demanded. Nigel Willington shook himself as his inner bravado quickly melted.

"It takes time," he pleaded. "We're investigating…"

"No!" Hartch bellowed, cutting him off.

He placed his thick hands on top of the desk, slowly pushed himself to a standing position, and leaned across the massive desk. Nigel Willington took a step back without realizing it.

"I don't want any more excuses. I want results." Nigel braced himself as the human blimp sucked in more air in order to deliver his list his demands. "I want discoveries that will place us in control of human evolution. I want new breakthroughs and modern weapons – not interesting antiques or some old-fashioned toys you found in the dessert."

Then Nigel Willington's corporate master narrowed his gaze and dropped his voice to a lethal whisper.

"Listen to me carefully, Mister Willington. I do not want yesterday's products. I want weapons and machines beyond human imagination, and I want them by the end of this year." He paused and dragged another breath deep into his massive frame. He raised his voice and pointed an accusing finger at Willington.

"Now get out. And don't let me see you until you come back and hand me something truly extraordinary."

Nigel gladly stepped around the papers and scurried through the office door. Several heads popped back inside cubicles. His confidence quickly returned once he was safely outside the office. Julian Hartch never bothered to speak with employees. Out here, it was Willington who ruled the world of research, planning and production. He noted a few individuals that had been listening to their conversation and made a point to pass by their cubicles on his way back to the lab.

"Smith. Martin." He barked. Two faces stared blankly back at him from behind the short walls.

"You two should have more to do around here than eavesdrop and gossip." Willington did not even bother to slow down as he decided to teach everyone a lesson.

"In fact, you will have plenty of time for idle conversations—from the comfort of your own homes. You're fired."

Willington pulled a sleek silver device from his coat pocket. The ViewComm allowed him to see, speak, and hear anyone working for the firm. It also allowed him to manage, or alter, their daily activity. It was the latest digital technology. At least it was the latest - today. He was certain his scientists would update the ViewComm with a newer version, perhaps one day using the technology they had "borrowed" from Cosmic Enterprises. He would use this device for now, and then throw it away when a better model was invented.

He easily selected the profiles for the two men. With two quick taps he made certain security would be up within minutes to help them move out.

Dark Matters Indeed

Alone in his office, Julian Hartch was well aware that Willington would take out his anger on the others. It was what kept everything in working order. A little fear keeps workers focused, he thought contentedly, the same way he used fear on Willington.

He dropped back into his chair and thought about the recent turn of events. Mister Willington's bumbling research teams. Idiots and thieves. Stasys Global Corporation was behind the curve, and he knew it. If he was not careful, humans would wake up to the fact that Stasys was loosing its edge. Then, maybe they would learn how to control their own destiny. That would lead to disorder and chaos for Stasys. That would not be good for Julian Hartch.

Someone, somewhere, was attempting to change the downward spiral he had so cleverly designed for humanity. But who or what was it? There was no one as powerful as Julian Hartch. He pondered the possibilities.

Ironically, the answers he sought now lay scattered across his office floor. An assistant scurried about on her hands and knees, gathering up the loose papers. He considered the worker with a disdainful eye before motioning for her to leave. With arms full, the employee quickly exited the opulent office and hurried to an inner wall where a small chute directed the bundle to an incinerator deep below the building. Within minutes, the original report and all of its secrets were reduced to a small pile of ash.

Julian Hartch slowly rubbed his chin as he thought. Looking at his fingers, he realized a large piece of skin had come off in his hand. He swiveled the chair and took a mirror from the top draw of the desk. Holding it up to his face, he could clearly see a black spot below his lip. It revealed a swirling black surface, as if his face masked a hole into space. He examined the piece of artificial skin in his hand as he opened a desk drawer. He removed a new piece of skin from a dispenser and frowned as he carefully pressed it into place.

He would have to visit the rejuvenation tanks again, very soon. He could not risk exposing his true identity. Besides, the others needed more time. Stasys would not reveal its plans for the Universe until all the pieces were firmly in place. He dropped the lump of old skin into a round cylinder and watched as it disintegrated in a flash of white smoke.

Yesterday's Dream

Low gray clouds swirled in the inky black sky above Trevor's head. Lighting flashed and thunder roared in his ears.

He tightened his grip on the leash, but Moke continued to pull him toward something he could not see. The wind was blowing so hard he thought it would surely lift him off the ground and toss him in the air like a kite. Lightning flashed again. Moke strained even harder against the leash. He looked down at Jay, who was working on the ground, near his feet.

"I can't hold her back much longer." Trevor shouted.

"Almost finished" Jay shouted back.

His face wore a look of desperate concentration and his braided hair whipped around his face like angry cobras. Jay returned his focus to his lap. He was struggling with a wrench as he tried to tighten a bolt sticking out of a flat piece of metal.

The sky flashed once more with jagged streaks of lightning.

This time the very air crackled with electricity as the ground shook from the thunder. Trevor looked off in the distance where Moke was pointed. He almost imagined he could see someone standing at the top of the bluff, but it was too dark to be certain. He focused on the spot and waited for the next round of lightning.

Pop. Pop. Pop. Lightning bolts strobed across the sky.

Trevor stared at the top of the bluff and saw the outline of a person. It was Sam. She was holding what looked like a branch or stick, and was waving it in front of her. Why is she doing that? Trevor thought, as a new round of lightning illuminated the scene in front of him.

"Oh my G—" He froze in mid-sentence.

Sam wasn't swinging a branch. She was holding a sword. And she was using it to fight off some kind of wolf. From a torso of matted hair and bony legs, two fearsome heads sat atop its mangy neck. The bloody mouths each snapped at her with razor sharp fangs. He could hear her calling for help as she fought valiantly against the horribly mutated beast.

"Sam." Trevor yelled.

Moke pulled against the leash and broke free as the cord snapped in two. She sprinted up the bluff directly toward Sam.

"Moke, no!" Trevor commanded his dog. The beast would surely kill her. It wasn't even a fair match. "Moke, come back."

Trevor was frozen with fear. He couldn't move his feet. He looked down at his shoes, and realized his feet were literally frozen to the ground. The forward motion of trying to walk caused him to trip instead. Trevor collapsed in a twist, landing on the ground next to Jay.

"Jay, please." he shouted to his friend.

Jay turned the wrench once more and then shouted in triumph. He stood, and pulled something up with him. It was Julie, or at least a life-sized doll of Julie. She was dressed in a bright pink dress with ruffles and bows, and her faced was painted white, with cherry-red spots for cheeks and lips. She, or it, was holding a large yellow birthday cake with both hands. Small icing-flowers covered the sides and top of the cake.

"Awesome." Jay proudly announced, pointing to the Julie-doll.

"You see," he yelled over the wind, "you wind the cake up here," he was pointing to a small hole in the side, "and the people come out here… and then everything is groovy again."

Groovy? Trevor stared at the robot and its maker in disbelief.

He didn't have time to waste. He turned and pointed to Sam and the wolf-beast. Moke was about to join them in battle at the top of the bluff. Jay simply had to understand. They didn't have time to bother with a cake. Then the Julie-doll began to speak as the flower blossoms snapped open and closed like deadly little mouths.

"Hey, y'all, " it shrieked in a very un-doll-like way. "I've baked us a secret!"

"Jay…" The sound of Trevor's voice was cut short by a shrill whistle. It started softly in the distance but quickly grew louder and more demanding. Jay and Trevor both cringed and covered their ears. The Julie doll simply tilted its head and frowned.

The pain was excruciating.

As they collapsed to their knees, a flash of lighting revealed Sam also covering her ears. Then Trevor realized that Jay was now lying motionless on the ground beside him.

"Do something!" Trevor screamed, as he struggled to his feet and turned to the bluff. Sam was gone, but Moke had just reached the top of the bluff. The wolf heads were frozen, mouths wide open

– were they the source of that noise? Trevor watched helplessly as Moke leapt at the wolf and... disappeared into the storm.

But now something demanded his attention: the ground around him was beginning to melt. The skin on the Julie doll started to wiggle, then quiver, and finally slide from its metallic bones. Only a brass globe with two blue eyes remained perched on top of a brass skeleton. As the whistle grew louder, the wolf's two heads began to peel away, revealing...

Trevor lost his balance as another rolling pass of thunder tossed and shook the ground. Now he was melting as well. As he fell back, he caught a small glimpse of a human face beneath the wolf's mottled fur. He was certain he recognized the face. He tried to get a better look, but couldn't. He was slipping backward, becoming part of the ground around him as it melted and drifted away. Rain poured around him. Small streams of water tugged at his feet as he slid into a canyon of mud. Now even his face was wet...

Trevor woke up as he hit the bedroom floor. Bed sheets were wrapped around his legs and had fallen on top of him in a heap. He was staring upside-down at giant red tongue. Moke was licking his face as if to say "Good morning, silly boy. It's about time you got up and took me outside."

That explained the rain. But his feet were muddy and he could still hear a shrill whistle.

Role Call

Trevor pushed aside clothes, stacks of books and old maps to find the source of the noise.

It was coming from the top of his dresser. His phone was chirping in the high-pitched siren of the dog whistle. He understood why Moke was so eagerly trying to wake him up. He tried to sit up as he reached up for the phone on the table next to his bed. He pushed the "send" button and collapsed back onto the pile of sheets.

"Hello?"

"Weeeeeeeeeeeeeee—" The pain shot through his head, another brain-piercing whistle.

Trevor jerked the phone away from his head as fast as he could, then tentatively moved it toward his ear again.

"Earth to Moon Child?"

"Julie," Trevor yawned, and closed his eyes. "What time is it?" He heard Julie laughing.

"Well that answers the question of whether or not you're awake," she said, as if she'd been instructed to find out on behalf of a Silver Lake sleep committee.

"Okay. Good night," he mumbled, dropping the phone on his chest without hanging up.

"Oh, no you don't. Not yet. You need to hear the latest news." Trevor could tell by her voice she was excited.

He rallied what little energy remained and focused it on his phone. This latest dream had wiped him out, just like all the others.

"Sorry, Kitch Witch. It's just…" How could he explain the weird dream? Or the mud on his feet? He decided not to share that just yet. "I had a long day yesterday and it's taking me a while to wake up." Yawning loudly, he sucked in fresh air, as if to underscore his point.

Moke placed her head on his stomach, taking advantage of the fact that he was on the floor with her long enough to beg for a belly rub.

"You're forgiven," Julie said. "By the way, I heard all about the fire. Congratulations on a job well done." she offered.

"Well thanks," Trevor replied shyly, hoping to change the subject. "By the way, I want you to meet my friend Jay sometime. I think the two of you'd have fun together—he's a good listener."

"Are you saying I talk too much? Wait, don't answer that."

Trevor clamped his lips together so he wouldn't say anything he'd regret later.

"Okay. So down to business." Julie was getting to the point of her early morning wakeup call. "Here's a quiz. What up-and-coming chef that you know" she began, "has been cooking since she was knee-high to a grasshopper and loves to make amazing desserts for surprise parties?"

"You." That was an easy question.

"And what talented young person might one day become a famous chef for a world-class restaurant?"

"You?" That one surprised him.

"Okay, you're two for two. And last, what fantabulously charming junior pastry chef is going to be featured on Channel 9 during *Good Morning Tri-Valley*?" Her voice was so full of excitement it forced him to smile.

"Julie, that's awesome." Trevor didn't have to see her face to know she was beaming. The young superstar chef sighed contentedly into the phone.

"When did this happen?" he asked.

Julie answered his question, at great length. "Well, it seems the people in charge of planning the big party mentioned my dessert to Chef Pauline Montreaux, who owns Café Patisserie, and Chef Pauline mentioned it to the owners of the Big Valley Diner, you know, the one on Maple Street, and they mentioned it to the mystery food critic, who isn't much of a mystery anyway, and he mentioned it to the producers of the local morning show, and they talked to the owner of the station and he said 'yes'."

Trevor could barely follow the long list of connections. Julie paused, very briefly, and took a deep breath before continuing. "So, I'm going to be a great big Tri-Valley megastar and I want you to be my assistant." she finished triumphantly.

"Me?" Trevor was stunned. "Julie, what the heck do I know about cooking?" It was like asking one of her imaginary vampires to guard the blood bank—just a bad idea.

But Julie remained firm. "Look, you already know what to do, and we've worked together on other projects. It'll be easy. Don't worry. Just listen, and follow my lead."

"Well . . . "

Julie took that as a yes.

"Trevor Kip, you rock. They are going to start taping at 10:00. I'll have to get all of the food ready, and then I will need a little help setting everything up. Can you meet me at the Community Center at 8:30 tomorrow morning?"

"Us? Meet? At 8:30? In the morning?"

"Great. I'll get started on my recipes right now. See you later," Julie concluded cheerfully, leaving Trevor listening to a silent phone.

Trevor sat up on the edge of his bed and looked into the mirror. Of course he would help her, but he would be the sleepiest kitchen assistant a TV audience had ever seen. He had to get a haircut soon or he'd start to look like Jay in that windstorm. He started thinking about his dream again. As if summoned by his thoughts, Moke walked over and nuzzled his arm and he gently rubbed her head.

For some reason, he felt drawn to the woods. Between the fire and another crazy dream he wasn't sure of what they might run into on the other side. He only knew he needed to find out.

Trevor stood up and stretched, and Moke jumped up on the bed and curled on top, her brown eyes following her master's back as he shuffled down the hall to begin another busy morning.

The Collector

Small circles of light broke through the leafy canopy and flickered across the alley's bricks. Nature dabbed points of color here and there, while painting the rest of her canvas in shades of gray. A gentle breeze turned leaves and gave flight to scraps of paper, while most of the town remained still.

Old buildings and garages lined the alley. A large maple tree had taken advantage of an empty space to spread its limbs over the years. Shadows from its branches enveloped the narrow lane, as if to mark its territory. No further. This area is mine.

The sole recent addition to the alley was a white pickup truck parked near the middle. The lone figure of a dark man soon appeared beside it. Crouching, poking and peeking, he slowly made his way through a maze of cans, boxes, and discarded kitchen equipment. No one noticed as he picked through the alleys of Silver Lake.

A random ray of light caught the man's face, illuminating a pair of kind brown eyes and a soft, lined face. The man wore a red plaid shirt with thin blue and green stripes, although the shirt's colors had also faded with time. Years of sunlight, sweat and washing had reduced it to a whisper of its original brilliance. He was also wearing a pair of blue overalls and a battered straw hat.

Henry Fox, the man known throughout Silver Lake as "Hank the Handy Man", now surveyed the alley behind Main Street.

He looked behind the nearest dumpster and spied an old blender. He walked over and picked it up, turned it around in his hands, and immediately thought of someone who could use it. Yes sir, the old blender would work quite nicely for her. After he finished poking around the alley, he would head over to the café, clean up the old blender, and offer it to the Chef Pauline.

Pauline Montreaux was one of the few people in the town who knew him. There were others, like Coach McCorkle, but he kept those secrets tucked inside his head, safely under his straw hat. Hank chuckled quietly, wondering how most people would have reacted if they had known their local handy man - the owner of Hank's Handy Hideaway - had once been an important scientist.

Hank chuckled to himself as he dropped the blender into the shopping cart. He wheeled the cart to the back of the old pickup truck and pulled a set of keys out of his pocket. Selecting a slender silver key, he unlocked the camper top fastened onto the bed of the truck.

"If only people realized what they were throwing out."

He shook his head. Everything has two lives, he thought, even this old junk. He reached into the shopping cart and transferred its contents to the back of the truck. This morning alone he had found two blankets, $9 worth of aluminum cans, a disc player, a TV, and of course, the blender. He set the blender on the ground next to his feet. He reached in and pulled a vinyl tarp across the contents.

He locked the camper top and wiped his hands on his overalls. Then he picked up the blender and cleaned it off with his shirt. He looked at it admiringly. He knew Pauline would enjoy his humble gift. "You got a dent or two, but there's more life in you yet. Heck, you might even make me a milkshake one day."

Hank had just turned around to leave when a black tank of a car barreled down the alley. The vehicle raced down the narrow lane, almost hitting him. Hank jumped back against the truck before it did, and stared at the two men sitting in front. The person on the passenger side leaned out the open window as the car sped by.

Move it, old man!" he yelled. Hank heard laughter from inside the automobile.

How could they be so reckless and mean? They might have hit him if he had taken one step forward. Hank felt anger rise up inside. He was about to yell something back, when he sensed a familiar presence. *They're here, Hank,* a familiar voice warned inside his head. *They are gathering now. You've got to hurry.*

Hank instinctively touched a gold pendant hanging around his neck and felt a sudden awareness surge inside him. He didn't have much time left. He checked to make sure he had his keys, gripped the blender, and started walking quickly toward Main Street.

New Orders

At the exact same moment in New York, Nigel Willington stepped out of a pair of gleaming office doors and onto a busy street, somewhat cleaner than the alley, but less colorful, moving quickly around his chauffer and into the waiting limousine.

The vehicle began moving rapidly toward the airport as soon as he motioned to the driver. Secure in his soft leather seat, Willington opened a silver briefcase and took out his ViewComm, flipping it open. The small screen offered him a number of options. He then withdrew what looked like a sheet of paper from his briefcase.

The DataSheet was made to be read by one specific person. When removed from its protective sleeve, the contents became visible to the individual with a particular set of DNA. Once that person released the sheet, it would evaporate in a small cloud of dust.

Nigel studied the sheet created specifically for him and retrieved from it the list of names he needed.

He spoke to his ViewComm. "Agents." The screen flickered to life with a very long list of names.

"Narrow Search," he said. "Collins, Sloan, Ferrill, Greer, Morgen, Slate . . . " He read aloud the names of the agents closest to the target – Silver Lake.

Then he tossed the DataSheet out of the car window. A small puff of white smoke trailed behind the long, black vehicle. The ViewComm now listed the names he had chosen, with short profiles and photos of each person.

"Voice Message," he said. Then, "Priority One orders. You are to proceed directly to the target location and coordinate your activity with our advance scouts. Use of disruptors is permissible only as needed to capture the subjects they have identified – four children. They are needed for their unique talent and expertise; therefore casualties will not be tolerated. Any agents injuring one of these children will be..." he paused briefly to select the most appropriate word, "terminated."

Willington selected and attached a digital file that included maps of the target location, background data on each child, agent assignments, required equipment and enough information to insure compliance with mission objectives. He also sent along the names of the scouts who were already on location.

He waited until the ViewComm display had refreshed, and then he said, "Transmit," and closed the device. Soon, his agents would receive his orders on their own ViewComms. Although they had been staged close to the target, he had withheld their final destination until now. He realized with some pride that even though they would have to scramble in order to converge on the location, the operation would be underway in less than two hours.

Nigel Willington studied the passing landscape. After a quick flight, he would be deep inside the European operations center for Stasys Global. It was the best place for him to coordinate field activities. It was also the best place in the world for him to work without constant criticism from Hartch. He knew his agents would succeed—they had to. If they failed, and he flinched at the thought, then someone would need to provide a backup plan. Or a secret place to permanently hide from Hartch.

Nigel's right eye twitched at the thought. He wasn't in the mood to deal with Julian Hartch any more than necessary.

The Explorer

Trevor stood at the back door to his house and sighed. He absentmindedly clipped a leash onto Moke's collar. Last night's dream really had him rattled.

He'd been trying all through breakfast to shake a bad feeling. It was as if a cold hand had wrapped its fingers around his imagination. He had never had dreams as real or urgent as these. He shook his head to clear it, double-checking Moke's leash to make sure he had actually fastened it.

Secretly, he hoped one of his friends would join him on his exploration. His brief journey yesterday through the wild woods and unpaved roads had not ended on a good note. He had been raised in the city. Born of concrete and asphalt. Throw him into the middle of a busy street, with all of its crazy drivers, fast-talking crowds and subway lines and he was on his home turf. Need to find the nearest deli? No problem. Want to get to the museum? Trevor knew all the turns and stops. Out here, Trevor still found himself getting nervous if too many birds gathered in the trees.

Life was different in Silver Lake. Until now, he and Moke had stuck to walks around Town Park, but he was determined to explore the forest on the other side of the lake. What's scary about a rocky coastline, ice-cold water and vast wilderness, he asked himself. The city side of his mind began to answer, but he knew it was silly to feel nervous about a simple walk around a perfectly harmless lake.

Still, he peered tentatively out the back window to the foreboding woods that surrounded his house. "Just use your head and you'll be fine," his practical side reassured him. His mind was made up.

He checked Moke's lead again and stared into her chocolate brown face. At least he had his dog to protect him from any wild creatures. The most loving animal on the planet stared back at him. Trevor changed his mind. Who was he fooling? She would probably try to lick a bear. Regardless, it would make him feel more secure to hike with his dog than no one at all.

Suddenly, a shrill whistle chirped from somewhere on top of the kitchen table. Trevor rushed over, pushed aside some papers, and snatched his phone.

"Trev, I got your text message. What's up?" It was Jay.

"Not much," Trevor said. "Umm, I was just wondering. How about a walk with Moke and me to the far side of the lake and back?"

Moke heard both her name and the word "walk" in the same sentence. Her ears folded up in the middle and her head cocked to the side. She began to follow his lips for any other important words that might tumble out, such as ball, squirrel, or cat.

Jay laughed. "For sure, but I have this teeny tiny science project to finish. You know, something about a Fortress of the Floating Warrior . . ."

"I thought you submitted the forms yesterday?" Trevor offered sadly, like a plea for help. From what he remembered, the only requirements were an entry form, a description of the design and some illustrations. Jay had sketched out his ideas yesterday. A scale model was optional. "You already sent in the sketches, didn't you?" Trevor heard his own voice and realized he sounded desperate.

"Uh-huh. But I want to nail this competition and I'll get bonus points if I build a model. So I asked my dad if he could help me build one."

"You're kidding me? Your dad can build a model of the building... from your sketches?" The image he had seen looked impossibly complex. Trevor was more than a little curious.

"It's crazy. But my dad says he has some old metal alloy poles that I can use for the frame, and a kind of plexiglass sheets I can use for the sides. I guess he has them stored in his warehouse."

"Wow. That's great, Jay," Unbelievable, Trevor thought, almost too good to be true. He wanted to ask Jay how his father could build something like that. His dad could barely manage to get a piece of plywood into the tree. He was about to open his mouth when he heard someone calling his name from outside.

"Hey-o!" a girl's voice announced.

Moke barked twice and raced for the back door, her nails clicking on the wood floor. She wagged her tail as Trevor walked over and scanned the yard. There was no one in the yard or the woods as far as he could see.

"Uhh…. Jay, I think there's someone in my backyard. I'll call you when I get back from the lake." He could tell Jay was already lost in thought, as he heard only a mumbled "uh-huh" before ending the call.

Trevor walked to where Moke was barking at the unseen visitor. He grabbed the leash, pulled her back and opened the door. He slipped outside and closed the door behind him, keeping Moke safely inside. Moke barked once more in protest, but to Trevor's surprise, the area behind the house was completely empty.

"Hello?" he called doubtfully into the dark woods.

Almost immediately, a chestnut-brown horse trotted out of the trees and into the sunny clearing, with Sam sitting high in the saddle, looking every bit the cowgirl in her boots and jeans.

"There you are." Sam smiled down at him. "I thought maybe you were still in bed," she added, laughing. "Major and I went for a quick run. I'm taking him back to the stable for a good bath and a brushing."

She patted her horse, and invited Trevor to pet him too. Moke stared through the door as Trevor inched cautiously up to the friendly brown animal and tentatively stroked its side. He had never been this close to a horse. Moke growled a low warning. Trevor petted the horse timidly at first, and then more confidently as the Major ignored him and focused on the grass near his feet.

"See? He's friendly." She confirmed. "So what are you up to?"

"I was just getting ready to take Moke for a walk around the lake. You want to come with us?"

"Sure, I'd love to. The horse trails go all the way around the shore. But…" Trevor's hopes sank. "After I get Major back to the stables I have to give a fishing demonstration at my Dad's new store. But maybe after that, I could grab a rental kayak and meet you on the other side. How about that?"

Trevor considered her offer. At least she was trying to find way to make it work... Wait a minute.

"New store? Your Dad owns Adventures-To-Go?"

Everyone in Silver Lake knew about the new store. It was the first one to be built in more than thirty years. Every kid in school had found more than one excuse to walk by and watch as the huge displays were installed on the store's exterior. Sam laughed.

"Not really. I wish. He's just the manager."

Trevor was surprised she had never mentioned her father's position at the store. It was an interesting turn of events.

"Just the manager." Trevor blurted out. "That's the next best thing to owning it. And, you're my new best friend. Well, you were always one of my new best friends, but now you're way up there." Trevor was thrilled to hear this news. Even he was eager to explore inside. All those fancy displays and aisles of outdoor technology… and maps! It was the closest thing to a big city store in the valley.

"Thanks." Sam cried with feigned injury. "At least now I know we'll only be friends as long as I have a store discount."

"Hmm, maybe." Trevor scratched one ear and played along.

Sam rolled her eyes. Trevor pointed back to the house where his dog was now staring at them through the back window.

"How will you catch up with me and Moke?"

Sam looked at her watch as she calculated the time each of her projects would require. "After I finish up the class, grab the kayak, wheel it to the lake, meet you on the other side... I could probably make it around noon. Is that okay?"

"I'll be on the other side by then," Trevor guessed. He had never been to the other side of the lake. In truth, he had never hiked anywhere, much less through a forest. What if it took longer? "Maybe you should call me when you get ready. We could meet somewhere near that old house..."

Trevor was referring to the large house that sat partially hidden, but still visible on the far side of the lake, nestled amongst the ancient trees of the Wilding Forest. Anyone standing at the edge of Town Park, below the statue, could easily see it with sharp eyes or a pair of binoculars. From what he had seen, the house seemed enormous: a stone monstrosity with two towers, more windows than he could count, and a broad porch that encircled the entire building. Everyone in town knew about it, but evidently no one ever went there. Apparently, he had also said the magic word.

"Awesome idea, Kipster! I've wanted to check it out since we moved here. Don't you wonder what such a big house is doing all by itself in the middle of the woods?" She leaned down from her saddle and whispered, "Everyone in town says it's haunted..."

Sam did not sound the least bit scared. But Trevor would be out in the woods by himself today, and he sincerely hoped none of the stories were true. "I'm sure there's nothing to it. It's probably just an oversized shed with rats in the walls and spiders waiting to crawl into your hair."

Sam shivered. "I hate spiders. I'd better bring a blowtorch," she added matter-of-factly. Trevor was certain Sam could teach a course in that as well.

"Okay, let's meet down by the shore in front of the old house, around noon." he offered. Sam calculated her schedule, adding the hours inside her head, before smiling back down at him.

"You got it." She made a loud clicking sound with her tongue, and Major reluctantly picked up his head from the delicious field of spring grasses.

Trevor watched them disappear over the hill and into the woods, then returned to the back door to find a very frustrated friend. He grabbed his backpack, shoving an apple, banana, and some water inside. As soon as he opened the door, Moke sprang into the yard, following the scent of the visitors. She circled the place where Major had been grazing. Trevor grabbed her leash before she could wander any further up the trail. He looked down at his loyal hiking partner.

"Okay Moke . . . " Trevor paused.

It was a game they often played together. Trevor would start a sentence and Moke would jump as soon as she could finish it.

"Do." He spoke slowly. "You. " Moke barked in response. She was onto his game.

"Want . . . To . . . Go..." He didn't get any further. She was ready for their walk, and now. Moke pulled on the leash, tugging him towards the woods and the lake beyond. Trevor laughed at his dog and then frowned as he peered up the hill.

This is going to be a great adventure, his brave internal voice announced, trying to convince the doubter inside. Forget the city. Don't be a wimp. Besides... Trevor paused at the edge of the yard, hitched the backpack up on his shoulder, and finished his last thought with a smile.

"Hey Moke, I wonder what we'll see out there?"

His dog barked joyfully in response and jumped forward as he stepped one foot into the pine straw and shadows that lay beyond his back yard.

Keeping it Real

Sam turned the corner as she walked from Wonderland Road onto Main Street. Major had been washed, fed, and was now resting comfortably in his stall.

She surveyed the downtown thoroughfare, with its quirky array of shops. Trevor had told her once how old-fashioned everything seemed, but she got a kick out it. Hargrove's Hardbacks – the only bookshop she had ever seen with ladders running up and down and along the walls of all three floors. Belle's Buttercups – a candy store full of tempting sweets and calories that Sam tried hard to avoid. Tefton's Drug Emporium – a pharmacy complete with enormous bubbling bottles of colored liquids and an old-fashioned soda fountain. Jolly Jules Gentlemen's Clothing, Hometown Hardware & Machinery, Sew Sweet Ladies Finery, Café Patisserie – many more than she could see from the corner - all were all bustling with tourists and local residents.

The tourists were busy buying trinkets, t-shirts and ice cream cones in flavors with names like Bearry Bonanza and Moose Poop Brownie. The locals were trying hard to avoid the tourists. Sam laughed and continued walking. The entire scene seemed so odd, and yet, somehow familiar and comfortable like an old pair of mittens. Maybe, she thought playfully, a big scoop of Moose Poop could help change Trevor's mind.

Sam walked a few steps further and then paused in front of Pinnacle Properties, the local realtor's office. She looked at the pictures of various houses posted on the window and realized with a jolt that Jansen's Farm was for sale. Where would she put Major if the farm was sold? Maybe someone nice would buy it and keep the stables. She made a wish and crossed her fingers for luck.

She took one of the flyers from a display rack and turned around, watching the tourists and viewing her new hometown with a sense of pride. True, the buildings had not changed in years and years. Yes, the small shops didn't sell the latest toys or gadgets. Even the brick streets and the gas lamps that lined them seemed to be from another time or place. But it wasn't as if *nothing* had changed. Most of the people here also owned cell phones, used microwave ovens and drove electric cars. The difference was Silver Lake had stayed the same while the people came and went, like clouds drifting over the hills.

Sam resumed walking with a slight hop. She walked faster as her thoughts flipped between catching up with Trevor to her Dad's new store to wondering if the stables would be around tomorrow, when she turned the corner and bumped headfirst into someone else. She immediately recognized Hank the Handyman. He looked surprised, as if she had startled him from a daydream. An old blender was gripped firmly between his hands.

"Sorry, Hank" she told him. "I wasn't watching where I was going."

Hank stopped, too, and looked at her. "Well now young lady, I sure am sorry too." He tipped his hat to her and Sam giggled. "How I could miss seeing a pretty girl like you is beyond me." He usually wanted to talk for hours. However, today he was in a hurry. He smiled, tipped the straw hat again, and turned to leave. "You have a nice day now, okay Sam?"

He waved goodbye as he resumed walking in the opposite direction along Main Street. Sam thought about their encounter. She rarely giggled… She wondered why she had acted so shy. It was probably the gift. She remembered the week after they moved here and she found an old canoe paddle leaning against their hotel room door.

A card taped to the paddle read, "Welcome to Silver Lake. There's always something to do, and one day you might need this paddle to explore our lake. In the meantime, how about playing some soccer? Go see Coach McCorkle—he's already waiting for you." It was signed, "Hank."

Back then, Sam couldn't figure out why someone would leave her an old paddle. Now, his gesture made sense. So what if it was odd for a stranger to leave a welcome gift? Hank was just like the old town – nice, relaxed, and just a little old-fashioned. Besides, now she also knew Hank somewhat better. He was the Handyman - always fixing things up and giving them away. Sam smiled at the memory and kept walking. She'd probably use the paddle today.

In a few more steps, her father's new store appeared at the bottom of the street.

Go Fish

"Grand Opening!" A large banner proclaimed across one side.

Adventures To Go looked like an oversized log cabin built for some giant woodsman.

A diorama attached to the front of the store extended up and over the top of the roof. It depicted a smiling man in a kayak, a bear on its hind legs taking a swipe at some trout that were jumping out of the water, another person casting his line into the water, and clusters of rocks and trees surrounding them all. The entire image was designed to set the mood for outdoor adventures, or at least for buying the adventure supplies available inside.

Smaller banners strung around the parking lot announced "Grand Opening" and "Open Today."

The parking lot was filling up quickly as a steady stream of visitors headed to the entrance. Employees stationed at the front door handed out maps and gave directions to activities and refreshments. Approaching the main entrance, Sam spied her father standing just below the left foot of the giant bear in the diorama, shaking hands with his new customers.

"Dad." Sam shouted as she squeezed though the people standing next to him. "What a crowd." Sam had never seen her father as happy as he was today.

"Sam. How are you doing, sport? You ready to teach these city slickers how to bag a trout?"

Mike Hudson gestured with his thumb to the interior of the store and all the people milling about.

Sam followed the direction of his thumb and looked into the store behind him. She had seen it while it was under construction. But now, every light was on, the merchandise was all in, and the displays were up and running. It was like a magical candy land for athletes and adventurers.

"Wow. It's incredible, Dad." Her father nodded in agreement.

"How about I give you a quick tour? Then I'll show you where you can give your demonstration." Sam followed her Dad as he began walking to the back of the store.

Giant murals identified the items that could be found within each section of the store. Sam and her Dad began in the running and hiking section identified by a giant hiker pointing into the distance while consulting an oversized map. They moved from there to hunting, where a mechanical hunter stood to peek through a blind and then crouched down to hide. The replica of log cabin signified the indoor shooting and archery range.

They continued walking until her father stopped in the very middle of the store. Beside them was a large rectangular hill made of artificial rocks and trees. Four enormous ponds surrounded the entire manmade mountain, each containing a different type of environment and species of live fish. A gigantic waterfall rushed into the center pond. All of the ponds were engineered so customers could see the fish at eye level. Her father led her to the pond on the north side of the store and pointed to a flat spot on the rocks at the water's edge.

"That is where you can give your demonstration." He said. He pointed out the trout swimming inside. Not only would people be able to watch her cast, she would be on the biggest natural stage she had ever seen.

"Now remember, just have fun, and don't worry about the technical details. There are plenty of salespeople nearby to give out advice on any of the equipment."

He gave her a pat on the back and a quick thumbs-up for luck.

"I will," she promised, as her father disappeared in the crowd.

She noticed people looking at their watches and beginning to gather around the aquarium. Sam went over to the counter where her father had carefully placed her gear for the demonstration. She knew her casting basics and had been practicing her presentation at home. Now all she needed was a stage. Sam paused to look around the store as she climbed the hidden stairs up to the platform. She estimated the crowd at around 200 people, and it was still early in the morning.

Then Sam noticed two men standing in the gun section. Compared to the other shoppers, they looked out of place. They wore pressed pants and dark polo shirts. They glanced around nervously without speaking as they eyed the store. Sam sighed. Some people just don't know how to relax, she thought.

She set down her fishing equipment and focused on the small audience that had gathered by the tank of fish. A few people had already purchased fishing gear and were holding it in their hands.

"Good Morning," she said to the group.

One man mumbled "hello" in return. A couple wondered if the young girl in front of them was joking or if she was really their instructor. Sam playfully scowled at them and cranked up her wake up call about 10 decibels.

"Good Morning everyone." Sam's voice grabbed their attention.

"Good Morning." They all shouted back at her.

"That's better." Sam beamed. "Isn't this store absolutely amazing?" Everyone nodded. A few people even smiled up at her.

"Well, my name is Sam, and today I'm going to teach you the basics of fly fishing."

Help Wanted

Julie was a mess, and her kitchen looked even worse.

Her hair was a tangle of flour and loose ends, and her apron was covered in about fourteen different sauces. She put her hands in her thick curly hair, adding sausage bits to the flour, oil and various spices that were already in there.

She had been trying different recipes all morning, so she could find the right one to use for her demonstration on television. She wasn't sure if she should make duck a l'orange, or game hens with sage stuffing, or possibly a dessert like chocolate soufflé, or an apricot brandy roll . . .

If her brain had been an oven, it would have been set to 'broil.' Her mind was a bubbling stew of fear, uncertainty, and doubt. Julie finally called her friend Pauline to see if she could offer any advice.

Pauline had immediately agreed to help.

Julie now dashed about the kitchen trying to gather up all the tools she might need. She knew any chef worth her weight in salt not only bought the tools, but also maintained and cared for them as well.

She went through the list of possible tools in her head.

She might have to crush some herbs to make a sauce. A mortar and pestle were still the best way to release their true flavor. She placed them in her chef's kit. Perhaps she would need to roll the apricot into a log… She grabbed a sheet of cheesecloth and placed it in as well. The recipe for duck required her to wrap them in herbs. She tossed a ball of twine into the box and then looked for a pair of kitchen shears to cut the twine.

For the next ten minutes she opened every drawer and cabinet. As hard as she tried, she could not find them anywhere. "Stupid shears," she said. "Where are you?" She started crawling around on the floor looking deep inside the lower cabinets. Julie's father cautiously stuck his head through the swinging kitchen door.

He watched helplessly from the sidelines, afraid to interrupt his daughter's frenzied search. He sighed and shrugged his shoulders. He had seen her like this before. "Well, now." He looked at his daughter in mock indignation. "My daughter has gone completely nuts. I knew the heat in the kitchen would eventually bake your brains."

Julie pretended not to hear him.

"Baby girl," he looked at his daughter with real concern "is there something I can help you find?"

In fact, he was trying to figure out exactly what Julie was doing. She continued to ignore him and kept her head firmly planted inside a cabinet, poking through all of its contents.

Patrick Meriwether took a tentative step into the kitchen. He leaned over the island counter and stared down at the rear end of his tormented daughter. Julie pulled her head out of the cabinet and looked up at him in protest.

"Daddy, don't just stand there. Help me."

Unknown to her, a couple of rubber bands and a scrap of paper had now become attached to the mess of hair, flour and sugar on top of her head.

"I have to find my poultry shears before I go over to Pauline's."

Julie stood up with her hands on her hips and looked around the disaster that was the kitchen. Her father worked very hard not to laugh and coughed into his hand before speaking.

"Now Julie," he coughed. "Chef Pauline is a good person. I know she will let you use her tools if you need them."

Julie sighed. "I know she would. But I want her to know that I am a professional. I want to be a great chef one day, and great chefs don't do this, this . . . *mess*." she looked at her father hopelessly.

He took a step closer, and picked gently at her hair.

"Little angel" he said softly, "every chef has a day like this, at some time or another. Do you really think she will be mad if you don't drag every spoon and bowl out of our kitchen?"

"No." Julie had to admit.

He pulled a lumpy strand of dough from her head and pretended to examine it.

"Honey, I could pop your hair in the oven right now and make us some biscuits. Are you hungry?" he said in mock seriousness.

Julie looked around the kitchen and laughed at the tangled mess she had made of both her hair and the room.

"It's just me being a dope, Daddy. I don't want to ruin this chance."

Her father opened a cabinet drawer and poked through its contents. He turned back to her, a pair of expensive-looking scissors dangling from his hand, and said, "Um, is this what you are looking for?" He winced. "I forgot to tell you I borrowed 'em a few days ago to cut up an old garden hose."

"They are not scissors, Daddy." Julie swatted her father's arm and retrieved her shears. Then she kissed him softly on the cheek.

"Thank you, Daddy."

Her father turned and walked upstairs. Julie could hear him muttering about farm reports as he retreated inside his office.

The Best Recipe

Julie finished packing and straightened up the kitchen. Then she washed her hair in the downstairs bathroom and put on a fresh uniform. She placed a chef's hat on her head and picked up her bag of kitchen tools and recipes. She gave the clean kitchen a final glance as she dashed out the front door.

Minutes later, she was still thinking about all the possible recipes as she approached Pauline's café. She paused to admire the restaurant from across the street.

Pauline Montreaux had opened Café Patisserie a dozen years ago and it had become a true Silver Lake success. Café Patisserie sat inside one of the historic buildings downtown and occupied two storefronts. Curving gold letters and decorative woodwork wrapped around the brick façade. On the left side was a bakery, with a long glass display case that offered a variety of yummy treats and fresh baked breads. The right side of the store was the café, where a few people now sat, enjoying a quick bite.

Julie crossed the road and was about to reach for the door when it opened in front of her. Hank the Handyman shuffled out. Julie knew Hank from his frequent visits to the Café. Chef Pauline always had some cold lemonade or pastry to share, and Hank would usually leave behind a kitchen tool or some little accessory.

"Well, hello, little chef" he said to her. Then he leaned closer. "What are the two of you going to make today? Or is it a secret?"

Julie played along. She looked at Hank through the tops of her sunglasses. "Hank, it's such a secret my lips won't even tell my brain. That's why I'm hoping Pauline can help me."

Hank burst out laughing and took a step back smiling, as if to thank her for his laughter. He offered a wave goodbye to Pauline inside, and then a nod to Julie. "I'm sure she will Julie. I'm sure she will." He gave Julie a wink and then hurried down the sidewalk toward the alley.

Julie stepped through the open door. Pauline was standing in front of the pastry counter wiping down an old blender.

"Help," Julie said in a small voice. "Please?"

"Oh, non. We'll have none of that sad face in my café, mon petite chef," Pauline answered, her French accent still thick despite many years living in Maine. She held up one finger and wagged it back and forth. She walked from behind the counter and wrapped her arms around Julie's shoulders. A couple of tourists peered into the glass display, eyes wide in anticipation of finding a sweet confection.

"Come. Sit over here." The chef led her to a table, keeping one eye on her guests. "Sit down and tell me all about your cooking catastrophe, hmm?"

Julie recounted in detail her disasters with both the duck and the desserts. She explained how, for her very first television appearance, she wanted to make something intricate and special...

Pauline motioned for her to pause, and then hurried over to slip a few pastries into a small white bag and ring up the sale. Julie watched the couple walk out the door, their hands eagerly searching inside the bag for the pastries. Pauline shut the café door behind them and flipped a sign from Open to Closed. She then slipped back into her chair at the small table.

"Okay, mon cherie" she began, "I will help you find both the answer and the recipe you will use. Do you remember what I have taught you about what people want to eat? Mmm? Three little words, like the Little Pigs, yes?"

Julie laughed out loud. Now she knew the answer. "Easy, quick, and delicious." She counted them off on her fingers. "Is that right?"

"You are wise," Pauline agreed.

"I was trying too hard," Julie said. "Wasn't I?" She couldn't believe all the time she'd wasted, trying to learn recipes this audience would never, ever attempt at home. Pauline nodded. "Tres bien. Now, let us see what we can make that is easy, quick and delicious." She got up and went to her little desk behind the counter, then brought back an old box stuffed full of recipes. Julie and Pauline began to flip through them as they began to search for the easiest, quickest and best recipe for tomorrow's show.

A Logical Connection

Across the street from the cafe, the Community Hall was buzzing with activity as workmen assembled decorations for the big celebration. Coach McCorkle admired their progress as he turned the corner walking onto Main Street. He stopped briefly in front of the Hall before turning toward the Fire and Rescue Department.

The section housing the fire trucks and firefighters had been built many years ago. It was made of old river rock and looked like many of the other old downtown buildings. The massive doors hiding the trucks were arched like doors to a cathedral. Over the years, ivy had crawled up and now covered much of the brick.

To the left, a more modern two-story addition had been added next to the older building. He walked to this side and entered the large wood and glass doors. The modern section had been built almost a hundred years ago. But by Silver Lake standards, it was practically brand new, and only the sports store would be newer.

The coach read several signs indicating offices and their location: Emergency Response, Fire Station, Forensics Lab. An arrow pointing up had been placed next to the sign indicating Fire and Rescue Management. He stepped inside the main entrance and walked up a broad set of metal stairs.

The walls of the second floor were covered with photos of firefighters and plaques and awards from past deeds and competitions. He stopped to take a drink from the fountain next to a vending machine. As he sipped the cool water, his eyes glanced across the headline of a Tri-Valley Tribune. He knelt down to examine the paper inside the vending machine.

The headline read: "Fire Destroys House, Occupant Missing"

He could only read the portion of the newspaper visible through the window of the vending machine. The reporter, Gavin Kip, explained that a woman had been seen leaving in an ambulance, but had not been treated at any of the local hospitals. The cause of the fire was said to be suspicious and under investigation by Chief Pierce.

He walked over to the door and waved to the man sitting behind a large glass window. A buzzing noise followed, and the officer inside motioned for him to enter the door. He pushed on the metal door open and walked over to the officer's desk.

"Hi Coach, she's waiting for you in her office. It's on the right," he said, pointing behind him, "...back there." Then the detective swiveled back around and resumed studying the computer screen on top of his desk.

He turned, and walked along the row of desks to the far end of the room. As he approached, the door opened and the Chief for Fire and Rescue stepped out to greet him.

"I read the newspaper Susan. I think it's time we took action," he stated bluntly.

The Chief glanced around and ushered him urgently into her office. "I'm not sure. I've been tracking recent Stasys activity, but I can't see any clear pattern yet. I still think we need to let the Professor decide on our best course of action."

"Hmm" the coach considered her thoughtfully before responding. "I am not sure he anticipated this turn of events." There was genuine concern in his voice.

Just like the main entrance, Chef Pierce's office walls were filled with photographs, certificates and plaques. There was a letter from the mayor and photos of thankful neighbors and local business owners. Behind the desk hung an especially large black frame that contained both a photo and a handwritten note.

Coach McCorkle glanced at one photo in particular.

The picture showed Chief Pierce standing beside a man and another woman with a little girl. The note was written in blue ink on crisp white paper. The paper had a familiar blue and gold seal of the United States at the top.

It read, "*Susan, Words cannot begin to describe our deepest thanks and gratitude for your heroism and bravery. Your courageous action not only saved our most precious daughter, it saved our family. We are forever in a debt we may never be able to repay. Our door and our hearts will always be open to you.*" and it was signed, Ethan Andrews.

It was a note from the President of the United States.

Chief Pierce went behind her desk and took her seat. She picked up a file with "House Fire" typed neatly on the label. She opened the folder so Coach McCorkle could see documentation and photos of the house. The images had been taken right after the rescue team extinguished the fire. The chief placed a photo on top of the papers.

He nodded. He recognized the face of the Stasys agent. "Stella Irvin" identifying the woman. The chief reviewed her thoughts.

"Here's the mystery I am trying to solve." She pointed to a photo showing the upstairs bedroom. "I'm curious about the exact cause of the fire. Our evidence points to this area, and to some type of explosive. But why would Stasys agents store explosives inside this house?" He closed his eyes briefly and opened them, slowly pulling on his lower lip. "It can only mean one thing – they are getting ready to make a move on us."

Chief Pierce turned in her chair and spun the dial on a small metal vault beside her desk. She opened the door, reached in and pulled out an amulet attached to a gold chain and an old, worn file folder. She put both on her desk. She placed a hand on each side of her jaw, just behind her ears, and pushed. It was a peculiar action, but one that was completely expected Coach McCorkle. The motion was followed by a slight click.

"This is Pierce confirming a visual. Coach McCorkle and I are certain Stasys agents are operating in Silver Lake." She removed her fingers and her jaw clicked again. She paused and glanced at the red-haired athlete. "Now, we wait for further instructions."

The Dreamer

The old silver trailer was swaying back and forth on its wheels as music played inside:

"Cause your brain's in the dirt. And it's all right . . . the kid's alright . . . Some people out there who disagree, They don't want to see . . . things could be better . . ."

It was as if some invisible hand was rocking it like a cradle. However, the kid inside had graduated from pacifiers to power tools many years ago.

The silver trailer had seen better days. What paint it had remaining was either faded or peeling. Thin curtains hung in the windows and plastic daisies were tacked along the windowsills. On top of the aluminum roof a rickety brass antenna struggled to stand at attention with the assistance of two concrete blocks. A cable snaked from the pole along the roof, down the corrugated metal of the trailer, and into a partially open window.

The thick black wire entered a small bedroom where Jay Fox was now dancing with his eyes closed, his fists pumping in the air. A curly black cord attached to oversized headphones ran from his ears to an odd-looking device sitting on his small desk.

A slender wooden box lay open on the desk's surface, its contents a combination of glass tubes, gears and colorful wiring. By any estimation, someone visiting Jay would have guessed it to be a collection of used parts rather than the fifth generation computing device it truly was. He had built his first computer when he was nine years old, quite by accident, just to prove he could.

It all began when a local shopping plaza held a competition for people between the ages of 8 and 80. It was the usual guessing contest, allowing only one hour for participants to turn in their guess. That year, each contestant had to guess the number of beans inside a giant clear container for a chance to win a new computer.

Jay was determined to win. Even though the rules prevented him from actually touching the jar, he wrapped a mental tape measure around it. He held an invisible ruler up to the glass and recorded the size of several beans. Based upon his mental measurements of the jar, the beans, and other conditions, including the thickness of the glass, distortion, and room temperature, Jay finally entered his answer with only 23 seconds to spare. He scribbled a number on the backside of a discarded gum wrapper and handed the wrinkled slip to a very skeptical, and somewhat bored employee.

Upon final tally by all five judges, Jay's guess was only off by a single bean. The astonished panel of local judges re-checked their tally of beans from the jar, bean-by-bean. They re-examined Jay's entry, scrawled on the loose scrap of paper. They interrogated his mother. They checked him for hidden notes and cheat codes.

"Statistically," one judge finally announced, "it is impossible for a boy his age to be so accurate."

"You cheated," another judge claimed.

"You're a moron," Jay countered.

Ultimately, the judges awarded the computer to a runner-up – whose guess was off by a whopping 97 beans – leaving Jay with an empty jar. At exactly that moment, he learned 1) that some people would try to keep him from winning, for no apparent reason and 2) if he wanted something bad enough, he could simply make it himself. And so he did.

He gathered books and theory on human computation. He studied early works that demonstrated how the human mind was the ultimate computer on Earth. Using spare parts from his father's warehouse, Jay fashioned an analog computer that worked on principles of thought process and chaos theory. Ultimately, he constructed a device that could still communicate with the digital world, but without all the associated risks, like viruses, hackers and poorly written software.

The first version he constructed caught fire. The second was never accurate due to magnetization. The third and fourth versions were functional, but too large. The version he now used – version five – was far more advanced than any computer sold in stores.

Jay realized his solution was the best, even if it wasn't the one everyone expected. It earned him good grades in school and praise from his teachers. It also earned him cruel nicknames and odd stares from some students…and the occasional "F" from a teacher who could not appreciate his unique perspective. He did not care. It worked.

He flipped two brass switches on the wood case. A small cylinder began to boil, causing small gears in the device to spin faster. The volume increased accordingly.

Jay was singing along at full volume and way off key. He could only hear music through the brass and leather headset. He didn't care—it was his room and his own private jam session.

" . . . *some people around say that I'm insane, they need someone to blame* . . . "

"Jay." A voice broke through his invisible wall of sound.

Jay turned around and opened his eyes to see his mother standing only two feet away. He laughed and took off his headphones. "How long have you been yelling?"

He was thinking about calculating the volume of her voice against the volume of his music, to see how loud he would have to play it so that he could not hear anything in the future. Her face looked pink and hot and she yanked her hair behind her ears.

"I've been looking all over for you," the words coming out in a staccato, like bullets. "I walked up and down the street. I thought you might be rummaging through that awful Dumpster."

Jay often went Dumpster diving to look for interesting items for his artwork. Most of it now adorned his walls. He wondered if he could ever sell it . . . Cindy Fox snapped her fingers in front of her son's face.

"Hello?" She threw her hands toward the ceiling. "I might as well be talking to the toaster." She snatched up some of his dirty clothes and stomped out of the room. Jay followed her into the living area.

"Sorry Mom." He meant it. He really liked his Mom. He knew she tolerated his eccentric behavior and creative streak. She walked over to him and gently placed a hand on his cheek.

"I know sweetheart." She said, calm returning to her voice. "You are my bright, shiny star." His mother always told him this. "Even if you sometimes frustrate the hell out of me." She didn't always say that.

Silver Lake had given his family a new start. Of course, they were still poor, but he was doing better in school, his Mom had found a great job at the local hospital, and his dad was selling recycled junk, or reclaimed treasure, as he preferred to call it.

"I need to wash some things before I go to work," his mother said as she continued to pick up stray socks and underwear. "What do you have planned?"

Jay looked at his watch. It was later than he realized. "Oh crap, Mom." She glared at him for using bad language.

"Sorry." He quickly apologized. "But I have to meet dad at the warehouse." He gave her a kiss and retreated inside his room.

She shook her head slowly.

"Just what we need. Another trash collector in our family," she mumbled to the air where he had just stood. "And while you're there, grab a handful of that junk and get rid of it," she yelled to the closed door.

Green Day Alert

Jay listened as his mother disappeared down the hall. He sat down at his desk and tapped a brass button on his computing device. A small screen came to life behind the wires. His version of an e-mail program displayed four new messages. Two of them were junk and he deleted them.

He opened the other two, both from Cosmic Studios. "Dear Mr. Fox: The review committee is pleased to announce the finalists of the Cosmic Studios summer science contest." That's strange, Jay thought. I only submitted the form yesterday. He continued reading. "The committee is also pleased to announce that your design has been chosen as one of four finalists."

He stopped reading. His design and sketches had made it to the finals. He knew a real model could still help him win, but this was impossible. How could they have evaluated all of the entries in one day? He scanned the rest of the message and printed it out, then opened the next e-mail. His smile faded.

The next message said, "Mr. Fox: My name is Professor Maximillian Gladwell, and I am the Founder of Cosmic Enterprises. It is a great honor for me to include your design as a finalist in our competition. You will be surprised to learn that more than one winning entry will be announced tomorrow. You will also be surprised, and I hope excited, to learn that we will be making this announcement from your hometown of Silver Lake. I have attached the location and time of our announcement. A representative will be in contact with you before tomorrow, and will provide additional details at that time. In the meantime, please keep this announcement a secret until our presentation tomorrow. I look forward to the pleasure of meeting you in person. Until then, I remain your most humble servant,"

The e-mail concluded with the golden electronic signature of Maximillian Augustus Gladwell.

Questions churned through his head. What kind of mistake was this? Certainly, someone had to be playing a joke on him. But who? Was it Trevor? How could anyone else have known about the contest?

Jay scanned the message again. "Most humble servant." That was so old-fashioned. He had heard that kind of expression spoken in old black and white films, but who talked like that anymore? Who even writes like that anymore?

He was about to close the briefcase when his Dimension 64 Message Board typed a new message. He was receiving a communication from GreenDayStriker1, another user on the network. His screen displayed a single prompt: Accept or Decline?

Jay thought about the invitation. He didn't have a public profile so it wasn't a random message or advertisement. He had heard of a band called Green Day but he was certain they didn't know him. He pushed on the word "accept".

GreenDayStriker1:

"JAY – NO TIME TO EXPLAIN, MEET ME AT HANK'S PLACE – HE NEEDS HELP NOW. DON'T REPLY, JUST RUN."

"What the hell." Jay jumped up from his desk as if he had been shocked. He heard his mother yell from the other side of the trailer, "Jay! Watch your language."

More questions. What the heck was going on? And how did this person even know he was going to his dad's warehouse?

His dad's shop was nearby, in the industrial park next to their trailer park. It was completely crazy, but Jay knew to trust his instincts. He closed his eyes and sorted through the facts. He came to his own conclusion: run.

Jay closed the homemade laptop and shoved it into his backpack. Ten feet or ten miles, he wasn't leaving his bag. He raced through the trailer and threw open the side door. His mother barely heard him shout "Later." as he bounced down the rickety metal stairs. The door slammed shut with a clang behind him.

The one good thing, thought Jay as he kicked up dust running down the dirt road, is that I don't live far from dad's shop. Morningside Trailer Park was located on the east side of town and north of Echo Park Industrial Center, a collection of warehouses and commercial spaces only two blocks away. Conveniently out of sight of any tourists or prying eyes. Although Jay was not ashamed of where they lived, he was smart enough to know both he and his family lived on the "wrong" side of Valley Road.

Jay cut diagonally through the trailer park toward the warehouse. He had just reached Sunrise Drive and turned into the industrial park when a dark SUV sped past him in the same direction.

Although the car was faster, he had the advantage of being able to cut through empty lots on his way to the industrial park. The SUV was parked in front of his dad's space. Jay turned and ran to the rear entrance. He found a dumpster and hid his bag underneath a few pieces of old cardboard. As he stood up, he pulled a baseball bat out of the canvas bag. Just in case, he thought.

He moved toward the door but was cutoff as a green jeep screeched to a halt in front of him. Jay brandished the bat and circled it above his head. Although he wasn't much of a baseball player, he could open a piñata with one swing. Jay imagined what he could do if someone tried to hurt his father.

Coach McCorkle poked a head around the car door and stared at Jay in surprise. Jay did not recognize the man since he never played sports at school.

"Jay, drop the bat," the coach said.

Jay didn't flinch. Perhaps it was some sort of trick?

"Jay, It's Coach McCorkle. I'm here to help." The coach fumbled as he tried to think of another angle. "How about GreenDay Striker 1? Will you listen to me now?" It worked. Jay relaxed and dropped the bat by his side. Coach McCorkle pointed inside.

"I think your father's in danger." He hurried to the front door, which was partially open. Jay held up the bat up again, and crept along behind the coach. Coach McCorkle glanced over at Jay and held out his hand.

"Here, let me take that. I might be able to use it more . . . effectively."

Jay hesitated and then thought about his request. Coach McCorkle could probably blow the warehouse down with one lung if he wanted. Jay handed him the bat. The Coach opened the door and they entered the warehouse together.

Jay stared in amazement. He never bothered his dad at work and he had never realized just how many things his dad had collected. The warehouse was full of gadgets and boxes and shelves reaching over thirty feet into the air. This isn't a junk shop, Jay realized. It's a laboratory.

He followed Coach McCorkle deeper inside the building. It was apparent the coach knew exactly where he was going, as he skillfully navigated the gigantic piles of metal and boxes. Then Jay realized that this path had been created deliberately. It was a labyrinth designed to hide the center of the workshop and slow people down as they worked their way toward the middle.

Jay was deep in thought wondering how the school's soccer coach knew the layout of his father's workshop better than he, when he heard the coach bark an order to some unseen intruder.

"Stop!"

Before Jay could look up, Coach McCorkle leaped over a stack of boxes six feet high, and sprinted toward the rear of the building.

Jay looked around for another way out. He turned the corner and stopped. The path had opened up into a wide clearing. A man lay crumpled in the middle of the circle. It was his father. Jay rushed over and knelt down. From outside the warehouse, an engine gunned as a car sped away. The metal building echoed with the sound of squealing tires.

"Dad!" Jay cried, "Are you hurt?" There was no reply.

He was wondering what to do next when he heard a loud scraping noise. A tall stack of steel poles at the edge of the circle began to separate. Rather than weave his way through the maze of junk, Coach McCorkle cleared a path directly back to them.

"How is he?" the coach asked anxiously as he set down Jay's bag. Jay stared at the bad he had hidden moments ago. The coach pointed to it. "I found this out back. It's yours, isn't it?" Jay nodded silently and then looked back at his father.

Coach McCorkle lifted Hank's eyelids and felt his pulse. "He's alive but he's taken a beating. We need a first aid kit." Coach McCorkle stood up and searched the many piles for a first aid kit, but there were no emergency supplies or medical kits to be found.

"Hold on" Jay said, and he opened his backpack. He rummaged through it and pulled out a small red box. "I thought I had one here." He handed it to a surprised coach.

Jay explained. "My mom makes me carry it, just in case." Jay shrugged. "She worries." Jay stood up and looked around while

Coach McCorkle sorted through the first aid kit. Jay reached into his pocket and brought out his cell phone. A strong arm locked onto his wrist before he had a chance to open the phone.

"Ouch."

"No. Wait." Coach said. He looked at Jay's concerned face.

"Shouldn't we call an ambulance or something?"

"It's complicated, Jay. I can't explain everything right now, but I'll make sure your dad gets the help he needs."

Coach McCorkle finally located what he was looking for and placed a small white cylinder under Hank's nose and then cracked it open. Hank immediately began to cough. Coach McCorkle continued watching Hank as he explained his decision to Jay.

"I need to ask your father a few of questions first. Then we can call for help." Coach said to Jay. Hank eye's fluttered and then focused on his son.

"Oh." Hank moaned slightly. His voice was as thin as a reed.

"I'm sorry Jay." He said feebly. "Seems like..." a short coughing spasm interrupted him. "...we might not get to your project today." he finished. Hank looked at Coach McCorkle.

"You scared them off, Sean." He said to Coach McCorkle. Jay looked at Coach and then at Hank. They know each other, he realized with a jolt. Hank stared into the coach's eyes.

"They thought Jay was here." Hank tried to roll to his left, but the pain was too great. He winced. "Stupid thugs. Those Stasys agents gave me more information than they realized."

Jay looked at his father and then at the coach. "Agents? After me?" Hank coughed softly and started to explain.

"Where are they?" Coach interrupted. Hank didn't provide the answer Jay expected. Instead of telling him where the agents had gone, he clutched his chest and pointed to a group of boxes nearby, and coughed.

"Over there, third box down. Pull it out and reach inside." He said.

Coach McCorkle stood up and pulled out all three boxes. He set them down between Jay and Hank. They were blocking Jay's view so Jay tried to push them out of his way. He could not make them budge.

The enormous man made it look as if he was stacking empty shoeboxes. Jay couldn't begin to guess how heavy they were. Jay crawled around the boxes and moved closer to Hank. Coach reached into the third box and pulled out a large envelope. He handed the package to Hank.

"They're gonna try to get Sam, too." Hank said. "At the store. You've got to leave, now."

Coach McCorkle turned and ran out of the building without looking back at Jay or saying goodbye. He was surprised the coach did not offer to stay and help. Jay turned and looked at his father.

"Well, son, I'm sorry..." Hank coughed and Jay waited for the spasm to pass. Then he pulled the envelope up and rested it on his chest. He placed his other hand on Jay's shoulder and smiled.

"I bet you have about a thousand questions." He panted slightly before continuing. "I'll try to answer all of them. But there's something I gotta do first." Jay watched as his father gingerly placed both of his hands behind his ears and pressed.

Two Brave Scouts

Caw. Caw. A monster screeched next to Trevor's ears.

Trevor jumped back and threw his arms defensively over his head, certain some hideous creature was about to peck his eyes out. He slowly peeked through his arms and looked around. Being alone in the wilderness was a new experience. It was good no one had seen him. He wondered what Sam would have thought about his reaction to a harmless bird.

Trevor looked over at Moke. Her ears were up. She tilted her head to the left and stared at him. Surely she now grasped the fact that her owner was not a man, but in fact an oversized city chicken.

Caw. He ducked reflexively as he heard the loud noise once again. A raven stared at them from her perch on a nearby log.

No wonder it sounded so loud, Trevor thought.

He waved his arms and yelled at the bird. The raven hopped back, but made no real effort to leave. Moke spied the creature and began barking at it. With a little coaxing from his dog, the raven finally flew up into the tall pines.

Go away, Trevor thought. Especially since you made me look foolish in front of my dog. Trevor resumed walking along on the path of pine needles.

"Almost there," he said confidently to Moke. Maybe he could regain his status as the Alpha dog.

Nah, he concluded sadly. I am probably Chicken Dog from now on.

Moke and Trevor were following a well-marked trail that encircled the enormous lake. The broad path was carpeted with old pine needles. This isn't so bad, Trevor thought to himself. It's like a New York street, only paved with leaves.

They had rounded the north side, and were almost midway around the eastern shore. Trevor left the trail and wandered closer to the lake. He paused on a small rise and looked around.

The sun was high over his head and the deep blue lake appeared to be covered in bright silver sparkles. He suddenly realized how the lake probably got its name. From what he had learned in school, Trevor knew that many thousands of years ago, a glacier had slowly retreated north, deciding to take up permanent residence in Canada. As the glacier left, it took the ice and left behind a huge crater. The crater was now a lake. Trevor crouched low and placed his hand in the lake. It was ice cold.

Perhaps the glacier never really melted, he thought. Trevor playfully imagined a mammoth wall of ice lurking somewhere near the bottom of the lake. He stood back up, and gazed at the distant shore. The eastern side of the lake's shore was covered with small rocks and low bluffs to the north and south. The shoreline gradually rose to a dizzying crescendo right below the town. Gigantic boulders and high rolling cliffs joined together at the base of Town Park.

Trevor shaded his eyes with both hands as he examined the canyon more closely.

He could almost trace the path of a small creek as it dropped under Town Park and into the canyon below. The little trickle of water bounced from rock to boulder before merging into the lake. A few rooftops and a couple of the larger buildings were almost visible above the trees. Seeing the town reminded him of his friends.

He wondered if Sam's presentation was going well and if Jay had all the materials he needed. He looked at the large distance between them. He would have a long hike back if Sam didn't show up with a kayak. Trevor decided to stay by the water and began walking along the shore. This side of the lake was serene and peaceful. It was privately owned land. No boats, no cars. Just nature. With the raven now gone, the air was quiet, filled only by the low shusssh of the wind as it passed through the pine needles high above his head.

He picked through some branches and climbed up the large rocks scattered along the shore. Moke circled farther inland near the trail to bypass the rocks. A tree had actually grown into the rock in front of him. Trevor stared at the tangle of roots that twisted and dug deep into cracks and fissures and into the very rock itself.

Amazing, he thought. Why would a tree grow here when a few feet over it could live in real soil and not have to work so hard?

He grabbed onto the gnarled trunk, and used it to pull himself over the largest rock. Just as he was close to the top, Trevor heard a yelp, followed by the sound of Moke barking wildly. He climbed faster and pulled himself over the rock ledge. He could see his dog ahead of him in the middle of a clearing. She was facing the largest, and the only, raccoon Trevor had ever seen. The raccoon was standing on its hind legs. It looked quite fierce as it bared its teeth and hissed. He had heard how wild animals sometimes carried diseases. Now he was afraid the nasty animal might be sick with rabies.

"Moke. Get back." She took a few steps back but kept barking. The raccoon had turned and was now hissing at Trevor. He jumped back two steps.

"Brave little devil, aren't you?"

He looked closely at the animal. The raccoon was holding something in its hand. It wasn't rabid; it was defending its lunch. Trevor picked up a branch and tossed it at the raccoon.

"Go on. Get." He yelled and stomped his foot. The raccoon dropped the item and ambled off into the woods, hissing in protest the whole way. Trevor hoped his brave act had raised his standing in Moke's eyes. They both moved closer to investigate.

Moke sniffed the area where the raccoon had been and Trevor walked over and looked down at the shiny object. It appeared to be a small silver pouch, the kind used for energy bars. The raccoon had already pulled out whatever had been inside the container. Trevor shook his head. Some irresponsible camper must have left it behind. He considered that for a moment. Camping was not allowed in the preserve, only day hikers.

He picked up the pouch and turned it over.

H-O-O-A-H was emblazoned on the silver foil. Trevor said it the word out loud: "Hooah." It didn't sound like any food company, candy, or energy bar he could recall seeing in the stores.

He stood up and looked around. About 10 yards to the west, closer to the woods, Trevor could see more objects lying on the ground. He walked over and studied them. More food packages. He gathered them all up in his arms. Might as well carry them out instead of leaving them here, he thought.

His stomach rumbled, reminding him that he had not eaten anything the entire day. Maybe he could find something good in one of the packages. He examined each of the packages as he picked them up, finding two unopened.

The label on a large tan package said *Meal Ready To Eat. Individual. Menu #20: Spaghetti with Meat Sauce. Stasys Global Corporation.* The label on the second, smaller package read *Strawberry Dairyshake Powder.* The thought of a powdered milkshake made Trevor wrinkle his nose in disgust. He looked at Moke as she watched his every move. She was certain something good would drop out of the wrappers and into her mouth.

"I can see why they left this one." Trevor said to his hiking companion as he held up the package containing the instant milkshake. "Who would want to drink a powdered shake when they get a fresh strawberry milkshake just across the lake?"

Trevor gathered the rest of the trash and shoved it into his backpack, and examined the unopened packages. He selected one of the snack bars and ate it hungrily. Not bad, he thought. He put the empty wrapper in with the rest of the trash and scouted the area for more debris. A section of rocks and branches caught his eye. He walked over and kicked at it with his feet. Although someone had tried to conceal it, the charred remains of a fire were visible.

Why would someone cover up a fire and then leave all this trash? He decided to look around further. *Caw.* His friend the raven had returned. *Caw. Caw.* Moke barked and stared up at the trees.

"Leave it alone, Moke." Trevor ordered, and continued to scan the ground around them.

Moke barked again and he scowled at her. He was about to scold her when he noticed her intense concentration. She let out a soft whimper. Trevor followed her gaze high into the trees until he was staring directly at a large canvas tent. He had seen these before: They were called blinds, and hunters used them to hide from animals. But this blind was very large and too high in the tree for hunting animals.

The brazen raven was perched at the opening of the blind with another pouch in its mouth. It picked it up and dropped it. The foil package fluttered to the ground where Trevor had retrieved the others.

"So that's how they got there."

One mystery solved. But there was still the issue of the hunting blind hidden about twenty feet above his head. Trevor knew this was both private property and a nature preserve—there was no hunting allowed. Trevor moved closer to the tree supporting the blind and began to search around the trunk. There had to be some way up. He could see clearly where the small plants and grass had been crushed around the base of the tree.

He knelt by the trunk and examined a small patch of dirt. The imprint of a boot was barely visible. He knew a rope or ladder had to be somewhere nearby. He leaned against the tree as he stood and felt something odd.

A slight ridge ran along two sides of the tree. Each was about 6 or 8 inches thick and ran all the way to the blind. Trevor ran his hand along the bumps and realized they were artificial. Something had been bolted onto the tree, and then pine bark had been used to cover it. He slowly moved his hand up the ridge. About six feet up, at the very edge of his reach, he felt something sticking out from the bark. Trevor stepped back and looked at the spot. He could see a small blue knob protruding from the ridge.

Walking back to the tree, he set down his backpack, reached as high as he could, and pushed on the knob. The blue button popped out of the ridge with a distinct *click*. At the same time, the ridge moved slightly out from the tree. Trevor tugged on the ridge and, to his complete surprise, a metal ladder unfolded. The steps expanded out as he pulled the ridge down. He continued pulling until the steps had been fully extended. The entire mechanism locked into place with a soft *thunk*.

"Whoa." This was a cool trick, especially for a pine tree.

It suddenly dawned on him. Not only was there a ladder in the middle of the woods, but also someone had gone to extreme efforts to hide it.

He looked around but could not see and hear anyone in the woods. Trevor placed one foot on the ladder as a test and found it to be solid. He began to climb quickly and as quietly as possible. At the top of the ladder he paused briefly and looked back at the woods.

Still, no one in sight.

Trevor peered cautiously into the blind. It was constructed from heavy canvas in a camouflage pattern. The fabric was stretched across a metal structure measuring almost 10 feet in all directions. This was practically a tree fort. He pushed aside the entry flap. The raven had used the same opening to steal the small packages of food.

Trevor noticed immediately that no one had been inside for a while. To his right, electronics and metal boxes were piled to the top of the blind. Directly in front of him lay a tangle of cartons and Meals Ready To Eat, courtesy of his feathered friend. However, his amusement did not last long.

Trevor caught his breath as he focused on the wall to his immediate left. Lined in neat rows of portable shelves was an arsenal of various weapons. His heart skipped a few beats and he felt weak inside. The hunting blind contained enough ammunition to take out a small city—a city like Silver Lake. He panicked. This was bad, really bad. He had to get back into town and warn somebody.

He pulled his head out of the blind and began to reverse his way out using the ladder. Trevor tentatively negotiated the small steps, but froze less than halfway down. He noticed two odd shapes moving through the forest about 200 feet away. He squinted and focused on the spot where the branches of a tall bush had just parted. Two men were heading for the very rocks he had just climbed.

They were soldiers. At least, they were dressed like soldiers. The men were both dressed in camouflage and their faces were painted shades of green. Rifles were slung under their shoulders. The first man had now cleared the rocks and was reaching back to help his buddy. Trevor was frozen in fear.

Caw.

Both men stopped and remained completely still.

Why would a silly raven bother them? Trevor wondered.

The raven called out twice more, directly to Trevor's left. He followed the direction of the sound but he couldn't see the bird. He looked back at the rocks. The soldier in front had crouched down and was slowly removing a pair of binoculars from his hip.

That's not a raven, Trevor's mind raced. It's a signal.

There had to be a third man moving in parallel with the other two. They had spotted him. He tried to think of as many options as he could. With all their weaponry, these guys would not play nice, Trevor realized. He had to run as fast as he could in the opposite direction.

Trevor also knew he would not win this game by stealth, especially since he was wearing a white t-shirt. He would be an easy target if he didn't move soon. He pulled his feet out from the rungs and placed them outside the pole. He immediately began a rapid slide to the ground, the rough bark scraping the inside of his hands.

He hit the ground hard and stumbled back. Trevor heard one of the men shout an order, and the crash and snap of branches. With no time to spare, Trevor grabbed his backpack, turned, and began running south, away from the men. He looked down by his side expecting to see Moke close by his side. He skidded to a halt and turned around.

Moke had not followed him.

Instead, she was holding her ground near the clearing. The hair on her back was standing up. She determined these men were threats and was prepared to defend her master. However, Trevor knew what she could not: the soldiers would soon break into the clearing – and they would not treat her with kindness.

"Moke." Trevor screamed. Trevor crouched against the tree, helpless to intervene.

A soldier entered the clearing. It was the same soldier he had seen on top of the rocks. Moke bared her teeth and ran full-tilt at the intruder. The soldier was staring up at the blind and did not immediately see the dog charging towards him. Fortunately, he had little time to aim his weapon and fire.

Moke sprang into the air, aiming squarely for the soldier's chest. The soldier twisted his body at the last minute and reduced Moke's impact. She missed her target and bounced harmlessly off his arms. Her forward motion carried her directly onto the large rocks behind. Moke clawed at the hard surface in a desperate attempt to stop herself.

Trevor watched as his best friend slid helplessly across the rocks and skittered over the edge, falling hard onto the ground below. He heard a thud, followed by a muffled yelp, and then silence. The backpack slipped slowly from Trevor's fingers.

The scene played repeatedly in his head. Trevor covered his eyes; it was too painful to watch. Over and over he imagined himself being there to catch her as she fell. But he had not been there, and he did not catch her in his arms.

A sharp yell from one of the soldiers dragged Trevor back to reality. The hunt was on, and they were after him once again. He turned and stumbled through the brush, half-heartedly deflecting the branches as they slapped and cut his face. The pain on his skin was no match for the pain in his heart.

He lost his focus and tripped on a branch. Trevor dejectedly pushed himself up with both hands. Why bother? It seemed useless. Part of him knew that the soldiers would eventually catch him.

"No. They. Won't." a strong voice deep inside him replied. He clenched his fists. Trevor felt an anger he had never known before.

Trevor's city-survival instincts kicked into gear and he sprinted low through the bushes, aiming for clear passages free of branches and obstacles, running closer to the ground. He was so focused on running that he lost track of his location. He had only a vague sense of his direction - toward the old house. Stopping to think about directions was a luxury he could not afford.

Trevor twisted and turned in every direction in order to keep to the smoother sections of ground. The taller men in pursuit had no such advantage. He turned one way and then another. Pushing between a thorny patch of briars Trevor suddenly found himself standing in the most beautiful garden he had ever seen.

Only moments earlier he had been running through thickets of leaves, stems and briars. Now, he was standing on a thick carpet of grass, surrounded by neatly trimmed shrubs and rows of wildflowers.

The sharp transition stopped Trevor in his tracks.

In a strange way, he felt so relaxed he could have lied down in the grass and taken a nap. He looked ahead. The old house was in fact a large mansion. He was standing on the edge of an immense lawn that surrounded it. The trees concealed the house from town, but were not as thick as they appeared from across the lake.

Trevor was faced with a new challenge: He couldn't turn around and hide in the woods, because the soldiers would eventually find him. But if he ran out into the open space, his pursuers would definitely be able to see him.

He began to run forward again, searching for places to hide as he did. There were no big bushes or rocks he could see. It seemed his best option was to keep running and hope for more options. He scanned the grounds ahead. The house was too far away.

A gazebo stood to the right. It was surrounded by hedge of roses, but other than rose thorns, it would offer no real protection. On his left stood a massive dock built to accommodate many boats, but there was no boathouse, only more open space. Trevor heard the sound of men crashing through the brush behind him. He had to choose quickly.

He turned to the right, in the direction of the gazebo.

Although he could clearly hear the men shouting, he did not bother to turn around. He knew from soccer that turning around would only slow him down. They had already gained on him as he paused to consider his options.

He dug deep inside and turned on all his energy. It would be his final sprint to the goal. Ironically, his hard work at soccer practice was rewarded - off the field. Trevor quickly closed the distance between himself and the gazebo.

As he drew closer, Trevor realized with dismay that what he had assumed to be a gazebo was, in fact, a very large well.

The Wishing Well

It was the largest well Trevor had even seen.

In truth, it was the only real well he had ever seen. He had thrown dimes into the wishing well inside a toy store. He had also seen a movie about a boy who lived at the bottom of a well. But he had never actually seen one in person, nor one this large.

A large stone wall three feet high and twelve feet around surrounded the well. Four metal supports arched gracefully into the air and joined at the top. A rusted metal wheel hung near the top, but no rope or bucket onto which he could jump. There was a sign at the base, but Trevor did not take time to read it.

He ran toward a small clearing in the rose hedge.

Without pausing, Trevor sprang into the air, using his hands to vault over the low wall. It was like playing leapfrog, only with deadly consequences if he missed. As his legs came up to meet his chest, Trevor got his first glimpse down into the well. There was no water below – only blackness. It was too late to stop now. Just like his dog, Trevor was airborne, and his weight was carrying his body over the wall and down into the black hole.

At least I will see Moke again, the thought flashed through his mind.

Trevor realized he had closed his eyes, because they flew open the moment his body plunged into a pool of shockingly cold water. Trevor had fallen several feet inside the well. Gasping, he kicked and thrashed as he tried to keep his head above water. His breaths escaped in puffs of steam. He would have to hide in here until the men passed. The cold brick walls magnified every breath and splash. It sounded as if he was shouting. Trevor clamped a hand over his mouth and attempted to control his movements.

For some reason, one particular lesson from his aquatic survival class at the YMCA came back to him now.

Relax. Don't panic. Create a neutral buoyancy.

Trevor floated on his back and tried to slow his breathing with regular, shallow breaths. Aside from his trembling from the cold, Trevor remained absolutely quiet. He closed his eyes again as he tried to concentrate on the noises above. He could hear the men speaking in the distance. They were talking more softly now, perhaps wanting to remain hidden from anyone in the old mansion. One of the men seemed to be moving closer.

Or was he moving farther away?

Trevor stared at the circle of light directly above him, expecting to see a man's face appear over the edge. Instead, he noticed that the opening above him was growing smaller and smaller. Trevor performed a mental check of his body. He was still breathing air; all of his limbs seemed to be responding. He touched his cold face with numb fingers—it was still there and above the water.

The circle of light continued to shrink. Trevor tried to focus on the slimy green walls around him. Slowly, he noticed a pattern, a spiral groove, carved into the rocks.

"Those aren't grooves," the thoughts sloshed inside his foggy mind, "those are small steps."

The tiny steps spiraled all the way up to the top of the well. He was moving downward, toward the bottom of the well. Trevor was too cold to think clearly. Maybe the men had found a way to drain the well. He could picture them standing next to an enormous drain with a giant stopper in one hand and guns ready to fire as he shot out of the imaginary opening.

His frozen mental gears turned slowly once again.

If the well is draining, then there is a drain. If there's a drain, that means I am going to get sucked into it. Trevor rotated into a sitting position and tried to look down as he treaded water. The light from above was enough to illuminate a small circle far below. He was headed directly toward a drain.

"Remember your training," he thought calmly, "Don't panic." Trevor looked at the drain once more; it was moving closer every second. "Forget the training," the other part of his mind screamed. "Swim. Now. Anywhere but here!"

Trevor splashed toward the edge and clawed frantically at the wall. He grabbed onto one of the small steps. His hands immediately slipped off the slime and mud-covered stones. He tried again and slipped again. He tried several times with the same results: Grab. Slip. Grab. Slip. He swam closer to the wall and tried to place his entire body against it.

If two hands won't work, he thought, then two hands and two feet might be better. He used both hands and selected one step to hold on to. At the same time, he let the water pull his legs onto the step below. Then he rested his weight between his hands and his feet. The plan worked. The water continued moving downward while he remained leaning against the wet, bare wall.

"Yes." Trevor celebrated a major victory.

Two minutes later he looked down in disappointment. He had not stopped to consider what to do once the water completely drained from the well. Most likely, he would break his legs jumping or falling onto the slippery brick floor below. He shifted his weight and moved one foot out. He searched blindly for the next step in the wall. His foot slipped. He brought it back, but not before the shifting weight had loosened his grip. He felt his hands sliding down the step until he was holding on by his fingertips. There was no sense in beating himself against the slimy stones. He let go.

He didn't have very far to fall. The remaining water caught him well above the drain.

Once again, Trevor lay on his back and closed his eyes, awaiting the 'final flush'. He could hear the roar of the water as the drain grew closer. He wondered how many gallons were going out into the lake at this very moment. He pondered how long he could hold his breath when he suddenly, he realized he was lying on top of a metal grate.

A patchwork of metal bars had spared him from the largest flume ride in town. Trevor began to laugh, not caring if the soldiers heard. There was no way they could climb down the slippery walls.

With the water gone, they would have a much longer and deadlier landing than his. He'd like to see them try.

Trevor could barely see the opening far above, but he could discern a figure moving above it. He heard some rustling, followed immediately by an echoing clatter. One of the soldiers had thrown a rope into the well. To Trevor's good fortune it landed by his side and not on top of him. Although the rope did not hit him, it certainly startled his brain back into action.

Of course they have rope, Trevor scolded himself, they're soldiers. Pretty soon one of them would follow it down. Trevor rolled over onto all fours and began crawling around the floor like a rat seeking a way out of its maze. He probed the walls with his fingers. He pushed and felt each stone. It was too dark to see clearly, but he knew there was not a space large enough to squeeze into.

He was trapped, and the soldiers would eventually make their way down. He slumped down with his back against the wall. As he did, his hands slid against the slimy stone as he lowered himself onto the floor. One of his fingers touched a slight crack.

Trevor quickly moved his arm back up and felt the stones behind his head. There was a very definite and straight groove carved into surface above him. Trevor turned around and traced the line five feet up, five feet over, and five feet back down. He began searching frantically inside the lines.

He started feeling along the entire perimeter for a handle or anything to grab. He could find nothing. Trevor rose to his knees and pushed against the wall. He crouched and pushed again. Again, his efforts had no effect on the wall.

He looked up toward the opening.

The first soldier was now inside the well and descending rapidly. The man was far enough inside that his body almost cut off the light above. Trevor could also see that the soldier's face was covered in some type of mask. He turned back to the wall.

He closed his eyes and curled himself into a tight ball. He slammed hard into the wall. This time the wall moved ever so slightly. He looked up one last time. The soldier was no more than thirty feet above him now. Trevor leaned in and pushed once more, as a deafening roar filled the stone tunnel. He not only heard a tremendous rush of air, but he felt it as well.

The door opened so quickly the suction pulled him inward and threw him against a hard, dry floor. Trevor rolled several times before landing upright. Even though his ears were ringing, Trevor could hear the whir of machinery and a boom as the stone door closed with a hiss behind him.

He heard a muffled pounding on the stone, as the man outside tried to follow him through the door. Suddenly, the thumping on the door stopped. Trevor could barely hear frantic shouts as the man issued orders to his comrades at the top of the well. Several silent seconds passed before Trevor could focus on his new surroundings.

He was sitting on the floor of a stone vault. The room was not very large, at most fifteen feet wide and twenty feet long. The walls had been constructed from the same massive blocks that formed the well. Trevor stood and placed his hand on the cool stones for support.

A small pile of clothing lay neatly stacked on top of a small stone bench. The only other object in the room was a round door set into the far wall. Trevor walked over to the bench and examined the clothes carefully. He expected to find discarded rags or old clothes left behind by some long-retired workman.

Although old and somewhat dated the clothes were actually wearable and, more important, they were dry. They were even the right size, or close enough. Trevor quickly stripped out of his wet clothes and changed into the plaid shirt and dry pair of jeans. Some mysterious person had also left behind a pair of socks and leather shoes which he immediately placed on his feet.

Trevor reached into his wet pants to retrieve his cell phone. He stared at the foggy display as beads of water dripped from inside the plastic case. Images and letters flashed briefly and then the screen faded to solid gray. It was ruined.

"Great." The word raced around the curved ceiling.

He dropped his phone on top of the wet clothes and walked to the round wooden door. Trevor placed his hand on a brass metal wheel set in the very center. Immediately, he heard several loud clicks, followed by a slight hiss. The small wheel turned and the door swung inward. Trevor stepped back as the door opened silently into the vault. He waited, and then peered into the space beyond. Nothing. No one had opened the door. Beyond the opening he could barely discern a dim narrow passage. Electric torches placed at regular intervals along the walls illuminated the floor and walls.

Trevor stepped over the low threshold into the hallway. Immediately, the door closed automatically behind him. He watched as it settled into place and the little metal wheel spun quietly, closing the room behind him. He heard the now familiar hiss as the door sealed itself once again.

He examined the door from the outside. It appeared to be a normal wooden door, but it operated as a kind of hatch. A bright light switched on inside his head. Of course! The doors were designed to seal the room, like pressurized doors on a boat or submarine. He touched the door. No response. He turned around and peered down the long hall. He would have to find another way out.

Trevor stepped forward and felt his way along the corridor, passing his hand along the stones for balance. Or security. He was fairly certain he wouldn't lose his balance. The stone all around him was perfectly smooth, as if something had melted, rather than carve it. There were no lines, grooves or mortared joints. Trevor squinted and looked for the end of the tunnel as he moved cautiously forward.

His journey ended in less than ninety steps. He found himself standing in front of another wooden hatch. Pulling his hand off of the cold walls, he moved toward the center of the hallway. He reached out his left hand and paused. His fingers hovered over the wheel, a mere three or four inches above the handle. He considered his choices. Stay here? Move forward. Forward into what?

He looked back to the other end of the tunnel. The other hatch was barely visible in the gloom. He knew that way only led to an empty chamber, a very deep well and men who, for some reason, were intent on hunting him down like an animal. Besides, he was certain he couldn't scramble along those slippery stones or pull himself up the rope. He leaned his head against the door. He could hear nothing, except the thumping of his heart.

Now or never.

He lowered his hand and let his fingers rest lightly on the brass wheel. Hiss. He stepped back slowly as the second door began to open.

The Cosmic Blender

A wisp of cold, stale air stroked his face, causing the hair on his arms to stand up. He remained in the doorway with one hand on the edge of the frame and looked inside. The space beyond was much darker. It took a few minutes for Trevor's eyes to adjust.

Five small points of light glowed dimly in the distance. Leaning in ever so slightly, he could see a rough, rocky wall to his left... Much different than the tunnel. Another wall curved away to the right. From his place in the doorway, he could not see the farthest wall or any kind of ceiling. He could, however, see a solid floor on the other side of the door. He was standing on the threshold of an immense underground cave.

He took two tentative steps over the doorframe, moving from the relative safety of the tunnel into the dark and unfamiliar space beyond. As he crept inside, the five points of light suddenly sputtered and roared to life. Trevor watched anxiously as the small points of light exploded into large cauldrons of flame. Soon, five gargantuan brass torches completely illuminated the area in front of him. Trevor stood still, as the overwhelming size and scale of the cavern filled his senses.

He jumped as the door closed behind him. Thunk. The tiny wheel spun and then stopped. The way back was closed. That left only one path: forward into the belly of the enormous room.

He tiptoed directly from the doorway into the massive structure. The torches crackled and roared, drawing his eyes upward. At first, the ceiling above looked just like the walls - ordinary rock. Trevor blinked. The space over his head seemed to somehow blur and soften. He closed his eyes tight and then opened them, focused on the ceiling. The top of the cavern was now smooth, forming an immense golden dome high above him. As if on cue, the entire room was soon bathed in the soft orange glow of the torches and light bounced off the dome onto the walls and floor around him.

An underground cave with a golden dome for a ceiling. And so far above... Trevor's head began to spin. He forced himself to look down, away from the dome. He focused instead on the wall closest to him.

The jagged surface rose up from the floor to support the dome above. The sides were cracked and pitted, just like . . . Trevor rubbed his eyes. The walls, which only seconds ago had looked like ordinary rough stone, had somehow become highly polished black marble. They had transformed, exactly like the ceiling..

He blinked and looked again. Five walls, like a pentagon. Each wall had three sections: a lower section of gold along the floor, followed by black stone in the middle, with another band of gold at the top. Five massive columns stood between each wall. Large wooden doors were set into each one, like the door Trevor had entered directly behind. The bowls of fire that illuminated the chamber sat perched above each of the entryways. Five walls. Five stone columns. Five wooden doors. Five enormous torches.

Trevor walked over and examined the wall closest to him. One minute: rough rock. The next minute: a beautiful, smooth wall polished to perfection. The space was looking less and less like a cave and more like a cathedral. Slowly, he realized the black walls were not entirely black. Upon inspection, he could now see the walls were actually covered in images. He stared closely. Old people walking hand in hand. Children played in a park. Baseball players in the middle of a game. A young couple in love. A family eating dinner together.

He could only recognize a few of the images closest to the surface. The artist had painted each scene with such detail he could not see them all. He walked around the chamber examining the other four sections. Curiously, the last wall was different. Unlike the others, this wall was indeed completely black, without any images or scenes.

Trevor stopped and turned to look at the entire space. He was wondering which door to try next when he happened to glance at his feet. The floor was tiled in a mosaic that formed a ring around a low platform at the center of the room. The ring mirrored the dome above. He continued forward. Someone had placed a stone bench on top of the platform.

Trevor edged his way closer to the stone platform and looked down. The large dais on which the bench rested was composed of five types of stone, each one a different color. The perimeter of the platform was carved with symbols that he could not read. Without warning, the symbols re-arranged themselves and formed words that seemed to glow from within. Trevor walked around the entire platform as he read all of them aloud.

"Within Every Living Thing, A Universe of Possibility"

Trevor stepped cautiously onto the platform. Pop. It was as if a twig had snapped inside his head. The noise inside was followed by a series of clanks, clicks and whining noises around the hall. He bent over, wrapping his arms tightly around his chest. The sound hurt his ears. He waited until the cacophony faded into a gentle whisper. Trevor reached out and grabbed the far edge of the bench with one hand, and slumped onto it.

White Shirts

Back in Silver Lake, three black vans maneuvered into position at three separate locations. The men inside the vehicles wore crisp white shirts and dark, serious expressions on their faces.

With professional precision each man silently opened metal containers. Almost in unison, as if each van was side-by-side rather than miles apart, the men extracted tubes and parts from various cases and quickly assembled them. No one spoke. No signals were exchanged. The men were highly trained. Today was not a day for words.

The guns they assembled were quite odd, like toy water cannons with bright neon buttons. In reality, they were high-end molecular disruptors that could momentarily interrupt signals from the nervous system or, switched to more lethal settings, rearrange the molecules of any object.

The man in the passenger seat was the first to open his door. He covered his weapon with a nylon jacket and stepped into the street. All clear. The driver joined him. Across town, the routine was exactly the same. Each group paused briefly outside their vehicles and surveyed their targets before beginning the operation.

Operation: Croissant

Inside the Café, Julie placed her hands inside two oversized mitts. She flipped open a large metal oven door and retrieved a long baking sheet. On the sheet were a dozen tiny white bowls, each containing her easy, quick, and delicious dessert: *Tarte fine aux pommes*.

Julie imagined her father's reaction: "Darlin', those apple pies ain't got no crust." They looked perfect to Julie, and for that reason alone she felt delighted.

The apples had baked to a golden brown, and the delicious aroma of cinnamon filled her nose. She would display this batch during the show as the "final" product. She carefully set the hot tray down on the counter and turned to Pauline. Waving her mitts in the air, Julie announced her blessing on the new desserts.

"Chef Pauline," she crowed, "if people don't like my tarts, they can kiss my muffins." Julie laughed at her own joke and waited for the chef's reaction. Normally Ms. Montreaux enjoyed her little jokes and would have hurried over to inspect the latest batch of pies.

However, the chef did not speak or move. She remained frozen with a large bowl of peeled apples in her hands and a look of confusion on her face. Julie frowned.

"Yoo-hoo?" Julie called to get her attention. Her culinary teacher seemed to be somewhere else.

Without warning, the ceramic bowl slipped from Pauline's hands. Julie watched helplessly as it hit the tile floor and shattered. Sections of sliced apple and white pottery scattered about the room. She worried about all the apples she'd have to peel again.

As Julie bent over to clean up the pieces, Pauline spun on her heel and rammed her from the side, lifting her off the floor. She hit Julie with such force that the two of them rolled behind the pantry shelves. Copper pots and pans clanged to the floor around them.

Julie struggled to sit up, but she soon realized she could not move. Pauline was pinning her down with her left arm. The woman was much stronger than she appeared. At the same time, the chef used her other hand to search inside her blouse. Julie knew it was acceptable for southern women to act a little eccentric from time-to-time - some even communicated with dead relatives on occasion - but this was completely unexpected.

Julie opened her mouth to complain, but nothing came out.

Two strange-looking guns were pointed directly in her face. As her body went limp, her mind continued to process information. The guns looked like toys, but the men holding them were deadly serious. One of them had small ears and the other had a mole on the left side of an extremely muscular neck.

What a funny thing to notice before you die, she thought. Julie now realized the chef was probably trying to pull out a rosary or lucky charm. The gold pendant she held in her hand was glowing a peculiar shade of jade green.

Oh, Chef Montreaux, Julie thought. You were only trying to save my life. Then she hugged Pauline tightly and closed her eyes.

Operation: Redwood

Coach Sean McCorkle's vehicle bounced over the curb as he maneuvered it closer to the front door. He had to work hard to avoid hitting shoppers as they threaded their way into and out of Adventures To Go. He jumped out of his Jeep and looked inside through one of the store's side doors. Shoppers were checking out merchandise and admiring the store displays. They were shopping. Everything still appeared normal.

Good, he thought, maybe they haven't arrived yet.

A man who had had been frightened by Coach McCorkle's erratic driving was marching indignantly over to confront him.

It was clear to the coach that this man was intent on starting a fight. He couldn't afford to lose precious minutes in some meaningless altercation. He held up both hands as a sign of surrender. It was also clear from the look on the man's face that he was not ready to accept McCorkle's peace offering.

Oh boy, thought the coach. What a waste of energy. Why can't people learn how to manage their emotions? He shrugged. Some idiots just enjoy fighting. It was time for Plan B.

Coach McCorkle drew himself up to his full height of six feet, five inches and extended his chest. He had to struggle not to laugh as the angry little man skidded to a halt less than ten steps away. The man took notice of Coach's intimidating build and seemed to lose any interest in a fight.

Coach McCorkle leveled a stern gaze at the man and raised a single finger.

"Stop," coach announced in a clear, but controlled voice. It was as if he had scolded a bad dog. The man looked at him in frustration as if he still wanted to fight.

"Your kids are fine. Your wife is fine." He was focused and direct. "If you're smart, you'll take your family and leave as fast as you can."

Naturally, the man thought the coach was being arrogant and bossy. In reality his general health was in serious danger if he started a fight. Coach McCorkle gave the man one last, intense look.

The man muttered something under his breath, but quickly spun in the opposite direction and hurried back to his car. He could only imagine the conversation during the ride home. Coach McCorkle looked back at the store. He couldn't afford to waste any more time. More important tasks lay ahead. He sucked in a deep breath and opened the door.

Silver Lake's soccer coach had just stepped into a wonderland of hunting equipment and outdoor supplies. He wanted to look around. On a better day, he would have enjoyed shopping here. Right now, he needed to find Sam, and quickly. He scanned the store by gazing across the tops of displays within each department. Because of his height he could see most of the store and therefore, most of the shoppers. But he was unable to see around the large displays including the massive pile of rocks and waterfalls at the center of the store.

He was trying to form a plan when he noticed two men walk in through the front door. He knew them immediately. Stasys agents.

Coach began walking in a parallel direction, keeping himself between the men and the rest of the store. If Sam was somewhere behind him, as he hoped, then he would be the first to reach her. He continued to look around as he tracked the agents' progress. They were scanning the store. That was a good sign—they had not located Sam either.

Coach McCorkle caught the sound of a familiar voice as he passed by the large waterfall. Sam was kneeling on top of a rock formation. A woman wearing more fishing gear than a bait shop was watching Sam eagerly as she demonstrated, for the eighth time, how to tie a lure onto a line. He headed in Sam's direction as casually as possible. He didn't want to alert the men to his presence with any sudden movements.

"So now you have the fly fastened securely to the line," Sam explained patiently, "and you won't need to worry about the fish running off with your bait." Sam smiled at the woman and then noticed her coach walking towards them.

"Hey, Coach." she shouted and waved at him. He grimaced in reply. He would have to assume the agents had heard as well. He did not look back at the men but immediately sprang into action.

He pushed the tourist aside, scattering bags of expensive fishing gear across the stone floor. The gentleman inside him wanted to apologize, but only her pride was wounded. Instead, he focused completely on Sam.

He reached up and pulled himself onto the nearest rock. Sam had little time to react as Coach McCorkle jumped up and crouched on the platform next to her. His sudden behavior surprised her, but nothing prepared Sam for his next move.

Coach wrapped his massive arms around Sam and lifted her into the air. Using his momentum, he leaned backwards, pulling them both down into the huge freshwater aquarium.

Sam took a gulp of air as head broke the surface of the water. Then she felt Coach McCorkle's strong hand clamp down on the back of her head. Sam kicked frantically in an attempt to free herself and get out of the artificial pond. Customers yelled and pointed as they ran to the source of the noise and began to notice Sam's struggle.

Outside the tank, the two men had drawn their plastic guns, and were running directly for the tank. The customers' angry yells of protest quickly turned into screams of terror as the man began to fire their weapons. Customers began tripping over each other as they pushed through racks of merchandise to reach the exits. Someone pulled a fire alarm and water began to stream from the ceiling.

Racks of clothing and ruined displays were strewn about as if a herd of wet cattle had stampeded through the store. In three minutes a retail fantasy had turned into a shopping nightmare.

Sam heard a sharp whisper break through the noise.

"Sam." Coach hissed, "Keep your head below the glass and breathe through your mouth." Suddenly, Sam heard what sounded like gunfire. Only this type of gunfire seemed to vibrate the very air around them.

Sam turned her head slightly and watched in horror as two men fired directly at the tank. She recognized them from earlier. They were the same two men she had seen in the gun department. She knew for certain her father didn't sell anything like those two weapons.

She stared at the glass. The guns were firing small Jell-O-colored balls that stuck to the surface of the glass. Sam would have laughed if Coach McCorkle had not been so serious. Why are they trying to shoot us with gummy blobs, she wondered.

Suddenly, the glass on the tank started to vibrate. Soon, the water in the tank was rippling. The ripples turned into small waves and the trout began to jump out of the water and land on the floor. For now, the extra thick glass of the tanks seemed strong enough to deflect the green and blue blobs.

Sam suddenly realized how serious things had become. In fact, she noticed that the water was glowing red. Even the center of her coach's chest was bright red, as if he had been shot. Except the glow was coming from the pendant around his neck, and not from a bullet wound.

The men ignored the fish and the screams of the customers as they continued to discharge their weapons at the tank.

Coach McCorkle realized they had only seconds remaining, at most a minute. Maintaining his grip on Sam, he turned around in the water so his back was to the store. He had also positioned his body between Sam and the men. He placed both hands on her cheeks and turned her face so that she was now looking directly at him.

"Sam." he said clearly, but with a tenderness she found oddly reassuring, "Don't move. You and I will live to fight these people another day."

Operation: Trumpet

"Old Floyd was crazier than a junkyard dog, I'm telling you. But he still sang better than anybody else that night." Hank laughed softly. He smiled at his son from the floor of the warehouse. He seemed to be a little better now.

Jay had watched as his father had used some kind of invisible phone to contact some kind of support center. Although he could not hear their replies, only what his father said, at least they knew he was injured and needed help. His father had let them know he expected the intruders to return to the warehouse. That was the good part, thought Jay. Then he had told Jay not to call his mother. That was the strange part.

During a long and very intense conversation, His father shared with him a deep secret. He had lived a life he and his mother had never known. Jay wasn't sure he understood everything. But he was certain his father had once been an agent for Stasys. Now those same people were trying to capture Jay and his friends for some kind of experiment. His father stopped suddenly, promising to tell him more, later. And then, quite suddenly, he began talking about the years he played in a jazz band. Jay knew most of these stories.

"Oh boy," his father smiled. "What I wouldn't give to be back on stage." His father sighed deeply and looked at Jay.

Enough stories about the band, his dad, stated plainly. He wanted to share the real reason they had moved to Silver Lake. He opened his mouth to speak, and then stopped. His dad set down the old trumpet he had been holding and touched Jay's arm. Jay could hear the screech of tires outside the building.

"Well Jay, they're back. Just like I told you." Jay followed his father's stare to the front of the warehouse. "But this time I bet those men aren't gonna leave."

Hank looked anxiously at his son. "There is too much to tell and not enough time." He reached out one arm and grabbed Jay gently by the shoulder.

"Ah, you are too young to understand it all." he whispered. His father closed his eyes and searched for the right words.

"Remember this Jay. You have a hidden talent you haven't begun to use. That's why we all came here." His father opened his weary eyes and stared into Jay's face.

"There is a Foundation that…" the warehouse boomed as the front door was forced open.

Jay ignored the noise. He studied his father's tired face, the faded clothes and the worn shoes. For as long as they had lived in Silver Lake, he had only thought of his dad as Handy Hank, a collector of trash and old stories. But there was more to his father than he had ever imagined. Much more.

Now, his father absentmindedly fingered the pendant around his neck. A five-sided medallion hung from the end of a long gold chain. A large blue stone rested in the center. To Jay, it almost seemed as if the gemstone was glowing from within.

A piece of metal fell on the warehouse floor with a clatter. The men were closer, Jay calculated. Perhaps they were right around the corner. He did not want to watch them approach, but he wanted to be brave for his father. He turned around and sat down beside him. Hank placed a fatherly arm around Jay's shoulders. He whispered one last secret in his ear.

"Dad." Jay said softly without turning. Tears ran down his face. The older man's face looked nothing like the fragments of memories he had kept in his head. His father looked so tired.

He offered Jay with a gentle smile. "Don't worry, son," he said reassuringly. "It's going to be fine. You'll see."

Lights On!

Sitting alone in the dim light of the cavern, Trevor began to see dark shapes and muted colors flicker across the walls like moths inside a lampshade. The lower band of gold was now completely unbroken. It was…

A single thought entered his head like a thief into a house: he was completely alone. The word bounced around inside his head. Trevor paused. *Alone*. The word had not simply echoed inside his mind, his thoughts were echoing throughout the chamber. The space seemed to reverberate with the sound of his inner voice.

Alone. Alone. Alone.

The entire chamber was empty. The murals had disappeared. The golden bands along the wall were missing. Even worse, he suddenly realized that the doors into the chamber, including the one he had entered, had faded away. He looked down. Even the bench and the tiles on the floor were gone, replaced with an inky blackness that seemed to swirl underneath him like dark water. He looked up toward the dome. The once golden dome was now completely black, just like the floor below. Not just painted black, but deeply and completely black, empty of any texture or images.

Trevor stared as hard as he could, searching for any remnant of the former underground structure. He hunted for a familiar shape in the ceiling. A line, a beam, a fleck of color, anything, but he found nothing.

Okay, where do I begin?

This time his thoughts did not echo, but landed inside his head with a thud. He peered into the dark and strained to find anything: images, a door, even a wall. His eyes searched across the vast darkness and found nothing.

Trevor felt himself moving. Not just floating, but accelerating. He was falling up or out, he could not tell which. Any definition of up and down, left or right was now missing. He let out a little yelp as his feet slipped and began to drift away from their original position. He flailed around with both arms, trying desperately to grab onto anything that would help him stop. He twisted in several directions to stop the motion, but he was soon spinning out of control.

A simple thought broke through the panic. If there is no floor and no ceiling, and no up and no down. I can't fall. Relax. And so he did. The spinning seemed to slow down, even though he had no way to measure his rotation, other than his body's natural, and currently unreliable, gyroscope. Soon he noticed a tiny pinhole of brilliant light far out in the distance. The speck of light rotated in and out of view as Trevor continued to spin slowly around.

If only I had something to hang on to, Trevor thought, something to stop the constant spinning. On the next rotation, his right arm brushed past something more solid than the empty blackness. Trevor reached out and grabbed onto the object with his fingertips. He rolled his body in order to take a closer look. Trevor realized he had firmly secured his hand onto the pedestal. Trevor reached up and lifted himself onto the platform. He was now standing, but how? There was nothing below the small disk, as far as he could tell.

On the brighter side, Trevor thought, at least I'm not floating helplessly like a jellyfish. He took a deep breath, tried to relax, and looked around. With the exception of the tiny star, Trevor could see absolutely nothing around him. He could not even see his hands. Something else continued to nag at Trevor's brain.

It was more than darkness. Somehow the air seemed to have - substance. It felt like something more than empty space. He had the impression he was moving particles about, although he could not actually see them move.

Trevor turned and continued to gaze at the pinpoint of light. On impulse, he reached out his arm, opened his fingers and carefully cupped the tiny star in the palm of his hand. Then, ever so gently, he brought the light closer to where he stood. Trevor had assumed the pulsing dot of light was far away, when in fact it had been very close all along.

He leaned his head closer to examine the speck of light. A small unexpected "wow" escaped his lips. The 'star' was a mass of moving color. Microscopic objects tumbled and collided, moving and turning across each other. Spinning and writhing about, it almost seemed as though the tiny speck was alive.

As if responding to the sound of his voice, the objects inside the tiny speck began to spin faster and faster. The star began to pulse. Trevor could hear a hum coming from the light. The sound grew louder every second, but for some reason the noise did not hurt his ears.

Suddenly, a fantastic light exploded in front of his eyes. The contents of the tiny star exploded in an ever-expanding cloud of light, sound, and color. Trevor braced himself as the cloud came whirling toward him. He felt a wave of energy push, and then move through him. At the same time, a small whine reverberated within his bones. The noise and energy quickly moved by. Trevor turned and watched as the formerly black space around him now filled in every direction with flecks of dust and pieces of light.

A cloud of material was now churning in tight circles and bands under the dome. Some of the dust clung to his clothes like lint on a jacket. He watched as the particles randomly stuck to one another, grew in size, and then dropped off the tips of his fingers. Trevor soon recognized some of the swirls as small galaxies and solar systems.

He looked around the projector or machine that was making it all possible. He looked back at the particles around him. It was completely crazy thought. It looked real. But how? Nevertheless, he stopped moving; just to be sure he didn't destroy the tiny universe.

His head felt thick. It was as if someone had emptied his skull and then poured everything back in. He could see only space and stars around him. Real or not, he wanted to know where he was. More important, what was happening with Sam and the rest of his friends? He wanted to share this experience with them.

Most of all, he missed Moke…

Turning on the Blender

The space within the chamber suddenly shifted and changed. The chamber slowly returned to its former appearance, with three notable exceptions.

First, the dome above him was now filled with stars. Second, the floor below him was covered in grass. Beside the bench, there was not a tile or rock to be seen. Third, the images on the walls were no longer still – they were alive with activity. Instead of pictures, people were moving about in various activities as far back into the walls as he could see. Trevor could hear a steady hum, the drone of many voices. It sounded similar to the noise he heard when his little universe exploded.

The section of wall he faced was now covered with billions of people. Some were singing, some laughing, others painting. Trevor noticed a school lecture or two, and scientists frozen in the middle of a heated debate. His eyes wandered across each mural, trying to search for some meaning or pattern to the portraits.

He stared at the walls closely. On one wall, scientists debated a theory scrawled across a blackboard, researchers tapped intently on computer screens, a journalist interviewed another person, a young girl peeked into the empty shell of a turtle. He pivoted on his heels and turned to face the next wall. Swimmers raced within the lanes of a pool, a teacher was explaining a new concept to her class, a singer performed with a band, and on it went...

Trevor ran his eyes across millions of images as he turned, but nothing had prepared Trevor for what he saw next.

Life-sized reproductions of his friends were now standing, floating, sitting, and laying, each in front of each wall. They were not paintings – but fully realistic statues that seemed as if they could come to life at any moment. Trevor also noticed that each one of his friends was holding onto another person. He stepped off the platform and walked over to the statue of Samantha.

She was floating in midair while holding onto the shoulders of a man. Her clothes were wet and he noticed a flash of concern in her blue eyes. All of her muscles were tensed, and she seemed ready to leap at any moment. Trevor walked around the man's body to get a better look at his face. He could see immediately that it was Coach McCorkle.

Trevor jogged over to the next tableau. He found himself staring down at Julie. She was huddled on the ground, partially covered by... Ms. Montreaux from the Café. Her eyes were closed in total fear, closed as firmly as her grip on the older woman. Someone or something else was scaring her. Trevor sprinted over to the last wall and the final image.

Jay was sitting on the floor next to his father, Handy Man Hank. The older man held one arm protectively around his son. Whereas Trevor's other friends were frozen in looks of anger, fear, or confusion, Jay's face was somewhat sad, but completely at peace. His eyes were focused in the distance, as if he knew Trevor was watching. There was not a hint of worry in his eyes.

Trevor stumbled backward and looked at the four images.

"What... is this place...?"

Trevor's lips quivered slightly as he spoke to the darkened room. There was no response. The wax figure images of his friends sat quietly. Frozen in time. Waiting. He could not come up with a reasonable explanation.

He studied his friends again, more closely. They had, in fact, moved ever so slightly from when they first appeared. He looked from his friends to the images on the murals, the ceiling, and the floor. Patterns and shades of green grass below his feet swirled and spun, while the images closer to his friends barely moved at all. Trevor walked closer to Sam and focused his complete concentration on her.

"I wish I could see more." A normal, offhand thought.

The room replied. As soon as the words left his mouth, Sam's image shrank and more of her surroundings came into view. Trevor could now see the chaos and pandemonium within the store. He could see the two men firing their guns at the tank. Green blobs inched slowly through the air toward Sam and Coach McCorkle.

Trevor felt like he was watching a dream. Not merely watching, he realized, it was as if he had entered *their* dreams. He closed his eyes. He wanted to protect Sam. He envisioned chunks of heavy safety glass flying toward the men as hundreds of gallons of water knocked them to the floor. He dreamed that inside the café, the men firing their weapons at Julie and Pauline would slip and fall on sliced apples as they tried to dodge falling cans of flour and oil. Trevor saw a future where Jay and Hank were saved, as rows of steel pipes collapsed around their attackers.

Each vision revealed a new outcome – the future he envisioned. Attackers were disarmed and confounded, their plans obstructed. None of his dreams had ever ended this way before – perfect and complete – the dangers resolved and everything back to normal. For some reason, he knew in his heart things would happen as he dreamed them. As long as his friends believed in him. He looked at them one last time.

Even though Trevor could not hear his own thoughts, he sent his thought – a simple prayer and the same question being asked at the same moment by all of the adults – to each of his friends. They spoke in unison as their voices echoed throughout the chamber.

"Do you…" asked Coach McCorkle looked directly at Sam.

"Trust…" Pauline whispered into Julie's ear.

"Me…?" Hank sincerely asked Jay.

The images within the chamber floor swirled faster and faster. Trevor felt a presence focused within the center of hall – focused on him – waiting for his response. The question appeared to him instantly, like a brilliant point of light. Trevor had only one answer. His friends had the exact same answer as well.

"Yes," he whispered in unison with his friends.

Doorways

Trevor instantly knew everything had happened just as he envisioned it. He couldn't explain why or how – he simply believed – without any doubt.

He knew his friends were safe; the killers disarmed. But there was little time to celebrate. He watched as throngs of stunned onlookers peppered his confused friends with questions they could not answer.

"Who are these people?"

"Do you know them?"

"What happened here?"

"Oh my god, they have guns."

"How did you do that?"

His friends stammered and stared blankly, unable to answer because they had no idea what had happened. Trevor surveyed the attackers. They were not dead, only unconscious. Nothing would help his friends if they did not escape their attackers. And the curious crowds.

If it worked once…perhaps he could use the chamber to create another future. He imagined bringing them to this underground chamber in a flash, but that wouldn't work. What would the crowds see? What would they say then? The headlines in the local newspaper would be outrageous: Four kids magically disappear. Location: unknown.

His friends were moving in slow motion, as their mentors began to slowly secure and disarm the attackers. Trevor noticed the strange amulets around their necks were still glowing.

He needed a way out for everybody, some kind of path or doorway that would let them leave there discretely, and join him inside the chamber without causing more panic. A safe place, where no one would find them. A portal. A doorway. A new thought took shape inside his head.

"Of course, that's it!" Trevor snapped his fingers as he shouted to the room. "Doors." He looked excitedly at the five doors lined around the chamber.

He hurried over to Julie. Chef Pauline was tying the hands of both assailants with twine from Julie's cooking bag. He concentrated completely on the two women, imagining himself in that space. It did not take long before he felt as if he was inside the Café.

"Julie," Trevor shouted.

Julie jumped back, brandishing a wickedly large kitchen knife in her hands. Her nerves were frazzled. Trevor's ghostly appearance inside the Café did not help. He kicked himself.

He had forgotten that although he had been watching her, Julie had been focused on her pursuers. She had no idea he was even around – much less able to magically appear inside the café and speak with her. Strangely, Ms. Montreaux seemed unfazed by his appearance. She continued working on the knots that held each of the attackers. Trevor started over and spoke in a slow, calm tone.

"Pauline, its Trevor..." he tried his best to speak gently.

"Maybe you can understand. Somehow I have been able to watch and help you out – just a little." Trevor gestured to the men. Chef Pauline smiled, but Julie squinted as she tried to focus on Trevor's voice. He realized she could not see him, although he could see her. He needed to remember this fact when approaching the others.

"You need to walk into that storage room as soon as you can." Trevor pointed to a door at the back of the kitchen.

Julie slowly put her hands on her hips, but now Trevor could see a smile growing on her face. She turned to Pauline in slow motion as Trevor left them and walked to the next image.

Sam seemed to be moving faster than Pauline or Julie. Maybe it's because Sam is so athletic, he decided. But a quick glance back at the others showed him everyone was moving a little faster. Time was beginning to return to normal. Or perhaps he was processing information more slowly... Either way, Trevor understood he had to work faster.

"Sam," Trevor explained his plan rapidly, but as calmly as time would allow, "you and Coach have to run to the bathroom as fast as you can. You have to trust me. Leave now."

Sam was an action-oriented person, so Trevor's commands sounded more like helpful coaching. Still, Trevor could only wonder how his barked orders had sounded inside the store. Sam slowly turned to Coach McCorkle as she pointed to the door.

Trevor was relieved to be standing in front of the third and final scene. Jay had secured the men with shipping tape as he followed his father's instructions. Trevor quickly made his introduction. Jay did not seem at all surprised.

"Trevor." he said into the air. "What's up, dude?"

"Jay, I need you and your dad…" Trevor paused.

He could not see a door anywhere inside the warehouse and their attackers were beginning to stir. The pipes separated them from Jay and Hank, but would not stop them. Trevor looked around the warehouse in desperation.

"A door." Trevor was thinking out loud as he scanned the image of the warehouse. "I need a door inside the warehouse for them to walk through."

Over and over, Trevor scanned the scene in vain for anything that might even resemble a door. A voice suddenly broke his concentration. "No problem, Trevor-man." It was Jay. Trevor had forgotten his friend could hear his spoken thoughts.

"Is that the most difficult request you can give us?" Jay asked. Trevor watched as Jay turned and explained Trevor's request. Hank chuckled and pointed to the collection of odds and ends in the warehouse. They quickly set out to build a door.

Trevor stepped back and turned his attention to the other images. Safe place, he thought. A safe place for all of us to meet. He tried to maintain a visual link with all of the doors and all of his friends. He wanted to make sure the connections between them remained as strong as possible.

Events were now moving forward at normal speed. There was only a little time left before rescue workers, police, employees and curious onlookers would watch as his friends were rescued by some strange cosmic force. They needed to move through their designated doorways as soon as possible, and into the safe place.

He turned and his legs moved slowly Trevor looked down at his feet and the… sand? He was standing on a mound of pure white sand. Somehow, patches of white and creamy beach sand now moved slowly where patches of grass, and before that, colorful tiles had once been. Curious, but he didn't have time to be distracted.

His friends were still in front of him, moving inside their spaces. Trevor closed his eyes and focused on the images of his friends. He saw the doorway to his right outlined in vibrant green. Moments later, the door burst open and Julie entered the room. He knew who it was because he could hear her talking before the door even closed.

"Trevor… those men… it was so horrible." she hollered, but her voice quickly changed its tone as she looked about the chamber. Her next question sounded less fearful.

"Where on Earth am I now?"

Trevor could imagine her confusion as she stepped out of the small café and into the giant hall, but something else about her question startled him.

Trevor opened his eyes and looked to where she had entered. As usual, her hands were planted firmly on her hips. She was covered in sliced apples. That seemed almost normal. What did

surprise him was the coconut she was holding out in one hand…
and the row of palm trees behind her.

As Trevor tried to figure out the change in scenery, another
opening – to his left – began to glow fiery red. It was partially
blocked by a grove of coconut palms, and almost a foot deep in
clear blue water. Sam entered cautiously between the trees and ran
several feet through the water before skidding to a halt in thick white
sand.

Both of them walked over to where Trevor stood. He looked
down and noticed the platform and stone bench were also gone. A
small red crab scuttled between his feet. Trevor jumped to avoid its
snapping claws. The three friends glanced around the island, trying
to comprehend their new location.

"Thanks?" Sam finally stated, with apparent doubt.

Trevor turned back to the wall. Beautiful green-blue water
lapped at the space where Jay and Hank had been standing. The
wall itself, as well as the other four walls, was now barely visible.
White fluffy clouds floated on a blue sky where only minutes ago
stone walls displayed images of people.

Trevor stared at the door. Something was wrong. Jay had not
traveled into the chamber - or tropical island – with the others.
Trevor ran to where the wall had once been, leaving the others
watching from the sandy hill. He studied the beach and the sky. He
waved his arms, but could feel nothing but a cool breeze.

He could not feel a wall. He could not see a warehouse. He
had lost Hank and Jay completely.

Another Nightmare

"Stop." Trevor scolded himself. "I know they are here. They have to be here."

Trevor counted to five and slowly opened his eyes. This time he believed he would see them. Slowly, their images began to appear once again –standing in front of him where the wall once was – at the water's edge. However, they were now part of a collection of images in the sky. They were no longer life-sized people, but simply two small images inside billions more.

Somehow he needed to draw them out of the wall and back into the chamber so Jay could join the others.

Trevor concentrated those two out of the millions projected into the blue sky. Jay was opening and closing a piece of plywood - what roughly resembled a door. He and Hank had constructed a crude door from materials inside the warehouse. Hank was standing opposite Jay, holding up the pieces to form a doorframe. Jay continued to open the door in a futile effort to make a connection in the way Trevor had described.

To add to his growing frustration, Trevor could clearly see the attackers beginning to free themselves – far out of Jay and Hank's line of sight. He tried to relax. He closed his eyes and focused completely on the warehouse.

The two girls watched in amazement. Without realizing, they found themselves walking down to the edge of the water and stared on in amazed silence. Julie opened her mouth to ask a question, but Sam touched her arm and placed a finger over her lips.

Trevor's desperately searched his imagination for the connection. He swore silently that he would not lose them again. It was as if he had held a slender thread in his fingers and had allowed it to slip away... It was lost among millions of threads... A touch; a bond that connected him directly to Jay. His head began to ache as he searched frantically through millions of possibilities.

How careless, scolded the negative voice inside his head. Maybe you've lost them for good? He knew thoughts like those would only distract him. He had to ignore his inner critic for now.

Focus, the other voice in him replied. Find the bond – the thing that links you to Jay. Make a connection based on your friendship. The Library. Madam Butterfly. Funky clothes. The Fortress of the Floating Warrior... there! He found Jay once again.

He felt a slight shift in the atmosphere around him. He could feel the connection, like a gentle touch. In his mind, Trevor lifted the slender, but invisible cord and pulled as hard as he could. It was working. He had re-established a link between them. Trevor opened his eyes as he heard a chorus of gasps behind him.

He stared in horror at the scene now playing in front of him.

Life-sized images of Jay, Hank and the two assailants now stood in the space before them, just a few steps out into the water. It completely startled the girls. They jumped forward as Trevor jumped back, colliding into a huddle. No mere projection, it was as if the people were standing on the island with them. The small crowd watched helplessly on the sand, trying to avoid contact with the realistic images.

The two attackers had escaped the tangle of pipes. Armed with wrenches they had grabbed off the shelves, the men were once again searching for their targets. Trevor watched in horror as Jay and Hank heard them approach and turned to face their enemies. Sam could not control herself any longer.

She splashed through the water and charged down the beach toward the agents. She swung her fists furiously at them, but her blows simply passed through their images. Oblivious to her attack, the men inched closer to Hank and Jay. Sam ran back and looked at Trevor with fierce determination as she pointed to the images.

"Send me in there," Sam demanded. "Let me take them out. I've got to help them."

Trevor looked from Sam back to the images in front of him. He couldn't risk her life. Julie placed a fist over her mouth, as Trevor quickly evaluated the scene.

He instinctively knew there had to be a solution. The challenge was picking the right one. He closed his eyes again in deep concentration.

"Jay," he finally said quietly, but clearly. "You have to come through the door, now."

Jay heard Trevor. He started to move through the door and then hesitated. He looked through the doorway at Hank who was still patiently holding the pieces of the makeshift frame together. Jay realized the door would fall apart if his father tried to come through on his own. Hank shook his head. He understood the risks and still wanted his son to move through.

Julie screamed and pointed into the distance. The killers had turned an invisible corner. They were now in hot pursuit with wrenches held high over their heads.

Jay held the door open with one hand. All he had to do was step through. Everyone silently waited for him to move. Julie squirmed impatiently as Sam shouted at the attackers.

Only Trevor noticed the bright blue line that now ran from Hank's amulet, through the doorway and across the island. The door inside the chamber was soon surrounded by a blue glow. Hank and Trevor shared a single thought. Hank placed one large hand in the center of Jay's back.

"You've got to go on without me," he said firmly. There was no hesitation in his voice. "I love you son."

Hank shoved hard as Jay stubbornly gripped the frame with his other hand. He did not want to leave his father alone with the agents. At the same moment, one of the men had begun to swing a very large wrench. Everyone in the hall heard a crunch as it slammed into the back of Hank's head. The blow shocked Trevor into action.

He reached into the sky where the door stood. In his mind he knew he would find a door handle on the other side – and he did. He opened the door and reached into the warehouse. His fingers hooked Jay's shirt and pulled him out of the warehouse and onto the island.

Jay and Trevor collapsed on the sand in a heap. Everyone watched as the rag-tag door collapsed in pieces. The killers, as obeying some silent command, turned and ran from the warehouse. Jay and Trevor rolled to their knees, beside the slowly fading image of Handy Hank. Jay was the first one to speak.

"Hold on Dad. I'll save you..."

He looked at Trevor in desperation. Hank opened his eyes slightly as Trevor closed his. Hank had made a difficult choice. For a brief moment, Trevor thought he might be able to bring Hank through, if only...

"Pull him through just like you pulled me." A spark of anger flared in Jay's eyes. "I know you can do it."

But Trevor couldn't. The door was broken into several pieces. There was no one in the warehouse to help Hank. That meant the doorway was gone – even if they could still see the other side. Hank smiled feebly at the group. He spoke softly to Jay from the warehouse floor.

"Son," he said softly. "It's all right. It has to be like this – it's a balance. You'll see."

Hank's breathing was as shallow as the focus of his eyes. He sighed. The blue glow evaporated. Then Hank slumped to the floor and his image faded completely.

No one moved for several seconds. Their eyes remained focused on the spot where Hank had been. Finally, Julie left the little mound and walked over to Jay.

"Jay, I'm sorry," she whispered.

Jay held up one hand. He glanced at her, flashing a crooked smile framed by tears.

"Just leave me alone."

Jay left the group and headed into a cluster of palm tress. He threw down his backpack and slumped down near the top of the dune, his back away from the group.

Trevor stood quietly on the little mound of sand. He looked across the horizon in every direction. Nothing remained of the original stone chamber. They were in the middle of an ocean, on the tip of a large island. The point on which they were standing led up to the cluster of trees where Jay had retreated. Behind the palms, a dense forest of trees and vines marched up a ragged mountain peak. He could see a waterfall in the distance.

Trevor dropped heavily onto the sand and covered his head with both arms.

The Island

Only seconds passed before Julie began to shower Trevor with questions.

"Trevor where are we?"

"I mean, what the heck just happened?"

"Daddy says we can figure anything out... Right Trevor?"

Trevor watched her lips move, barely able to comprehend all the questions. He didn't know how to answer. What to say?

"Wait."

A sharp command cut through the barrage of inquiries. It was Sam. Trevor tried to focus on her face, her calm blue eyes.

"I'm sure Trevor's just as confused as we are, Julie."

"Trevor," she said calmly. "Can you tell me what happened?"

He took a deep breath, and shared his side of the story. He told them about the hike, the agents, the deep well, and his spinning, crazy journey through time and space. He described how it felt like being inside a giant blender. Sam listened carefully to every word.

"I realized that... that things I dreamed about or imagined inside my head actually happened where you were. I can't explain it very well, but it was as if I could reach out and touch any spot in town. That's how I was able to get you away from those men."

It even sounded crazy to his ears. He tried to explain it again but gave up. Trevor groaned and put his head back inside his arms. Julie slipped an arm around to comfort him. It was her turn to speak.

"Tell me," she said softly. "What did you see in your mind?"

"Well, I saw the three of you… And I remembered there were doors leading into the chamber…" They nodded as he spoke, encouraging him to continue.

"So, I imagined there was a connection between the doors in the chamber and the spot where each of you were – the doors you used to come here." He paused and looked at Julie, who raised one eyebrow in response.

"That's it? Nothing else?"

Trevor closed his eyes and thought back once again. "I remember wanting to go somewhere safe. Some place safe, and far away from those men. I was only trying to help."

Sam looked at Trevor in surprise and snapped her fingers.

"What is it? What happened?" Julie asked impatiently.

No one noticed that Jay had walked quietly over to join them and stood quietly behind the group. It was his turn to offer a suggestion.

"I don't think it's an accident that each of us were connected by people with amulets. Somehow, the chamber brought us to a place that Trevor either invented or dreamed about in his mind."

"Well sports fans," Sam nodded her head slowly and stretched. "we are probably as far away from those men as we can possibly be." Sam turned to survey the island as Julie sifted sand between her fingers.

"Thankfully you didn't dream up an artic winter."

Sam interrupted before Trevor could answer. "Sorry, but I'd like to suggest we scout around to see if we are inside the chamber or actually on a real island, and just in case we are somewhere else..." she looked around the island.

"I don't want to find myself at the end of those guns anytime soon. We also need to look for shelter and food."

Julie raised her hand.

"I'll take care of food. If it moos, clucks, oinks, or somehow grows, I'll make sure we can eat it without dyin' first." She spun on her heel and began scouting around for anything edible.

Jay volunteered to look for any type of shelter and immediately disappeared back to the cluster of trees. Trevor waited a moment and then followed Jay's path into the trees. It did not take long to spot Jay's colorful shirt. He had his back against the trunk of a palm tree and was throwing shells into the clear water. He glanced up briefly as Trevor approached his shady hideaway.

"Hey," Trevor said softly.

"Whatever."

"Hey, I'm really sorry. I wish..."

"I know dad said it had to happen that way, and I know he made his own decision, but Trevor, how could you just stand there and do nothing?" he demanded.

Trevor's heart sank. He was at a loss for words. Jay picked up a shell and tossed it. It skipped twice over the calm ocean before fluttering to the bottom of the lagoon. Trevor counted to five. He wanted to defend himself. After all, it was his father's decision to let go of the door, not his. What could he say that would not make Jay angrier? He thought about some of the things he had seen inside the chamber.

Jay spoke up before Trevor could reply. "Sorry Trevor. I don't want to take it out on you. It's just… you weren't there. You didn't get to know my dad. Nobody in town really knew him… I guess I barely got to know him too." He said, with a trace of bitterness, his eyes briefly filling with tears.

Trevor sat and listened for over an hour as Jay told him about his time in the warehouse with his dad. "If only he had told me all this earlier… when there was more time." He surprised Trevor with a soft, choking laugh.

"You know, I've always had a fantasy that one day my dad would come home and tell me we were secretly rich or special or something. Then we could all hang out together and do cool things, instead of living in a trailer and totally busting our butts just to buy food." Jay stole a glance at an astonished Trevor.

"Jay, " Trevor paused. "Your mom and dad are two of the nicest people in town. They actually like you. That's more than most kids can say about their parents."

Jay leaned back against the palm tree and dropped his hands into the sand. He located two more shells under the sand and tossed one into the air, watching absentmindedly as it bounced off the trunk of a nearby tree.

"How screwed up is that... and now my dad might even be... dead."

"I'm sorry..." Trevor studied his friend. "But, I'm not sure you've really lost your dad, Jay. Who knows what happened back there? Not after what I saw inside the chamber. I think that's what your dad was trying to teach us. Nothing really ends, it just sort of recycles. In fact, I'm counting on it."

Jay looked up at his friend. He threw the last shell in his hand and watched as it disappeared over a small dune. He stood up beside Trevor and wiped his eyes with his sleeve.

"Yeah Trevor, I think I get it." He said, shrugging. "Dad said something about it; that we'd always be together. He told me not to worry. I think he knew something bad was going to happen. He just didn't want me to get hurt." Then Jay flashed his friend a peace sign.

"So, I'm not going to worry." Jay blew out a heavy sigh and scanned the trees before looking back down at his friend. "I do know one thing for sure. For some strange reason I am incredibly hungry, dude."

He bent over and picked up a coconut resting on the sand by his feet. "Do you think we could crack one of these open with our teeth?" he asked with a half smile, as he tossed it to Trevor.

Termination

"You did *what*?" His voice sounded too shrill, revealing far more fear than he would have preferred.

Fortunately for Nigel Willington, the office was well below the surface of the Earth, and was protected from eavesdropping by several electronic devices. No one outside the room would hear him, as the thick stone and electronics did their best to cloak his little tantrum.

And best of all, no other Stasys employees, except the two people inside the conference room and the nine agents attending by satellite, had been able to hear the pleading tone in his voice. A strangled growl escaped from his throat.

He covered his face with one hand and slouched deep into the black leather chair. The large chair was an exact duplicate of the one in Julian Hartch's office. But here, deep inside the European Operations center, this chair was Willington's and his alone. It was a symbol that served to remind everybody that he, and not Hartch, really ran the operation.

He slammed his fist down onto the black table as another symbol. This one was meant to remind them of their fate should they continue to fail him.

"I pay you for results, not excuses."

At least one thing had gone right.

He tried to take comfort in the fact that all of his agents had been able to slip away undetected. It would be an enormous waste of time and resources to pull them out right away. He had to keep them focused on the task at hand. They would have one final attempt at their targets before things got too complicated.

"Morgen," he barked. One of the images projected onto the wall flinched slighted, then nodded.

"Yes, sir," the agent said.

"You are in charge of the operation from now on. I want you to go back and capture those children. Since the identities of our undercover scouts are now known," he glared at Ms. Irvin in particular, "they can be used to actively assist with your operation."

Morgen nodded in confirmation. Willington drummed his fingers on the surface of the large table as he considered more options. "I don't know what kind of device they used to prevent capture, but I want you out of there within 24 hours, with that technology, and a full report on my desk. You've heard my orders. Now get moving."

He turned to the two agents remaining in the conference room as he terminated the transmission. The agents nodded, but did not move. "I have reason to believe there is more to this town than meets the eye. I am curious to know if there is any connection between the Cosmic Enterprises equipment we discovered in the desert and that old house near Silver Lake." He placed an index finger firmly on top of the desk.

"For now, I will see what Morgen and those bumbling field gorillas can achieve with their heavy-handed approaches." Willington frowned. "Frankly, I do not have much faith in their ability to complete this operation."

Willington stood as he appraised the man and woman in front of him. "However, I believe you would agree that sometimes it is easier to catch flies with honey. For now, I want you to remain hidden. Do nothing until instructed. It may be days or months before you hear from me again." Both agents stood quickly and left through a side door. He watched their backs as they left the conference room.

He suppressed a smile. He had no doubt these two would succeed where others had recently failed. He wouldn't resort to bully tactics anymore. Rather, he was confident that once the two new agents were in place, Cosmic Enterprises would simply hand them the keys to the front door.

Today's failures would not dampen his good mood. Hartch would be in a rejuvenation tank for at least two more weeks. Nigel would inform him of his change in plans, sometime after he emerged. The short break would give him time to refine his new plans. For now, he felt like celebrating. He scanned his ViewComm and randomly selected a name from the long list of employees.

"Feels like a good day to terminate someone insignificant. Let me see . . . Rose McGowan, you'll do," he said, tapping a series of keys to dismiss her. *Permanently.*

A Window Closes

Jay and Trevor made a short trip through the palm trees, collecting any fruit they could find along the way. They returned with two large banana leaves full of coconuts, red berries, a large orange fruit, and several bunches of bananas. They placed the food on top of the sandy dune.

Eventually, the entire group was gathered on the sandy mound.

Sam had gathered enough wood for burning and some larger pieces to make a shelter. She carried the large pieces to the grove of trees while Jay began assembling the smaller branches for the fire. Julie proudly displayed three large fish she had speared beneath a waterfall. She held one up for inspection.

"It looks like some kind of sea bass," she said, turning the blue and silver fish around in her hand. Then she looked at the mound of fruit and smiled. "I can make some tasty fish with coconut milk and mango." She took the mangos and left the boys to figure out how to crack open the coconuts.

As Jay searched for a couple of rocks, Sam held out a closed hand to Trevor. "For starters, we are not inside your magical cave..." she began.

"Blender," Trevor corrected her. Sam sighed, and waved her closed fist in front of him.

"Blender. Cave. Magic Genie Lamp…" she continued. "Whatever you want to call it. We are still on good old planet Earth, buddy. I found this while I was looking for wood."

Sam grabbed Trevor's hand, opened her fist, and dropped a small, flat rock onto his palm. Trevor looked at her for an explanation.

"It's a man-made tool Kippy. It's some sort of knife for chopping food," she explained impatiently. Trevor picked up the stone with his other hand, and examined it closely.

"Don't you see? This means there might be other people on this island." Then she pointed upwards. "Also, have you noticed," drawing Trevor's gaze skyward, "that there aren't any planes in the sky? No white clouds trailing behind any jets." She looked back at him, smiling. "So, Kiptonite," she asked softly, but with a hint humor, "do you remember wanting to go back in time as well?"

He sat down on the soft white sand. "No", he said slowly.

It was too unbelievable. As if transporting everyone to some tropical island wasn't enough… Now he had to consider that they might be stuck back in time, without any way of getting home. Trevor sat up suddenly.

"I remember focusing on all of you, and everyone being safe," he said. "I'm sure I didn't think about going back in time, just to a safer place." Sam thought about this for a moment, shrugged her shoulders, and seemed to accept his explanation. She strolled over to the grove to help Jay build a shelter.

Trevor looked down at the stone in his hand. Well, the same hands that had managed to get them all here would have to keep them safe, he decided. He struck a coconut with the stone, and a chunk fell onto the sand. Good start, he thought. He struck at the husk again, and within a couple hours he had opened all of the coconuts and several large chunks of white coconut meat were stacked on a broad green banana leaf.

Julie collected the coconut juice into a shell and used it to baste small pieces of fish. Sam stayed busy weaving the strips of palm fronds over the lean-to shelter. Jay added the final touches as he placed banana leaves on the ground underneath. Eventually, each of them paused to admire their little island home.

In a less than an hour, the smell of cooked fish and coconut drifted across the warm breeze. The group stared hungrily at the juicy fish as it sizzled over the flames. Julie knew her customers could not wait much longer - even she was starving. She stared back at the impatient crowd.

"As Chef Pauline would say," Julie said, and then offered her best imitation of her teacher's French accent, "it is almost time we serve our little meal, mon cher." She waved them in the direction of the seats under the thatched roof, and continued in her normal accent, although it too was equally difficult to understand.

"Ya'll can just settle down. This magic's gonna take time."

They all found a seat and waited in anticipation. Slowly, like a curtain opening over a stage, the mood shifted within the small group. Hunger was replaced by an overwhelming sense of awe. From their spot on the beach, they watched as clouds of bright white, pink, and gray formed and re-formed in a sky of deep blue. The sun splashed the sky with waves of orange, red and purple. They tracked the sun's progress as it slowly released its grip on the sky and slid under the horizon. No one talked about food, no one asked for water, and not one of them complained about the sand. The small fire popped and sent small sparks into the air, as the sky grew dark around them. Sam leaned back against Jay's upraised knees.

"I feel like I'm watching the first sunset on Earth."

Everyone shared her thoughts, except for Trevor. He was enjoying the view, but hoped with all his heart that this was not the very first sunset on Earth. The show ended when Julie stepped in front of them holding a large banana leaf piled high with fish. She had been watching from beside the shelter until the final rays of the sun had evaporated from the sky.

"It may not be the Ritz," she said quietly, setting the leafy tray down in the middle of the group, "but it's gonna be the best fish you've put in your mouth today, or my name isn't Julie Meriwether."

With her invitation, everyone reached toward the leaf and pulled off a small piece of fish. Within minutes, the entire leaf was empty. Julie jumped up and quickly returned with pieces of fresh fruit in coconut shells, topped with slivers of coconut. It was the perfect dessert for their island dinner.

"Julie." Sam said with pure satisfaction, "That was amazing." The rest heaped on their praises as well. Julie made an "aw shucks" gesture and leaned back against a tree trunk.

Darkness covered the sky like a blanket as thousands of glittering lights poked through. Meteors struck the atmosphere and blazed fiery trails across the black sky. There was no single place where they began or ended, the trails of fire went everywhere.

Trevor's mind was a flurry of thoughts, like the streaking fragments far above him. He continued to watch the sky show even as his friends drifted off to sleep. He watched their faces and listened to the soft breathing sounds. He could not stop his mind from racing. He searched for clues inside a jumble of thoughts. What will we do tomorrow?

He looked across the lagoon. Phosphorescent foam bounced gently over the quiet surf, like ripples of electricity riding across a distant storm. He licked the salt from his lips and closed his eyes. He leaned back into the sand and rested his head on the green banana leaves. Within minutes, his mind was free from worry. And, for the first time in a very long day, he relaxed. Even his dreams would not scare him tonight. He would walk through them happy and unafraid, as he and his friends floated across the universe on waves of energy.

Unseen, an old man stooped by age and time, watched the slumbering group from a distant dune. He blinked only once as he observed the four sleeping figures. Then he smiled a peculiar smile and faded back into the starry night.

The Gift

Cindy Fox walked through the dingy living room of the small trailer and placed her ear against the closed door to Jay's room.

She lifted a long strand of her brown hair and tucked it behind her ear, perhaps because it was bothering her, but most likely not. Perhaps at a deeper level she thought it would help her find her son.

She closed her eyes and listened. She waited for the tap of a pencil against a notebook, a small cough, or a yawn. But his room remained silent and empty. She slowly straightened her aching back and placed a hand above her hip. It wasn't as easy working the late shift every day.

She missed her husband. But when he left on wild adventures, she knew he would come home safe. Now Jay was missing as well. She would do anything to protect them, but she didn't know where they could have gone for so long. What have you gotten us into, Hank?

She bent down and picked a pair of Jay's jeans off the floor, old clothes she could no longer afford to replace, but only patch. She had just left the room and closed the flimsy door when a knock at the front door broke the silence.

A curious old man stood at the trailer door. He was wearing what appeared to be some kind of old-fashioned adventure costume. He tipped his hat and then invited her to join him at the large house across the lake.

It was not like Cindy Fox to completely trust a stranger, but for some reason she found herself instantly trusting the oddly dressed man. Within a few minutes, they had traveled around the lake to the far side, and quickly entered the large house. Inside the formal parlor, she met other parents, three couples in all. The old man made a short presentation and tried to set their minds at ease. But what he asked of them was no small request, and of course, they all had more questions.

Like the other parents, it didn't take her long to realize the old professor's unique offer was also the key to her child's destiny.

A Door Opens

Trevor lifted his head off the crumpled leaves and brushed sand from his face. Then he spit. There was sand in his mouth as well.

Maybe Sam can help us make hammocks, he thought, as he picked pieces of grit from the corners of his eyes. He wouldn't want to sleep on the sand every night. He stood up and stretched, and felt the muscles in his body loosen and several joints popping in relief. Ah, that feels good, he thought sleepily, as he noticed Jay and Julie waking up at the same time. He looked down at Julie and stifled a laugh as he watched her trying to remove the sand covering her face, one tiny grain at a time.

"Hey Kitch Witch," Trevor suggested, "why don't you just wash off in the lagoon?"

As he turned to indicate the place she could bathe, he froze, with one hand pointing west and his eyes facing the ocean. Julie was too busy brushing herself off to notice his stunned expression. Keeping his eyes fixed firmly on the horizon, he tapped frantically on her shoulder.

"Um. Hey, uh—look, Julie." He began waving frantically. "*Look, everyone.*"

The others got to their feet and followed his gaze across the lagoon. It took several seconds for them to realize what Trevor was so excited about, but then, there it was, clear to all of them: a large black shape slicing through the water, just beyond the coral reef.

"What is that?" he asked I a whisper, without taking his eyes off of the horizon.

They watched the dark shape grow larger. It was definitely approaching the island. Everyone began to stir and shift nervously. Sam disappeared unnoticed through the back of the hut as they strained to get a better look. Suddenly, the shape changed and began to rise up from the water. This is no fish, Trevor thought. This is man-made. So much for being lost in time.

Sam motioned for the group to move behind the shelter. The group moved backward, toward the shelter, and huddled there as they watched from a safe distance, hidden in the top of a tall palm tree. A smaller boat had emerged from the larger shape, and was headed their way.

She stayed in front, the ambassador for their small tribe. Soon the boat was only a few hundred yards from shore. She shouted over the noise of the breaking surf. "I see a man in a small boat, and he's headed right for us." She could not determine whether the odd craft was made of wood or metal, but from a peaked bow, the sides of the sleek black vessel tapered down to its stern.

As it approached, she could soon see a tall dark man dressed in an old-fashioned sailor's suit standing in the rear, carefully steering the boat through the reef. A soft rhythmic "shuh,

shuh, shuh" sound proceeded the small craft as it entered the lagoon.

Jay and the others studied the small craft closely from their place near the shelter. He could barely make out letters printed along its side: Cosmic Enterprises. Then he smiled. With a small yelp, he sprinted past Sam, across the beach, and splashed into the lagoon to greet the boat. The group slowly stepped from behind the shelter and joined Sam as Jay scampered down to the shore. They watched in silence as he waded through the shallow lagoon and grabbed onto the front of the boat. It bounced gently in the waves, and he made his way back to the stern, where the pilot greeted him.

"The professor sent me on a rescue mission." the man's deep voice sounded as if boulders were tumbling over each other to form the words. He inspected Jay with sharp eyes and serious intent.

"You look perfectly healthy and safe to me."

He turned and glanced at the faces lining the shore, smiled broadly and saluted.

"It's a fine morning," he rumbled. "Would anyone else care to go sailing?"

The Fin

Julie fluffed her hair and pushed her way to the front of the group. With her usual directness, she pointed to the stranger as she marched up to the sleek boat. "Mister, if you can get us off this island and back home, I'll hug your neck and name my first child after you."

The pilot helped her onto the platform at the back of the boat. Julie stepped up and faced her rescuer. "So...?" she demanded. The man seemed surprised by such a spunky passenger so early in the morning. "Well ma'am," he chuckled, bowing as low as his voice. "Parker Thomas, Captain First Class, at your service."

Julie nodded approvingly at the name she would one day give to her child, and plopped unceremoniously onto one of the built-in benches. Sam shook her head as she navigated around the impulsive young chef and sat down. One by one, they made their way onboard and stationed themselves at the front of the boat.

Trevor, who had been standing in the water helping the others, suddenly shouted, and ran back through the water to the shelter. They watched as he frantically searched the ground, finally pouncing on something that he jammed into his pocket. He dashed back through the water and onto the boat. Sam gave him a quizzical stare as the pilot helped Trevor onboard. He pulled the object out of his pocket, revealing the flat piece of rock she had found earlier.

"I wanted a souvenir. Just to prove we were here," he said turning the rock over in his hand. "And besides, who knows if we'll ever come back?" Sam gazed fondly at the island that had been their home for one night.

The pilot closed the door to the platform and returned to the small wheelhouse near the back of the boat. He pushed three small levers forward and the vessel began to glide almost silently through the water. With a muffled shushing sound, the craft began its return trip through the lagoon to the larger vessel waiting beyond the reef.

The ship waiting for them appeared to be a larger version of the smaller rescue boat. It was sleek and streamlined, its jet-black hull topped only by a flat deck. The black metal was punctuated rivets and windows, and an ornate metal fin formed a ridge along each side of the top deck. Unlike most boats, it had no railings, no masts, or any other structures that could be seen from the skiff. Like a stealthy shadow, it floated quietly offshore, safely beyond the reach of the sharp coral reef.

Captain Thomas reached behind his jaws and pressed.

"Mister George," he commanded to an unseen person, "please prepare the Fin for docking, and have the 'punks rig her for sailing." A magical transformation began to unfold on the larger vessel.

They watched as a section near the back of the ship began to rise up out of the water. At the same time, three black poles shot skyward from the deck, as luminescent sails automatically unfurled from the rigging. A brass railing rose appeared as a half-moon section of the forward deck rose slowly from within the ship. In fewer than ten minutes, the submarine-like craft had converted itself into a proper sailing vessel.

The skiff wound its way through the waves and drew alongside the newly transformed vessel. Sam judged its length in terms of her favorite sport: longer than a soccer field. At the same time, Jay offered his rough estimation: The ship was almost 280 feet long. The pilot smiled proudly at Jay's uncannily accurate guess, as he steered the little skiff from the ship's bow to its stern.

Once in back, he executed a series of turns that aligned the smaller boat with the back of the larger one. Everyone could now see directly inside the ship. The open space was filled with ocean water. Although it looked like the interior of a dark cavern, Trevor could see rows of tiny white lights flickering to life inside the large hanger.

The captain steered their small boat into the belly of the larger ship. Julie held her breath and squinted as they moved inside, like a small fish being eaten by a bigger one. Sam gaped in wonder as she examined all of the massive doors and walls of the container. Once inside, they heard the sound of water rushing past, and with a gentle thud, their skiff soon rested directly on the hull of the larger ship. Captain Thomas lowered a collapsible ladder and motioned to his guests.

"Welcome onboard the Fin. I will now show you to your rooms…" he smiled grandly. The group followed closely behind.

Their guide soon came to a closed hatch at the end of the platform. The captain placed his hand on the door and it hissed softly as it opened. The group followed, leaving the large room and the little skiff. They found themselves stepping from a steel hanger into a pleasantly decorated hallway. The hatch closed silently behind as the last person stepped across.

Captain Thomas led them down the narrow hallway and into a large, oval-shaped salon. Four Victorian chairs and a small table sat neatly between two closed hatches to the left and right. Electric light from several brass lamps cast a blueish glow across the room. The captain turned to address his small audience.

"I believe you will want to clean off and shake the sand out of your clothes. Better yet, you may want to put on the clean clothes that are waiting in your guest rooms." He waved toward the closed hatch on the right. "You will find your cabins through that hallway. Take your time. When you are ready, you will find me waiting for you in the main salon located at the end of this corridor."

He pointed down the open hatch, to the hallway beyond. "You will see a set of stairs at the end of the hall. Meet me inside the room at the top of those stairs," he said, smiling. "I have a very special welcome planned for each one of you." The captain spun on his heel and quickly disappeared down the long corridor.

Sam opened the hatch to the right of the salon and peered inside. A short interior hallway led to six more doors, three on the left and three on the right. She moved into the short hall and proceeded to the first door on the left. The others followed her inside as she pointed to one of the doors.

"Look," she said, "this door has your name on it, Kip."

She moved to the next door. "This one says Hudson" She opened her door and stepped inside. The others quickly found their rooms and followed Sam's example. Trevor stepped over the threshold and looked around the small room.

His cabin was lined in dark mahogany paneling that rose midway up the wall, exactly like the hallways. Black and white photos were arranged neatly on the space above the wood. Each of the room's four walls contained images of smiling people from distant lands. Across from him, a bunk bed had been pulled down from a compartment in the wall. A small wooden box sat on top of crisp white sheets, near the edge of the bed. Above the bed was a window framed in shiny new brass, through which Trevor could see the clear morning sky. To the right was a compact but well equipped bathroom, complete with a sink, shower and toilet. Inside, neatly stacked next to the sink was a set of clothes and a small travel bag. He would check out the rest of the room later. Now, all he could think about was washing the sand out of his hair.

Trevor quickly stripped off his sandy clothes, the ones borrowed from the underground cavern, and hopped into the shower. This time, he patiently waited until warm jets of water replaced the cold. When he was clean and sand-free, he dried off and reached for the shirt on top of the short stack.

He scanned the pants, shoes and socks. These were his things, from inside his closet at home. How did they get here? Trevor slipped on a bright red shirt and pair of jeans, and was tying the laces to a familiar pair of blue Converse shoes as he puzzled through the possibilities.

A soft whir and three sharp metallic clicks suddenly intruded on his mental deliberation. It took him a few seconds to realize the noises were not part of the boat's normal mechanical hum or tremor. In fact, the Fin seemed abnormally quiet for a seagoing vessel. These noises were much closer and more distinct. Trevor and pushed the bathroom door open just enough to peek out, into the small room beyond.

A pair of large blue eyes stared back at him from across the room.

New Friends

"Hello, Trevor."

A 3-foot-high polished steel globe was speaking to him in perfect English. He opened the door wider.

The metal ball was in fact standing on two bronze legs. Another pair of tubes extended from the middle of the globe, each ending in five metal fingers. Resting on top of the globe, a smaller black ball was bolted tight by a series of metal straps. A pair of large round eyes floated inside the dark orb. The blue eyes blinked twice as if to confirm the greeting.

Trevor blinked back. "Hello?"

The metal snowman took four awkward steps and held up its right hand. A symphony of whirs and clicks propelled the mechanical man forward. Green eyes floated upward and focused on Trevor, as it waited to shake hands. The metal fingers at the end of its arm fidgeted slightly as Trevor hesitated. The eyes pinched in slightly at the top, as if curious about the delay. Finally, Trevor extended his right hand and was rewarded with a firm, but gentle handshake.

"That is better," the odd-looking machine replied, sounding relieved. The blue eyes widened with delight. "For approximately 2.7 seconds I was worried you did not want to be friends." The metal ball began to totter toward the bed as a thought formed in Trevor's mind. The black orb on top seemed to spin as the blue eyes returned their focus on him.

"That is correct." The metal hands gestured to the globe that held them. "I do not possess a vocal device. What purpose would that serve when you and I can share our thoughts more efficiently?"

Trevor opened his mouth, but was cut off by the mechanical man's voice inside his head. "I am a rover, model Muk1357." There was a brief pause. "Ah, I see you have never heard of Rovers. Well, I imagine that is no surprise, since you have never before met one." A brief whining noise, like the spinning of a top, and the metal body tilted slightly forward.

"Our inventor viewed us as toys, and nothing more." Trevor heard a soft sigh between his ears. "If only the world knew how many rovers he actually created..." The rover's eyes seemed to brighten. "Regardless, the Professor has continued to improve our functionality and I now possess many significant upgrades since the time of my creation."

It speaks in such formal English, Trevor thought. The little ball... what was it called?

The rover straightened its metal legs and looked at Trevor. Its eyes seemed to dance. "My name?" it asked brightly, after hearing Trevor's thought. "Why, Orbit sir, and glad to be at your service."

The mechanical joints softly hissed and clicked, as Orbit executed a graceful bow. There was a brief pause as Orbit tried to understand Trevor's next unspoken thought.

"Why, of course. I almost forgot about the box."

Before he could think of another question Orbit resumed his journey toward the bed. Metal fingers clicked as they grasped the wooden box. Then the two mechanical legs whirred as Orbit returned and held the box up for Trevor's inspection.

Trevor unclasped the small brass lock that held the lid securely on top. He carefully lifted the top of the box and gasped as he stared inside. Nestled in a bed of red velvet was a gold chain and pendant. He reached into the box and carefully lifted the chain up for a closer inspection.

"Do not worry," the rover announced as it lowered the box to the floor. "You cannot break it, and besides, it is now yours."

Trevor slipped the pendant over his head and watched as light in the room bounced off a white stone set into the center of the pendant. He had seen one like it before, but where?

"Yes," Orbit said almost reverently inside Trevor's head. "Each of your mentors was wearing one of these today." Another pause. "Who are the mentors? Well, perhaps it is a good time to let Captain Thomas explain..." Orbit waved a single metal arm toward the door.

Trevor returned down the hall to the parlor, followed by Orbit. The small room was crowded with the animated discussions of his friends and the mechanical whirs and hisses from two other rovers. Looking around, he realized everyone had pendants. A blue gem gleamed from the center of Jay's and green sparks leapt from Julie's. All of them, that was, except Sam. Trevor counted three rovers in the parlor. One missing.

"Sam?"

"What?" Her reply was sharp and direct.

"Umm. Didn't you get a pendant? Wasn't there a rover in your room?"

She crossed her arms, holding her thoughts tightly inside. Trevor noticed Sam shuffle one foot. Jay coughed softly, and Julie suddenly seemed interested in patterns in the wallpaper. Something was wrong, and he was obviously the only one who did not know what happened. Trevor looked at Orbit who simply shrugged. Apparently, Orbit could only read his mind.

"Well, how was I supposed to know?"

Sam flung her arms around as she gestured at the other rovers assembled in the room.

"It surprised me. What else could I do?"

Trevor spun on his heel and raced back to Sam's room. The clacking and whirring of rovers echoed behind. He skidded to a stop in front of Sam's room and pushed the door open. Inside, pieces of gray metal and black stone littered the room. A crumpled rover lay in a sad heap near the bed. Trevor tiptoed over the debris as the other rovers strained to look into the room.

From behind, he could hear Jay snickering as Julie's laugh quickly turned into a series of guffaws, sniggles and snorts. Trevor reached out and plucked the box containing her pendant off the bed. He backed out as the other mechanical devices made way for him.

"It's not funny," Sam said. "I thought it was attacking me. How was I supposed to know it was friendly?" Her protests only made the others laugh even harder. Jay jumped in surprise as Sam swiped one muscular arm at him.

Trevor could not suppress a giggle of his own as he handed Sam her pendant. Appropriately, flames from a fiery red stone sparkled from its center. Orbit and the other rovers had also returned to the parlor.

"Yes, you are correct Trevor," Orbit answered his concerns about the other rover. "Sam's rover, Andromeda, can be easily repaired by the Foundation."

Trevor smiled and patted Sam on one shoulder as he walked away. Despite his mechanical friend's assurances, the other rovers gave Sam plenty of distance as the group proceeded towards the main salon.

The group walked quietly, gazing at the many portraits of persons unknown that lined it, until it finally opened into an enormous foyer with a staircase at the center. Both sides of the staircase curved gracefully toward the landing above. Two doors were set into the fourth wall, between the two stairways. Trevor paused, then twisted a large brass handle on one of the doors and stepped inside.

A furry brown missile immediately knocked him to the floor.

Family Reunion

Trevor couldn't stop laughing as Moke placed two large paws squarely on the middle of his chest and licked his face. He noticed scrapes and stitches under her fur as he hugged her close. Someone had worked very diligently to heal her injuries.

Two familiar figures hovered above him and his loyal companion. He peered around Moke and saw the relieved faces of his mother and father. He jumped up and hugged them hard. The entire room was filled with shouts of laughter and jubilant conversation as his friends were reunited with their parents. Hank, although battered and bruised, gingerly embraced his very relieved family.

The rovers waddled in behind and assumed positions along the rear wall. Clicking and hissing noises faded as the rovers stood motionless. They seemed content to observe the group rather than wander through the crowd.

The noisy reunion soon gave way to hushed exploration.

Treasures from a variety of eras and cultures were arranged on wooden tables and books of all sizes filled shelves along each wall. One table displayed an assortment of charts and scrolls. On another, a tribal mask rested precariously next to a purple crystal vase, while an ancient map of the world hung on the wall above an exhibit of rare gems. Odd brass and metal devices were standing, propped or hung in almost every part of the room. An enormous fireplace commanded center stage against the far wall.

Trevor and his parents stared through a large glass window as the ocean passed quickly beyond the outer deck. The fast-moving Fin was now far away from the island, with only water and clouds on the horizon. They had traveled many miles without any sense of motion.

A voice from behind caused every head to swivel toward the rear of the room.

"The Fin is the fastest vessel on Earth, no matter if she travels over the waves or under them," a man's voice announced. The captain appeared, entering through the large double doors. Two stewards followed behind, bearing silver trays on which were perched goblets of fruit punch. Everyone soon held a drink in his or her hand.

Julie glanced around the room, looking for additional servers carrying food. She wagged a pudgy finger at her father and whispered loudly, "If this were my party, I'd at least serve some sandwiches or ice cream, or for goodness sake, a tray of vegetables." Everyone standing near her smiled and Trevor nudged her gently in the ribs. "Well," she protested, crossing her arms, "I would. It's the proper way to entertain guests."

Undaunted by the junior chef, the captain lifted the last goblet off a tray and raised it in a salute. "Welcome aboard the Fin..." he smiled. "Here's to daring adventures on an uncharted sea."

The Enterprise

After serving refreshments, Captain Thomas waited patiently until everyone sat down, which took several minutes, as their ongoing explorations had scattered them about the room.

"First, let us first dispense with the obvious." he gestured to the room. "As you can see, this is not an ordinary boat." Everyone chuckled at this understatement. "Mr. George, myself, and our hearty band of steampunks, as I like to call my crew, work for an organization known as Cosmic Enterprises... which Jay correctly identified this morning as Cosmic Studios." He gestured to Jay, and then shuffled his feet before continuing. "I apologize if there has been so much secrecy surrounding our organization until now."

Trevor noticed the captain glance at each of the parents, except Hank. He remembered that Hank had been wearing a medallion, and seemed ready to deal with the agents. He obviously knew more about Cosmic Enterprises than his own parents. Captain Thomas straightened his shoulders and continued with a more confident smile. "But it's time for you to learn everything about us, and how you wound up here, on our submersible ship."

Then quite unexpectedly, the captain and the two attendants walked to the rear of the room and quietly closed the doors behind as they exited. Without a sound, curtains silently lowered around the windows as the lights in the room dimmed to a soft glow. After a few seconds, the face of teenage boy appeared in the stone directly above the fireplace. He had dark skin, black hair with deep brown eyes, and was wearing a very proper business suit.

"Hello." The smiling boy positively beamed at the group. "My name is Sachin Singh, Director of Research for Cosmic Enterprises. I am sorry I could not join you in person," he added with a soft British accent.

"Rest assured, the crew of the Fin will take excellent care of you during your journey home. It is my goal to explain a few facts and help answer any of your questions. In doing so, let me also shed some light on some very important things that have occurred this week."

Photos of the SUVs, the attackers, and their locations flashed across the wall above their heads. Trevor hesitated. This type of projection seemed vaguely familiar, almost multi-dimensional, like the murals on the walls of the underground chamber.

"These people are employees of an organization called The Stasys Global Corporation." The name now appeared under the photos.

"As you may already be aware, Stasys Global is one of the world's largest corporations. They make everything from clothing to combat gear, from crops to prepared meals. However, you may not be aware that they are also dedicated to the sole domination of the Earth." He paused as new images appeared.

"They will do anything to control world production—anything, including murder. In fact, it was their bold actions that forced us to contact each one of you." Sachin's smiling face reappeared on the screen. "Trust that I did not anticipate meeting you for the first time, as you traveled under the ocean." Smiles and polite laughter rippled across the room.

"Let me introduce you formally to Cosmic Enterprises, and those of us who work for it."

A series of friendlier images appeared on the wall. Scientists, doctors, technicians, and teachers were accompanied by images of actors, politicians, athletes… more people than they could track with their eyes. Finally, a single image of an elderly man replaced all the others and remained on the wall.

"We are all part of a global organization created more than two hundred years ago by Professor Maximillian Augustus Gladwell."

Sachin Singh gestured to the portrait. White bushy hair crawled down the side of his face, forming two very large sideburns that were connected to a neatly clipped goatee. His brown jacket covered a pair of tan trousers, each leg of which was tucked inside two brown leather boots. A gold chain was clipped to his breast pocket, leading to a small gold watch, at which he now peered intently. Julie and Sam smiled with amusement. The man reminded them of a cartoon character.

Meanwhile, Sachin continued his story, hesitated, and then paused altogether as he waited for the visitor to speak.

"Good Heavens," the man exclaimed. "Look at the time. It's well past 1910." He smiled and winked to the audience, as if everyone else was in on the joke. He peered intently at Sachin, who was staring down from the wall in amusement, as he examined the younger man's face and clothing. "Rather formal attire for a cruise, isn't it Mr. Singh?"

Despite his darker complexion, Sachin visibly blushed and glanced at his suit, before giving his lapels a reassuring tug. He opened his mouth to protest, but was cut off as the old man leaned a hand on a large chair and pointed at the audience.

Jay scratched his head in surprise. The younger boy just said the Professor had created the organization more than two hundred years earlier, and yet he was now standing in the room with them… He raised his hand slightly to ask a most obvious question. However, the two hundred year old man seemed unaware of the request and inhaled deeply before beginning his story.

"Ah… I was just going to explain our the nature of our operations, scientific research, and…"

"Ear wax and shoestring," the professor interrupted, thrusting both hands into his coat pockets "let's tell them why they are here. He waved his arms as if clearing a path through an invisible thicket of leaves.

"You see, many years ago my team and I were on an archeological exploration deep in the forests of North America - the exact spot where the town of Silver Lake is now located. Our group had recently uncovered evidence of an ancient civilization. Naturally, we began to excavate the site, removing hundreds of years of dense foliage as we explored the terrain."

The old man became even more animated as his voice rose with excitement. He inhaled deeply, his chest expanding to the point where Trevor thought the buttons on his jacket might pop open – before continuing his story.

"Try to imagine how very different it was back then. No trucks or roads, and no electricity or digging machines. It was hard work just moving equipment into the area. On the fourteenth day of excavation, I was working alone near the base of an enormous block of granite. At one point, I leaned against a particularly large boulder to rest and accidentally tumbled hundreds of feet down a hidden shaft. The only thing that saved my life was an equally deep pile of rotting debris that cushioned my fall."

He made a motion with his arm, tracing his fall into the leafy cushion. Everyone was now completely focused on the old professor's story.

"I looked up. The vertical shaft was completely smooth, with no apparent way back to the surface. I began to search the bottom of the shaft and finally found a small, narrow passage leading deeper into the mountain. At first, I thought I had stumbled upon an ancient waterway or sewer, but I knew I was mistaken – there was no prior evidence of this type of construction in North America."

Trevor gasped. It sounded like the very same well he had fallen into. The professor's eyes twinkled with amusement.

"I followed the tunnel deeper and deeper until I found myself standing within some vast underground chamber. It took some time for my eyes to adjust to the gloom and the meager light provided by my small lantern, but once inside, I still could not believe the vision my eyes beheld."

The storyteller leaned forward and paused dramatically before allowing his small audience to hear the next part of his journey.

""At first, I thought it was a Mayan temple or perhaps some ancient mine." Professor Gladwell breathed in heavily. His eyes remained locked on the group. Everyone now sat on the edge of their chairs and stared back in anticipation.

"However, there were sounds of machinery all around me. In fact, the clicks and whirs seemed to vibrate from within my very bones. Although it didn't look or feel like any human device, it was…or rather is, a veritable clockwork of the cosmos. Something not fashioned by man or beast." He paused to make sure all eyes were focused on him.

"I can still remember the exact moment, as if it all happened yesterday…"

144 Years Earlier

The old professor directed the workers as the last piece of scaffolding was carefully removed and secured inside its container. The underground crew consisted entirely of employees and associates from his company, Cosmic Enterprises. Despite his occasionally odd behavior, it had been a relatively routine job for his experienced archeology team: searching an ancient chamber, sifting through rocks, collecting samples, installing doors and devices to help them work more efficiently, while ultimately finding little noteworthy in what was an otherwise ordinary looking cave.

Once the box had been sealed, he called out and motioned for the last of his employees to leave. They immediately gathered their tools and the remaining crate, and headed for the only shaft leading up to his newly constructed manor. The professor noted that one of the workers had left behind a small pile of clean clothes. He made a mental note to take the bundle with him. Then, the professor heard the elevator doors clatter shut with a clang, and listened to the distant chugging of a steam engine as the metal cage was pulled slowly back toward the surface.

Minutes later, he stood alone at the center of the vast underground chamber, with only the flickering light of the five brass torches around him. He listened to the silence, imagining he could extend his hearing beyond the empty space. He heard nothing. No messages. No ghostly whispers. Absolute silence. He asked himself the same question he had been asking since the day of the discovery. Why am I so convinced of another presence inside this chamber? Only the cavern walls heard his reply.

"By gum, I believe you are here," he shouted. "I don't know what you are or who, or even where you are hiding. But there is something special about this chamber and all of its mysterious energy…" he waved wildly to the rough-hewn walls.

He felt lost in a sea of conflicting information. He was a scientist, a man of reason. Yet here he stood, in a place both foreign and familiar, somewhere between the known and unknown.

Although he could not actually define the energy around him, it was palpable - he could almost *feel* it. Amongst all his team members, only he could see the fuzzy images that floated on top of the walls - too many for him to clearly discern. He knew the only reason they had not committed him to an insane asylum before now was because they trusted his judgment completely. Or so he hoped.

The weary professor stepped toward one of the walls. There was only one image among the billions that he could see clearly. He moved to it now and watched in fascination. It repeated over and over.

It was the image of a small boy, standing inside the chamber, using it to command the entire universe. The professor realized the chamber was showing him one image – this boy - a child who would harness its power. In that moment, the professor resolved to let no one else visit the underground chamber until the boy arrived.

He turned, forgetting the bundle of clothes, and walked toward the elevator sent to retrieve him. He stepped inside and slowly closed the iron gates behind, watching the brass lamps flutter and dim, as he ascended from the cavern in a shroud of darkness.

Human Analog

Back onboard the Fin, the professor stood quietly near the fireplace, his story told, and blinked twice. He slowly focused on the group in front of him as if trying to emerge from a deep sleep. "We have accomplished much since then. And every day, I have waited for the boy I saw on the wall to appear. In fact," he looked straight at Trevor, "my long wait ended only yesterday."

Every person in the room, including his friends, the adults, and even the image of Sachin Singh, stared directly at Trevor. He looked at his feet, desperately searching for some little piece of lint or scrap of paper to distract him from their scrutiny. After what seemed like an eternal silence, Professor Gladwell cleared his throat with a loud "harrumph". He stepped forward within the room. One by one, the small crowd turned their attention away from Trevor and back toward the Professor.

"So now you know about our chamber. However, there is one very important fact you need to understand... about yourselves." He inhaled softly and continued. "The four of you represent a continuation of mankind. It is something my team predicted years ago: humans will one day move beyond the confines of this universe into fantastic new dimensions in space and time."

Julie wrinkled her brow into a frown and crossed her arms.

"Oh yes, my dear. It's true." Professor Gladwell did not have to be a mind reader to sense her doubts. "Would you believe there are 64 dimensions within our infinite Universe, Julie?"

Professor Gladwell looked at her and smiled, pushing his hands deep into his coat pockets. Julie seemed unconvinced. "My dear Mrs. Meriwether, how else would you propose to carry on a conversation with a man who should have been dead for more than one hundred years?"

He arched a bushy eyebrow at Julie and quietly puffed on the unlit pipe. "You see… inside each of us is a special piece of genetic code. It's only a trace amount, but enough to make us very special creatures. What my foundation predicted years ago is that a few humans would receive more, while others would receive less, while most would obtain none whatsoever."

No one in the room moved, as they waited for him to continue. Instead, Sachin Singh spoke from his place on the wall.

"The professor's team accurately predicted that humans with exceptionally high levels of this code would slowly gravitate toward their place of origin. In this case, you and your parents have subconsciously, yet not accidentally, chosen to live in Silver Lake. Exactly where Professor Gladwell discovered the chamber many decades ago."

The old professor put a finger to one eye. "Have you ever looked closely into your eyes?" He waited almost joyfully as the group excitedly began examining each other's eyes. Sons, daughters and parents began pulling their eyelids down in order to stare into each other's eye sockets. Julie couldn't help but giggle as her father playfully leaned close to her, practically sticking his nose into her face. After a few cursory inspections Sam sat upright and looked back at the professor.

"Wait a minute. What exactly are we looking for?"

"You each possess small flecks of gold in the iris of your eye. They are fragments of the human analog – the "non-digital" - as we like to say. That's why each one of you has exhibited specific talents, normal human abilities, only amplified to a higher level." The Professor paused as they stared into each other's eyes in order to confirm his statement. The old man pointed a finger to Julie.

"Trevor was right, Julie. You are a witch of sorts in the kitchen. You have the unique ability to unlock hidden chemistry within ordinary ingredients. As you have discovered, this can result in some very interesting recipes." He then turned to each of the remaining four students.

"Jay, you have shown an ability to think visually. You can form amazing designs and construct objects from the very molecules in our atmosphere." Jay sat up in his seat.

"Dimension 64… the game." He smiled. "Your studio named the game after the 64 dimensions." The professor nodded quietly. "But how did you know I would play it… or even like it?" he asked, puzzled. His father Hank looked down at his feet shyly as the professor responded with a wide grin.

"Let's just say our design team had some inside information to work with…" Jay shook his head slowly and admired the level of secrecy his father had kept all along. Meanwhile, the professor turned to address Sam.

"You have the ability to perform on any stage: the field, the stage, the air... You have athletic prowess that would rival any Olympian. Even if," he wrinkled his mouth in thought, "you did destroy one of our best rovers." Sam covered her face with one hand and slumped into her chair as her father raised one eyebrow and shook his head.

"Trevor you are... well I confess, you are still a mystery to us." The professor shrugged, somewhat puzzled by his own lack of understanding. "Of course, the chamber foretold your arrival, but not much else has been revealed to me. It is obvious you have done something extraordinary. While I can only see fragments of images, you," he gestured to Trevor with open arms, "have actually activated the chamber, or as you so aptly named it, a "Cosmic Blender". Beyond that, I am not certain how or when you will be able to harness its full power."

Great, thought Trevor, as he leaned back in his chair. No clue to what it all means. Professor Gladwell stood silently and Sachin watched Trevor's reaction for a few seconds.

""The Fin should be arriving at Gladwell Manor shortly." Sachin carefully chose his next words. "The professor and I spoke with your parents earlier today. They support our request to let you study at Gladwell Manor, where you can further explore your unique abilities, our manor, and of course, the chamber."

"I am certain that's why the Stasys Corporation has begun its nefarious campaign to stop you," the professor interrupted. The old man pounded the air with his pipe, and an unusual look of anger flickered across his face. Sachin nodded and then continued.

"Each of you has great potential —that is, if you choose to use your talent wisely. Please consider our invitation. You can also choose to walk away if you want. The choice is yours." He smiled, without any hint of force in his voice. He motioned to the Professor and then waved farewell to the group, and soon his image faded completely.

Sam rolled her eyes. She looked at Trevor and groaned, "What kind of kid wants to study *after* school?"

The old professor did not seem to hear her comment. He beamed proudly as he looked over the group. They all sat for a moment without speaking, the adults whispering quietly to themselves. The professor's eyes followed them patiently as they each considered the invitation. He began softly humming a song while he awaited their reply. Julie was the first one to break the silence.

"How's the food?" she blurted out.

Sam, Trevor, Jay and Mr. Meriwether all groaned in unison. Professor Maximillian Augustus Gladwell simply clapped his hands in delight and roared with laughter.

Welcome Home

Several minutes and many questions later, they all held on to their chairs as the Fin bumped gently to a stop.

"No need to worry," the Professor assured them. "We've arrived inside our underground port."

The Fin had traveled from the ocean through an underground tunnel, and was now underneath Silver Lake, beside Gladwell Manor. Before anyone could ask how that was possible, a side door to the lounge hissed open. Captain Thomas' face peered inside.

"Welcome home... almost," he said with a friendly smile.

Trevor noticed as Sam examined the sports watch on her wrist. "Do you realize that the Fin traveled from the ocean and somehow underneath Maine to get us here in... under two hours?"

Four kids, their parents, and one happy dog made their way through the wooden doorway, down a short ramp and into a small stone vault, much like the one Trevor had entered from the deep well. He heard a familiar voice and turned. The rovers waved goodbye from the Fin - they were remaining onboard for now.

"Goodbye, Trevor." Orbit said inside Trevor's head. "I hope to see you again soon. I'll be waiting for you."

He saw his friends quietly turn and wave farewell. They had been communicating silently with their rovers as well.

Moving inside, Trevor noticed this vault was filled with more antique devices, made from silver, brass and wood. Everyone wanted to stop and inspect the antiques. Despite everyone's apparent interest in the odd-looking machines, Captain Thomas managed to herd the crowd forward. That didn't stop them from wondering about the odd and distinctly retro-mechanical devices.

"What are those things? They look like antiques."

"I don't know. Did you see the one with the wheel on it?"

"Betcha that big one was some type of weapon..."

"I've never seen anything like this before."

The captain opened the door to the underground hallway and led the group through the tunnel and into a massive chamber. Trevor frowned.

"What is it?" his mother asked.

"This is the..." He paused, trying to accurately describe the change to her. "It's the Cosmic Blender, but it doesn't look same. It's similar, but now it looks more like a cave."

He shrugged as his mother looked ahead to a group in the distance. Near the center stood Chief Pierce, Chef Pauline, and Coach McCorkle. Henry Fox moved through the group of parents to join them. Professor Gladwell cleared his throat and placed a hand on Hank's shoulder as Jay hugged his father tightly.

"Henry Fox... I sure am grateful you survived, thanks to the same medical wizards who repaired Trevor's dog. Our little enterprise would not be the same without you. Of course," he added, with a wink, "you realize we have a lot of work to accomplish in a short amount of time." Hank nodded as if it was what he had expected and the professor turned back to the assembled group.

"It is still early in the morning, and if I am not mistaken, I believe all of you have some very important plans for today…"

The four kids stared at each other in disbelief. They had almost forgotten about the soccer game, the television show, the design contest, and the town celebration. Somehow their old plans didn't seem important anymore.

"It's time we rounded up some very bad Stasys agents." He continued. "But you will also have to honor your previous commitments at the same time. Quite an interesting challenge, isn't it Trevor?" The professor smiled as he looked at the shy student.

"So far, we have been able to capture six Stasys agents." Chief Pierce gave them her latest update.

"The men that attacked you in the store, the café, and the rescue station are now being held in one of our secure chambers in the manor above. However, Ms. Irvin, the Stasys agent that accidentally started a fire in the abandoned house, the agents who broke into Henry's warehouse, and the Stasys scouts who chased Trevor into the well, are still loose in the valley. I believe they will make their next move sometime during tonight's celebration. My goal is to prevent that from happening.""

Chief Pierce surveyed the crowd as she lifted up the small gold medallion that hung on a chain around her neck. "Each of you has been provided with a small piece of the chamber, disguised as a gemstone on these pendants. If you are anywhere near a pendant, you can communicate with your mentor, Sachin, the Professor Gladwell or anyone else at Cosmic Enterprises. Coach McCorkle will show you how to use your pendants before you leave. At least we can keep you safe while we…"

Trevor suddenly snapped his fingers. "Wait! I've got an idea." As soon as he realized how loudly he had spoken, he turned sheepishly to the old explorer.

"At least I think we can do more than just dodge them." he motioned to his circle of friends. "But we'll need some help. Professor Gladwell, could I ask a big favor?"

Bushy eyebrows arched over the old man's eyes like two white rainbows over green meadows. He roared with laughter, and then leaned closer to listen as the boy who was alternately brave and shy mapped out a very bold plan of action.

The Dream Machine

After finalizing their new plan, the group followed Professor Gladwell toward the elevator shaft that led from the chamber to the manor above. Once on the surface, they would spit up to begin working on various assignments. A chorus of excited voices echoed about the chamber as the group continued to discuss their various roles and activity for the day.

"I know the answer to *your* question Trevor," he said suddenly, smiling. Trevor frowned. He had been deep in thought, staring at the walls as they walked. He was the only one who had not asked any questions. The professor ignored his confusion. "All you have to do is simply turn the Cosmic Blender on."

"I don't remember turning it on before."

"Oh but you did, my boy. You just didn't realize what you had done." The older man gestured up to the jagged rock above and paused near the center of the chamber. The group listened in on their conversation, curious to learn more.

"Look up, Trevor" he instructed. "Focus outward, on the world around you, not inward on yourself."

Trevor looked up, and inadvertently thought about the people around him. The group listened as the air around them seemed to wind up in a symphony of whirs and clicks. The cavern quickly came to life with an energy no one could describe. Almost instantly, the chamber Trevor remembered – a beautiful space with smooth walls, intricate murals and an immense golden dome full of stars and galaxies - resolved into view. After a few minutes Trevor lowered his eyes. The Professor smiled as the chamber resumed its former state, the rocks once again rough and ordinary.

"One last thing, Trevor. Those are no mere dreams, my boy." The professor kneeled to be closer. "You have visited at least four other dimensions since moving to Silver Lake. Visits you made before you found this chamber…or more accurately, before the chamber found you."

Trevor tightly gripped his mother's hand. So that explained the mud on his feet after the last dream. His mind reeled. He had so many questions, especially, "why me?"

"You will understand soon enough," the professor spoke softly this time, gently guiding Trevor and the perplexed visitors toward the elevator. "In time."

Letting Go

Trevor jumped out of the van marked "Cosmic Enterprises" and waved to the driver before shutting the door. He darted down the walk, ducking under the vines that crowded the gate and opening the front door with his key. He sprinted up the stairs two at a time and disappeared into his room. His parents took a slightly longer route, exiting the van and walking around the vines as his father discussed events from the morning.

"Annie, I feel like I've been on some crazy Coney Island ride."

"Tell me about it. The most I had planned today was to throw a couple of bowls on the pottery wheel," she agreed, slowly shaking her head. "I think I was the one on the wheel today." Gavin Kip stopped, reached out one hand and firmly held his wife's arm. She turned and looked up at her husband.

"Are you sure we're doing the right thing?"

A storm of doubt flashed briefly across his dark blue eyes. He sighed and touched her face gently with his hand. "Hard to tell, baby. We'll just have to trust Trevor on this one."

Back inside, Trevor pulled on his soccer uniform, grabbed his gym bag, and raced into the garage in record time. His mother and father, still standing on the front lawn, opened their arms to him as he rode his bike up to the yard. His mother grabbed his shoulders and kissed his forehead.

"We'll see you at the field, kiddo." She paused, and then added softly, "Be careful, and keep your eyes open."

Trevor jumped back on his bike and was soon bouncing down the bricks on Vivada Street. Minutes later, he was pacing in front of the low wall near the sidewalk, between the Community Hall and the Rescue Center. A Channel 6 news truck, a bulldozer, two enormous dump trucks and two white panel vans were parked on the street behind him. The Community Hall looked great: the decorations were still in place and ready for the town's celebration. Pauline's café was a disaster.

He could see Chief Pierce standing at the far side of the cafe, supervising crews who were trying to repair a gaping hole in the wall. The bakery was ruined. It looked as though a giant tornado had pulled the walls down around the room. He was amazed at the damage the seemingly innocent blobs had caused. The thought made his heart skip a beat.

Trevor glanced at the road as a girl in bright white pants and matching jacket sprang out of a car that had just pulled up to the park. She waved to the driver inside and skipped along the sidewalk as red curls bounced up and down with each step.

"Chef Julie is here to save the day," Trevor announced. "I hope…"

She plopped down on the wall beside him. Her shoes knocked against the stone wall as she kicked her feet and dramatically flipped a thick strand of hair over her clean white collar.

She clasped both hands in her lap. She took turns staring at Trevor and the cafe. Julie had a secret to share, and she couldn't hold it much longer.

"I think Pauline and I have created a recipe that will save the day. Want to know how we did it?" She waited in silence, smiling and bouncing her feet, until Trevor couldn't stand the suspense any longer.

"Kitch Witch," he scolded. "Don't hold out on me."

"Well…"

Julie took in a big breath, filling her lungs so she could deliver one of her infamously long-winded stories. Without warning, she grabbed Trevor's wrist and yanked it closer. He had no choice but to fall over as she stared at the cell phone in his hand.

"OhmygoshTrevor…" she stammered. "It's almost 9:45. We have got to get in that hall right now. Our show is about to begin."

Julie practically lifted both Trevor and his bike off the ground as she turned to leave.

"Sorry Trev," without sounding remorseful at all. "You'll have to wait until we get inside," as she dragged him toward the hall. In a few more steps, they had disappeared completely behind the newly decorated doors.

Real Magic

They entered the large room and stared in wonder at the sight. The hall was now another room in another time and place.

A camera crew had set up equipment in front of a large wooden table. An ivy-covered wall behind the table set the scene. They hurried toward the crew and the table. They overheard a news reporter speaking with her crew as they approached.

"So let's wrap this up as fast as we can, "

The woman stabbed a brightly polished fingernail at the backdrop, as she checked her makeup in a small mirror. She dabbed powder over her eyes and barked more directions.

"Then we can head next door and get some shots of that destruction across the street. That's just the type of star-building report I need for my career." She skillfully ran a tube of lipstick across her lips. The reporter glanced into her mirror and noticed Trevor and Julie waiting patiently beside the table.

"Oh. Hello Sweetie." the reporter burbled, flashing two rows of brilliantly white teeth. Julie wanted to shield her eyes.

"I am so delighted you're here."

She didn't need to say 'finally'. They both caught the true meaning behind her tone. She placed her hands on their shoulders and forcefully shoved them behind the table. The reporter saw Julie's segment as a speed bump on the road to a much larger story.

"Listen sweetie, can you set up the desserts all by yourself? That's a good girl."

Her head bobbed up and down as she examined the rows of small pies on the table. The reporter talked to Julie as if she was a lost four-year old. Julie just bit her tongue and smiled. Not getting the sweet reply she expected, the reporter turned back to her crew and barked some more orders. The sound technician and the cameraman both motioned to the reporter. They were ready.

"Okay sweetie?" she crooned as she positioned herself between Julie and Trevor. They stood stiffly behind the table lined with rows of little pies.

"Let's get this over as fast as we can, okay?" she barked to the crew. "Okay sweetie?" her blond hair bounced up and down, as if by nodding she could convince Julie to wrap up her segment as fast as possible.

"Lady," Julie could not control herself any longer. "You call me sweetie one more time and I'll take that wig off your head."

The reporter had met her match. She stared at Julie as if a bee had stung her on the nose. Trevor could only control himself by staring down at Julie's pies. The reporter finally blinked and regained her regal composure.

"Oh… really?" The reporter hissed quietly at Julie. "You're nothing but a country bumpkin who knows how to microwave a burrito. Don't tell me…" She had begun to raise her hand when someone on the crew interrupted.

"…and you're live." the cameraman whispered.

Trevor could only imagine what people had just seen on their televisions. This time he actually laughed. However, the reported quickly recovered and turned on her charm. She continued to raise her hand and wave to the television audience as she beamed one of her biggest smiles directly into the camera.

"It's the Mid Morning Show." she crowed.

"I am your host, Nancy Todd, joining you live from the Silver Lake Community Hall…" The reporter beamed at Julie as if she had just laid a golden egg.

"We have a very special guest with us today, and this very special girl has made us a very special dessert." Nancy's emphasis on 'very special' informed the audience it was a miracle Julie could walk and talk at the same time.

Trevor glanced nervously at Julie. He was surprised to see her calmly watching Nancy Todd as she waited patiently for her turn to speak. He knew as soon as this was over, the reporter would race next door for shots of the damage in the cafe. She was more interested in breaking hard news than breaking bread with some precocious country girl and her precious apple pies.

"So sweetie, tell us exactly what you've made for us today."

Nancy Todd smirked just a little through her smile, as if to say, "gotcha." Unfazed, Julie turned to the camera and spoke directly to her audience.

"Well Nancy," Julie sounded truly professional and friendly. Trevor was impressed.

"Today I have made arte fin aux pommes for our audience." Julie turned and looked sweetly at the reporter. "Savez-vous des recettes françaises?" she asked the stunned reporter.

Nancy paused for a moment as she tried to translate French into English. Julie jumped into the empty space without given her a chance to respond. The game was on.

"No problem Nancy, I'll help you." Julie turned back to the camera. "I'm going to show everyone in Tri-Valley a quick and easy way to make tasty apple pies, the French way."

Julie proceeded to explain preparation, assembly, and baking instructions. A very upstaged Nancy Todd stood by helplessly and watched. She did not even interrupt to ask questions. At the end of her dazzling performance, Julie reached down and picked up one of the little pies from the table.

"Voila," she exclaimed with a flourish. "The finished pie. And let me tell you folks, they sure are *yummy.* That's bumpkin for 'tres bien,' Nancy." It was Julie's turn to gloat.

Now even the camera crew was smiling. Not only did the pies sound great, but also the cute little girl had just slain the dragon lady. Trevor realized Julie could probably host her own cooking show, tomorrow. However, Julie was not quite yet finished.

"Here Nancy, please try one." She said coyly, as she handed one of the tiny bowls to Nancy.

The reporter studied the pie as if it were a dirty diaper. She tried to figure out how she could take a bite, look professional, and not ruin her makeup. Julie also handed two pies for Trevor to give to the crew. He walked the desserts around the table and to the men behind the camera. All three took a small bite of Julie's apple pies.

Nancy followed her first bite with another. Then she took even bigger bites until the pie was stuffed completely inside her mouth. A look of pure joy spread across her face.

"Tmhis snis sno fmgoodf." she cried.

Her muffled praise came out, along with little flakes of pastry. The reporter tried to catch them all and shove them back in. Lipstick was smeared across both of her cheeks.

Trevor's mouth hung open in shock. He looked at the camera crew. They were hovered by the table stacking pies on their arms. Julie stepped closer and placed a hand over her stash of desserts.

"Sorry boys." she said, "only one pie per person." They looked heartbroken. Julie quickly extended her invitation to the audience.

"However, I will be giving away free samples of my pies at Town Park, the soccer field, and Adventures To Go, throughout the day." The crew was smiling again.

The sound technician suddenly looked up from his equipment.

"And... we're off the air." he shouted with surprise.

"That was simply amazing." Nancy Todd gushed as she fawned over her new favorite chef. Julie nodded modestly. Nancy looked back at her crew as she picked piecrust from the front of her jacket and popped it into her mouth. "That's all for today, let's pack up and head back to the office." She collected her things and started to leave.

Trevor opened his mouth to interject. Nancy stopped and waited for him to finish. Julie's elbow caught him sharply in the ribs. Only a puff of air escaped from his lips.

"Never mind" he wheezed.

The crew shook Julie's hand and congratulated her on the dessert once more. Then they packed the equipment and hurried behind Nancy as she pushed open the front doors of the hall and led them back to the van. In minutes, they were gone. Trevor looked at Julie in amazement.

"But…" he stammered. "They forgot all about the damage next door, and all the repair crews…" he finally exclaimed.

Julie was packing pies into a cardboard box. She paused with a stack of pies in her arms.

"Now Trevor… isn't that what we wanted to happen?" she confirmed with a wink and a nod.

Mother of All Pies

They left the Community Hall and walked into Town Park.

A festively decorated stage sat near the middle of the park. Placed at the center of the stage were three very large cylinders of different heights that seemed to be made of black plastic. Trevor assumed the contest winners would stand the cylinders during the science presentation. Pauline was busy arranging pies on top of a table to one side. Julie guided Trevor and his armload of pies toward the table.

"I saw the morning show." Pauline informed them with a frown. Then she smiled. "That rude woman should learn some table manners, non?" They both laughed with her as it finally occurred to him why Julie had baked these particular pies.

"Will there be enough for everyone?" Trevor asked Pauline. It certainly did not seem to be enough to feed the entire town.

"Let's just say…" she said with a wink, "that Julie has a very special way with food. I can't wait to see what she and I will be able to create together. But yes, for today, I am certain there will be plenty of pies to help everyone feel better and forget all about the unpleasantness of yesterday."

She reached down and placed another box of pies on the table. Trevor noticed a stack of identical boxes sitting next to the white vans parked behind the stage. Just like yesterday, these vans were also marked "Cosmic Enterprises". It seemed likely they contained enough pies for several small towns.

"I better head over to the soccer field." He looked at them hopefully and winced. "Care to watch me perform on the field of agony?" Julie knew he was not a very good soccer player. Trevor was hoping to find a friendly fan that would cheer him along. She looked eagerly at Pauline.

"Yes," she agreed. She looked at her young student. "You may go. But be back here before noon. We have many pies to give away."

They headed through the park, across Main Street, towards the Silver Lake School and the soccer field. Along the way, Julie told Trevor how she had used the enormous kitchen inside the Professor's mansion. Trevor felt a twinge of jealousy – he had only seen a glimpse of the big house as they departed earlier – and he tried to catch every detail as she described it. She was now telling him about her recipe. Even though he knew today's plan by heart, he was confused – he could only understand fraction of everything she told him. Julie stopped walking and stared directly into his blue and gold eyes.

"Trevor, it's as obvious as the freckles on my nose." she exclaimed. "The four of us are able to do things we could never imagine before you moved here. Somehow you've given me the ability to stir my thoughts and hopes right into my recipes. If I want a river of rice pudding, that's what I get. If I want people forget those pesky Stasys agents and think happier thoughts, then that's what's gonna happen. Don't ask me why, but I believe it'll work. You've just got to trust me."

Julie's part in the original plan was to help everyone relax while they enjoyed her fresh apple pies. The recipe she and Pauline had created had obviously gone much further. These pies resulted in two very pleasant experiences for anyone who ate a slice. First, they seemed to forget anything bad or unpleasant from the moment they ate the pie to the day before. Second, and most important to Julie, they also thought her pies were terrific.

Trevor witnessed firsthand how her pies had worked magic on Nancy Todd. One minute she was an ill-tempered tiger and, within seconds of eating some pie, she became a mild-mannered kitten. He was beginning to realize just how little he understood about the power of Julie's southern charms. He stopped. Julie also stopped and watched as he surveyed the field, his shoulders drooping, as a frown pulled his face downward with them.

"Don't worry Trev, you will be an amazing."

He smiled at her nervously, and then turned and walked toward his team's bench as she waved goodbye and blew him a kiss for luck.

Field of Champions

Although the Silver Lake Sharks had gathered by the home bench, Sam and Coach McCorkle were not among them. According to the plan, they were going to round up the agents and secure them inside Hank's old warehouse before coming to the field.

Trevor scanned the people sitting and the stands and spotted his parents. They waved back. He pointed at the field.

"Do you know where Sam is?" Trevor mouthed the words. His father shook his head and shrugged "no" in reply.

Meanwhile, Julie was next to a small table, guarding her pies. Her father stood nearby, helping keep people away from the magical treats. As planned, she was asking them to come back after the game for their free dessert.

The referee blew his whistle and called the team captains out to the field. Trevor looked at his team. They had no captain. A few whispers and rapid glances told him everything he needed to know. Thinking quickly, he gathered the team around the bench. How could the shyest kid try to lead the team, he wondered? Several players began asking about Sam and Coach McCorkle.

"Okay everybody." Trevor wished Sam were here. He could only imagine what she was doing right now, even though he could not share those thoughts with the team. "I know Coach will be here soon. So…" he stumbled, trying to find the best words. "Umm… go out there and play hard." He tried hard to sound confident. A row of blank faces stared back at him. He wondered what Sam would do next. An idea suddenly formed in his head. He put his arm into the center of the group and fifteen more arms followed. He smiled at his team as they all began to cheer.

"Hoo-ah!" Trevor shouted, "Let's go kick some Sky Park butt."

Everybody laughed at the bold words coming from the shyest player. The kid closest to Trevor slapped him on the back. They were just waiting for me to step up, he thought proudly.

"Hey kids." A referee called to the team. "I can see your parents but I haven't seen your coach yet. You don't have to play today. You can forfeit the game if you want." The referee gestured to the Sky Park coach and then looked at his team for an answer. He proudly stepped forward.

"I'm the team captain sir," he said in a deep, clear voice. He stepped over to the referee and shook his hand. "Our Coach should be here any minute. Silver Lake is ready to play."

The referee shrugged and blew his whistle as both teams ran out onto the field. A loud roar from the bleachers accompanied the players onto the field. The game went well for the first 20 minutes. The Sharks managed to keep Sky Park from scoring. Knowing that if they could at least score one goal, they might win their first game of the season.

Trevor was about to begin a drive toward the Sky Park goal when three dark blurs caught the corner of his eye. Two men and a woman ran from behind the trees near the edge of the track. They were dressed in black jeans and black shirts, and were headed straight for the field. Another man burst from under the bleachers and quickly joined up with them. Trevor didn't recognize the men, but he instantly recognized the woman. It was Ms. Irvin, the woman that he had tried to save.

The game immediately came to an abrupt halt. By now other players had noticed the intruders and were slowing down to watch them as well. The agents continued running directly towards the field… and Trevor. His mind raced as he tried to think of options.

Sam and Coach McCorkle burst onto the field from an alley off Main Street. They had flushed the Stasys agents out of hiding, and the chase had brought them here. Trevor could hear Sam shouting, but could not understand what she was saying. The agents were now closing in on the midfield. The referee began blowing his whistle and the other coach yelled for the strangers to clear the field.

"Run, Trevor." A familiar voice spoke to him, although no one was standing nearby. He looked around in confusion, momentarily forgetting the agents.

"Wake up Trevor." He finally recognized Orbit's voice and absentmindedly fingered the small medallion around his neck. "I am communicating through your pendant. You must run to the park— now." Of course! The park. As he turned to run, he almost tripped on the soccer ball. That gave him another idea.

Trevor wheeled and quickly lined up a shot. He kicked hard and low, directly at Ms. Irvin. His aim was better than the day before.

The ball flew up and into her face. He had little time to celebrate, because the other agents were still barreling toward him. He turned and ran towards Town Park.

Trevor's kick had given Sam the time she needed. She made a final dash and leapt into the air while Ms. Irvin tried to avoid the soccer ball. Sam seemingly flew fifteen feet before landing directly on Ms. Irvin's back. The agent collapsed in a heap at the midfield mark.

In any other soccer game, Sam's tackle would have been a major penalty. However, in this game of life or death, Sam had just scored a major victory.

Coach McCorkle blew past Trevor in the opposite direction. He was running directly toward the other four agents. Trevor had never seen him move so fast. He wished he could have watched his coach in action, but he tucked his head down and continued running out off the field as the coach closed the gap on one of the smaller agents.

The agent tried unsuccessfully to avoid him and immediately lost his balance. He tumbled unceremoniously to the field as Coach McCorkle wrapped his arms around the agent's left leg. The referee placed a foot on the downed man's back and dropped a red flag onto the ground. Coach McCorkle paused beside the two fallen agents. He shouted over at Sam, who remained on guard over the fallen Ms. Irvin.

"I've got to help Trevor. He reached behind his ears and activated his communication device as he ran. Trevor would need help from as many people as possible.

Fortress of the Butterfly

Trevor knew the remaining agents were closing in on him. His only hope was to reach the Cosmic Enterprises team working in the park. As he sprinted up Main Street he could see Town Park in the distance. Pauline was gone. The workers were gone. The stage was completely empty.

The agents dodged the trap before we were ready, he thought in dismay. Trevor panicked. He would have to deal with the agents on his own. Suddenly, he heard Coach McCorkle's voice clearly inside his head.

"Trevor, run for the stage. Everyone else, meet me at the Park, *now.*"

He looked at the stage again. This time he noticed Jay waving to him from beside three cubicle towers. The tallest was over eight feet. The black cylinders looked familiar somehow, but he didn't have time to concentrate on why. Jay reached down and touched the bottom of the largest cube and... disappeared inside. Trevor was confused. He can't leave me now, he thought.

Trevor reached the steps and bounded onto the stage, but wasn't certain where to go. He turned to face his pursuers and backed away from the edge of the stage until he bumped into the largest of the black cylinders. The agent closest to him was now fifty feet in front of the stage and running hard. Further back, Trevor saw Coach McCorkle turn the corner and enter the park. His coach was too far away to help him now. The agent leapt straight for the stage.

Without warning, a pair of hands darted out from behind the large cylinder and pulled Trevor inside. Trevor suddenly found himself lying at the bottom of the largest cube as a small door snapped close with a *snick*.

He was still breathing hard as he stood and looked directly into Jay's eyes. "We…" Trevor panted. "We've got… to get out of here… the agents, " Trevor looked back where the front of the stage had been. Why isn't Jay worried? Trevor wondered. That agent could probably knock the cylinder over with one hand. Jay calmly placed an arm on Trevor's shoulder.

"Hey, little man, take a deep breath. You looked totally stressed." Jay smiled. In comparison to Trevor, he looked calm and relaxed.

Relax? Trevor thought. Jay's part of the plan was to set up his entry, the Fortress of the Floating Warrior, on stage for the science competition. His role would be to distract people from the agents, while Sam and Coach did their part. This could only be a model of Jay's design, not the real thing. Or could it?

"Don'tcha remember, Trev?" Jay smiled. "My Dad was there in the chamber with us. He showed me how to build my model with supplies from his warehouse."

Trevor began to smile. This wasn't a science project anymore, it was the most realistic working model of any building ever created. He studied the inside of the cylinder. He saw metal tubes with flexible joints and an exterior skin made out of a glossy black film.

"Wow. A real fortress… But what about the Stasys agents? Coach was supposed to guide them into the warehouse…" Trevor was confused. Jay simply shrugged.

"No worries, dude." he replied casually. "They can't harm us in here. This tube will simply absorb anything they can throw at us. In fact, you can't even hear them yelling at us right now."

Trevor looked through the cylinder's legs. Jay was right. Outside the cylinder, two agents threw themselves directly at the tube. The other agent pounded on the outside of the cube with both fists. The tower had not moved an inch. They all seemed confused by a complete lack of progress. However, inside the tower, and true to its design, the tubular legs were flexing slightly as the fantastic structure and its unique materials redirected every bit of force and vibration.

Jay and Trevor looked at each other in celebration. Perhaps it was best that the agents could not hear laughter coming from inside.

Unfortunately for the agents, they became so preoccupied with the cylinder they forgot everything else. They did not notice as two white vans parked silently in front of the stage. Coach McCorkle leaped quietly onto the stage, undetected as well. In one fluid motion, he rolled between the men, popping up between them and the cylinder.

"Hello boys. I'm sorry, but I'm afraid you weren't invited to this party." He lifted one agent off the ground and pushed him toward a van. Two Cosmic Enterprises workers quickly scooped the man up and tossed him inside.

The second agent had more time to react. He leaned back and threw a punch aimed directly at the coach's face. Coach McCorkle turned slightly and deflected the punch. Then he grabbed the agent's arm and flipped him in the direction of the other van. The rear doors of the second van opened and once again an agent disappeared. He rapidly cornered the last agent. Coach McCorkle pointed to the last van. Knowing he was outmatched, the agent walked obediently inside. Coach McCorkle jumped inside and shut the doors behind him. The vans quickly headed away from the park to pick up the agents remaining on a very crowded soccer field.

Back on stage, a man stepped from behind the nearest black cylinder. He was wearing a simple white jumpsuit, the kind worn by construction workers, emblazoned with a patch that read "Strand Studios". He reached down and pressed a small button near the bottom. The small door reappeared, and two faces soon peeked out through the opening.

Jay stood and marveled at his creation as Trevor sprinted down the steps toward the soccer field.

By now, a small crowd of kids, parents and Cosmic Enterprises staff had walked over from the Community Hall and were now gathering around the stage. They were here to set up for the science competition. Parents chatted amiably as the three other finalists began rearranging tables and placed their entries on stage next to Jay's tower.

The staff could not have timed their arrival any better. No one in the park had seen Coach McCorkle rounding up the agents, and the guests simply assumed the vans were part of the stage crew. Jay quietly took a seat in one of the chairs as if he were the first contestant to arrive for the competition. The worker who, upon closer inspection looked like Hank the Handyman, pretended to adjust the microphone attached to the podium. Then he walked behind the stage and disappeared from view.

Meriwether Magic

Coach McCorkle was loading a defeated Ms. Irvin into one of the vans parked near the edge of the soccer field. Trevor ran up to Sam and tried to catch his breath as he watched.

"We've got an angry mob on our hands," Sam pointed to the middle of the field.

Parents were comforting scared kids while jabbing accusing fingers toward the officials. The Sky Park coach marched over to confront the coach from Silver Lake. Coach McCorkle closed the van door and addressed the crowd.

"Now, folks," he sounded forceful, yet calm. "It's all over now. Everyone please try to calm down."

Out of the corner of one eye, Trevor noticed Julie pick up something from the bleachers as she left her table to join them.

"Hey," the Sky Park coach yelled, pointing a finger at Coach McCorkle. "Just what the heck is going on here?" He fumbled in his pocket as he tried to locate a phone to summon the police. A pie appeared between his mouth and his eyes.

"Oh coach," Julie said in her most angelic voice. "I know this might seem like bad timing, but I really have to give away these pies before they spoil."

She stared at the coach with puppy eyes. He could not refuse her. No one could. The angry coach pulled his hand out of his pocket and grabbed the pie. Julie nodded as he took a small bite. Then she held up a megaphone she had grabbed from the bleachers, and pointed it at the gathering.

"Hi ya'll." She exclaimed. She didn't have to shout. The sound of her southern twang bouncing across the Maine hills was enough to make everyone stop in their tracks. Several of the younger children giggled at the foreign accent. Julie just smiled back at them.

"I hope ya'll won't let a little fuss get in the way of our town celebration. We have all worked so hard to make today very special." She pointed to the now ecstatic face of the Sky Park coach.

"Just ask your coach how fabulous these pies are." He was nodding so hard, Trevor thought his head would snap off his neck.

Trevor looked around the field. Mr. Meriwether was wading through the crowd, handing out pies as fast as he could. It looked as if he and Julie would have enough for every man, woman, and child. Trevor punched Sam in the ribs and giggled. The Sky Park coach smiled blissfully and laughed along with him. Within minutes everyone had enjoyed a pie, leaving them free to walk back to Town Park.

A Much Deserved Rest

Trevor and Sam wove their way through the Town Park, handing out pies as they neared the stage. Trevor listened to the end of the presentation, and watched with pride as the town's Mayor handed a large crystal sculpture to a very emotional Jay Fox.

"And for your inspired approach to architecture," he was saying, "with apologies from the director of Cosmic Studios who could not be with us this afternoon, I am honored to present Jay Fox with this award. He has indeed earned this award with his creativity and hard work."

Chief Pierce, the Mayor, and Jay turned for pictures and to receive applause from an audience that could not remember a more wonderful day. Julie, Sam, and Trevor raced behind the stage to congratulate Jay in a profusion of hugs and cheers. Cindy Fox joined them and repeatedly showered the top of his head with kisses. Chief Pierce soon joined their little celebration.

"I have a suggestion," she began. "Why don't you all go home and relax for a little while. Coach McCorkle, Pauline and I will clean up any loose ends. Then you can meet us back here tonight for the big celebration."

As if on cue, all four of them sighed in unison. They looked at each other and laughed. Between yesterday and the day before, they were call completely exhausted and could think of nothing better than some time at home. Across from them, Chief Pierce looked at her watch before slipping back into an unbelievably happy crowd that was now picking through the remains of Julie's apple pies.

'A' stands for 'Apple"

Two large white vans pulled up to a tall dark skyscraper. Behind row after row of windows labored employees in the New York headquarters of the Stasys Global Corporation. The driver pulled as close to the entrance as possible and parked in a loading zone. Eleven people jumped out of the vans and huddled on the sidewalk.

"Do we really have to go back to work?" one of them asked with a pout.

"I have a better idea," another agent said excitedly.

The remaining agents gathered closely to hear his plan. Coach McCorkle stepped out from a passenger door and watched in amusement. He looked at the eager, nodding faces now reaching out for the boxes he held in his hands.

"Now don't eat them all," he advised, "and pass them out to as many of your coworkers as you can." He handed the boxes over to the agents. Then he produced a large white envelope from his pocket and handed it to a very happy Ms. Irvin.

"Make sure you give this note to Nigel Willington after you give him a pie."

Ms. Irvin smiled warmly at Coach McCorkle as she took the note, clutching a pie firmly in her hands. Then she waved goodbye as she skipped to catch up with the other agents. Coach McCorkle watched as they hurried inside.

Coach McCorkle smiled as his van pulled away from the curb. He could only imagine the meeting Nigel Willington would soon be having with his agents.

Carnivale Intrigue

Silver Lake's frumpy Community Hall was now a Venetian castle, bathed in the glow of a hundred shimmering torches.

Trevor and his parents stood briefly outside, watching guests take rides in the Venetian canal that had been so painstakingly reproduced in the alley between the bank and the hall. It wasn't a very long ride, but with a little imagination, Trevor's neighbors were transported to another place and time. Girls sighed and snuggled closer to their dates. Men acted more gallant than they ever had before.

They joined the rest of the crowd moving toward the hall and were handed festive masks near the entrance. Trevor chose his mask, a lion's eyes and ears. His parents each took a mask, slipped them on and joined in with other masked strangers, attempting to guess their identities, while leaving him free to enjoy the sights. Just as he began to wonder if his friends would ever arrive, he felt the presence of someone standing beside him. A soft voice spoke into his ear.

"Quite magical, mais ouis?" Chef Pauline mused, her thick French accent tinged with awe and excitement. Trevor turned to see the chef standing beside him in a glittering dress of ruffles and beads. Her face was partially obscured by a sequined mask. Trevor waved slightly. Chef Pauline turned and moved into the hall. Before he could follow her, a pair of soft hands covered his eyes.

"Good evening, mister Kip." Julie was wearing a costume ball gown that was similar to Chef Pauline's. Her face was covered in a mask that gave her huge cheeks and a permanent laugh. Only her eyes, mouth, and waves of curly hair were recognizable behind the mask. Julie snapped open a large fan and began to wave it rapidly.

"Well fiddle dee dee." she exclaimed in her thickest southern accent. "But I do declare that you are the most boring man at the ball." She waved the fan in his direction. Trevor wanted to protest – costumes were not his usual idea of fun.

"Sorry, but there's no way I could…" he began. Julie cut him off, using her old south persona.

"Sorry?" she retorted playfully. "Well I won't listen to any pity parties on the night of our biggest celebration." She reached over and placed her arm inside Trevor's as a cue for him to escort her into the Hall. They strode through the doors arm in arm. Several guests smiled and stepped aside to allow them to move through the doors. She turned to him once they were inside the hall.

"The reason I am dressed like this," she said in her normal voice, "is that I am helping serve a most delicious dessert tonight. I think you may remember it…" She looked at Trevor with a meaningful nod to the desert table and then ruffled her costume.

"Besides, don'tcha just love these rags?" She twirled around once, and then giggled before hurrying over to where her rice pudding was being offered to the guests.

Inside the hall, Trevor slipped the mask over his face and carefully examined the decorations and the guests. He continued scanning the energetic crowd as he scored a soda from the top of a serving tray. It feels like something big is going to happen, he thought idly to himself.

He wandered to one side of the hall and listened as a band played from a small stage in the back of the room. Trevor stood on the tip of his toes to get a better look. His eyes widened as he counted one, two, three… the band consisted almost entirely of rovers. There were only two humans on stage with Orbit and his friends. Jay was playing keyboard and his father was playing trumpet. Trevor mentally added that mystery to the long list of questions he would have to ask the professor. Jay looked up briefly and waved enthusiastically.

Trevor nodded back, keeping rhythm with each nod of his head. He hummed the tune as he wandered about, slipping in and around conversations and adults who barely noticed him passing by, until he caught a glimpse of two very familiar faces.

Coach's Confession

Trevor found Sam standing near the center of the room, her face partially covered by a princess mask. He almost spit out his drink from the shock. He could no more imagine Sam dressed as a princess than Julie transforming into a football player.

She was saying something funny to Coach McCorkle, who leaned back in laughter. The coach was wearing an eagle mask that looked two sizes too small for his muscular face. Trevor moved through the crowd to where they were now deep in conversation. He waited for a break and then coughed loud enough for them to hear him.

Sam's face lit up like one of the party decorations.

"Kipmo!"

Trevor groaned at the latest variation on his last name. Sam ignored his reaction and hugged him tightly. Standing back, she tilted her head slightly in Coach McCorkle's direction. "Coach and I were just talking about our trouble rounding up agents. I hope we didn't scare you too much."

"Nah." Trevor did not want to make a big fuss over it. Then he realized he didn't know what coach had done with the agents.

"What about the agents? How did you take care of them?"

"Hah! Wait 'til you hear." Sam's eyes sparkled. "Why don't you tell Trevor, too?" She grinned hopefully at their coach.

He briefly retold the story of the agents and the condition in which they arrived back at Stasys headquarters. Trevor could only imagine what kind of chaos Julie's pies had created inside that building.

Coach McCorkle leaned back and enjoyed their laughter. Sam and Trevor eagerly waited for him to continue. He noticed as the coach's eyes drifted away, as if considering something else to say. He slowly returned his gaze to Trevor and shook his head in apology.

"About the agents..." For the first time ever, Trevor detected a deep thoughtfulness in his voice. "Well... Let's just say there is a good reason so many of us know so much about Stasys and its agents." After a moment, his smile returned and he pointed to the stage. "I promise I'll explain later, I promise. But right now, why don't we just enjoy the party?"

The Main Event

On stage, Jay and his Dad took turns exchanging improvised solos. The whole room was now listening to the band. People jumped and swayed to the music. The song ended on a flourish and the entire hall erupted in applause. The father and son team, along with their metallic backup band, took their bows and waved as they exited the stage.

Trevor and Sam watched as a single spotlight moved to the left side of the stage, next to a replica of the tower in St. Mark's plaza. Chef Pauline's beaded dress and tiara captured the beam of light and shot it back in a million splinters as she moved to the microphone near the center of stage.

"Bonsoir, and hello everyone." she gazed about the assembly. "Tres magnifique, non?" she waved her arms, proudly embracing the festive event. A loud cheer erupted throughout the hall.

"I am so glad you could join us tonight for our very special occasion. Not only is our little town turning two hundred and twenty six years old, but our Mayor is adding another year too." She laughed and held her hand up to her eyes as she peered into the crowd.

She located him, hiding near the back of the room. A spotlight pivoted to reveal a very surprised mayor who waved back gamely to the audience.

"I am pleased to add that he is not quite as old as our town…" A few people chuckled and one man standing next to the mayor slapped him on the back. "…but he is equally handsome." Everyone applauded and cheered again.

As if on cue, Julie entered from a side door pushing a cart. On the cart was an enormous and elaborately decorated cake. A lone candle shimmered brightly from the very top of the cake. A spontaneous chorus of "Happy Birthday" began and the mayor stepped forward to blow out the single candle perched on top. Then Julie and the mayor wheeled the cake to one side of the hall, slicing it into smaller portions for everyone to enjoy.

The spotlight returned to Ms. Montreaux.

"Now it is time for you to meet our newest arrivals, and to welcome them into our little family." She looked over the crowd as if trying to locate someone.

"Jay Fox," He raised his hands in a surfer salute as Chef Pauline gestured for him to step back on stage. "…and congratulations on winning the science competition today." The hall cheered enthusiastically as Jay reached center stage.

"Julie Meriwether?" Julie waved from her place beside the cake. The mayor gave her a little nudge inviting her to join Jay on stage.

"Samantha…" Chef Pauline quickly corrected herself. "Sam Hudson?" Sam smiled and sprinted through the crowd, skipping the steps, and leaping directly onto stage. There was scattered applause as everyone cheered her impromptu performance.

"Trevor Kip?" Trevor waved to his parents, and then joined his friends on stage. He quietly took his place with a quick wave to the crowd. Now all four were assembled on stage around Chef Pauline. Ms. Montreaux proudly gestured to each of them, as she spoke to the audience.

"On the occasion of the anniversary of the founding of our town and," she added with a smile, "our Mayor's birthday, I am also pleased and honored to introduce the newest members of Cosmic Enterprises. As Captain Thomas would say..."

A voice from the audience cut her off with a raucous yell.

"Three cheers for our newest voyagers!" Captain Thomas roared. "Hip, hip..." he led, to which the entire hall responded with an ear-shattering "Hooray!"

Sam, Jay, Julie and Trevor grimaced in surprise, but were spared further embarrassment as a musical blast drew everyone's attention away from the stage. The crowd parted as a pair of rovers played trumpets and another pair opened the front doors. Trevor laughed as Orbit awkwardly rolled a red carpet into the hall.

"Ladies and Gentlemen. Please follow me to Town Park where we will conclude tonight's celebration."

With her announcement, Ms. Montreaux left the stage and proceeded along the carpet. The assembled guests inside the hall began moving politely, but noisily through the doors. It would take several minutes for everyone to leave the building. Before Trevor and his friends could move, Chief Pierce stepped up to the stage and gathered them all together.

"Okay, my little voyagers," she said in a stage whisper "you can take off your masks. We will be taking a secret route to the ceremony. Follow me." She walked off the stage toward the replica of the tower of St. Marks as they all shed their masks. A hidden door in the side of the tower popped opened as the group approached. Julie practically squeaked. "An elevator! I just knew these sets were more than ordinary decorations." She beamed back at the group. Chief Pierce laughed, nodded her head, and gestured toward the opening.

"After you, Ms. Meriwether."

Julie led the group into the tower. Once inside, the door closed and dim lights came on inside the small room. The group giggled nervously as the floor lurched slightly and the elevator began to move upward. Almost as quickly as it began, the elevator stopped and the door opened once again. They could now see a small bridge between the community hall and the roof of the adjacent bank.

Following Chief Pierce once again, the group moved quietly across the bridge. Jay ran his hand along the brass railing that ran around the edge of the buildings and the bridge. It occurred to him how much it looked like the inside of the Fin. Meanwhile, the Chief opened a wrought iron gate and everyone spilled out onto the open roof of the bank. The Chief shepherded them onto a large platform containing five chairs near the edge of the roof.

Julie was the first to step onboard. She moved cautiously to the center, her hands frantically searching for a spot furthest from the edge. As the others approached, she locked her hands onto Jay's arm and dragged him into the seat next to hers.

After a few minutes Trevor's gaze drifted over the buildings, to the trees and people - over the entire park. Soon, he realized he could also see the entire town, the lake and to the edge of the dark hills that surrounded the valley. At the far edge of the park, he noticed the familiar statue keeping its vigil, arm pointed across the lake. He finally recognized the statue as Maximillan Gladwell. It was the mysterious professor's bronze likeness that invited visitors to look over the canyon, toward his home across Silver Lake.

"Look," Sam pointed, as Trevor focused his attention back down to the streets below. "All the lights just went off." Jay whistled softly. "Not just here," his voice filled with awe, "but everywhere." He was right. The entire valley was now darker than it had been in hundreds of years. No streetlights, cars or televisions. The decorative torches had been mysteriously extinguished. Not even the glow of a single cell phone illuminated the night. Aside from the occasional murmur and cough from the crowd below, it was as if every city had disappeared from the planet.

Julie edged closer to the railing and peered briefly into the inky blackness. She quickly sat back and shut her eyes as if seeing the dark space would cause her to fall over. However, Jay had not joined the others near the edge of the disc. He remained in his chair, simply staring up into the night sky. He drew everyone back to the center of the disc with another exclamation.

"The stars... they're so awesome. Just like the island!"

The night sky was full of stars. More than stars, it was filled with the entire Milky Way galaxy, and some galaxies beyond. Julie opened her eyes just a peek, and then fully, as she witnessed the spectacle above. Several shooting stars went by before Chief Pierce interrupted the show.

"As William Shakespeare once wrote, 'we are only players on a stage." She glanced upward. "But, oh what a marvelous stage it is."

She paused before leaning slightly forward and pressing a small red button placed deep into the scrollwork of the brass railing. From somewhere above, a soft spotlight focused on the platform. The crowd below looked up with excited faces. A hush descended like the quiet center of a storm.

"These students have proven themselves truly worthy of Cosmic Enterprises, as well as our little community. And, now…"

There was another pause as Chief Pierce surveyed the faces gathered below her. Trevor almost detected a slight waver in her voice - a rare show of pride and emotion from a proven hero - as she requested a favor from the one person not in attendance. She pressed the same button, which now blinked green.

"…and now, if you would be so kind, may we have some fireworks Professor?"

Infinite Possibilities

Almost immediately, the night exploded with light and color. Everyone's eyes were immediately drawn from the platform to the sky above. Any thoughts of Stasys agents were forgotten - for the moment.

Trevor leaned back as fireworks filled his vision. He laughed quietly. A cosmic explorer. A few months ago he was sure his parents had sentenced him to hillbilly hell. A few hours ago, he felt certain his life was over. Now his world was... very different. He glanced at his friends.

Jay was pointing out various constellations to Julie, who had released her death grip on his arm, and applauded at every new explosion. Sam roared a primal shout and Trevor covered his ears. He watched in awe as a cluster of fiery blue sapphires shimmered and fell from the sky. They broke harmlessly on the roof around them, leaving behind only a brilliant sparkle, like ice shattering on a frozen lake.

His thoughts drifted down from the show above. The strange village seemed to hold more secrets than a treasure chest. He had only visited part of the professor's mansion. But what he had seen – the Fin, the rovers, the chamber below it... He wanted to grab his friends by the hand and race back around the lake this very night. The professor had promised them a proper tour of the mansion. Maybe not tomorrow, but hopefully soon, and he wished it with all his heart.

He looked back up and smiled as a swirling white ball exploded high above his head and expanded into uncountable points of light. He followed the miniature universe as it bloomed over his head, growing beyond their town, past the lake, and almost to the shore where the mansion stood silently against the Wilding Forest. He was surprised to see a light on in one room of the house.

"Nice to meet you, professor," he murmured, as if the old man could hear him. Perhaps he could.

Catching only the sound of his voice and not his words, Sam looked quizzically at Trevor, and then laughed softly as she leaned her head gently against his shoulder. Then they sat quietly in the dark and watched as the universe wheeled about them.

The Next Day

President Andrews walked down the narrow hallway, followed by a phalanx of staff members, assistants and cabinet members. In front of him, a team of highly trained CIA agents made sure no one interfered with his progress.

The crowd filed through a doorway and into and large meeting room. Monitors lined three of the walls and a large desk sat in the middle of the room, surrounded by leather chairs. All the attendees waited for the President to sit before lowering themselves into a chair. One-by-one, the monitors flickered to life as images of generals, admirals, and directors of multiple scientific agencies filled each corner of every screen. The room fell into an empty silence while everyone waited for President Andrews to look up from the materials neatly set on the table.

"Gentlemen. Ladies. Would someone please tell me what was urgent enough to bring the First Lady and me in from a round of golf with Chairman Ming?"

Several people shifted in their seats and all eyes turned to look at General Martin, one of several men in uniform looking down from the monitors.

"Mr. President. I apologize for the timing of this meeting. But unfortunately, we felt this news could not wait any longer. Sanders, please display the images now."

A uniformed clerk entered a few commands on the keyboard buried beneath the table as a large screen descended in front of the wall opposite the President. A series of fuzzy images appeared in rapid order, and then repeated, a total of sixteen photos in all.

The effect was almost like an old-fashioned movie created by flipping images rapidly to show movement.

"This is a series of images captured by our deep space research satellite," the general began. The usual of galaxies and stars shined brightly on a field of black.

"General. I know what outer space looks like, but I have no idea what on Earth you are trying to show me."

President Andrews looked somewhat disturbed by the prospect of abruptly canceling a diplomatic outing to watch a poorly produced slide show.

"My apologies, sir. Let me clarify the situation. Sanders, please magnify the last image by a factor of one hundred."

Sanders entered several commands on a hidden panel. Seconds later, more than 250 miles above Earth, a telescopic satellite adjust its focus on a point deep in space.

The President now realized he was watching real-time images and not last year's photos. The images jumped slightly and the center or dark space grew to fill most of the screen. The show repeated once, twice, and then a third time. The darkness grew and then returned to its original size with every loop. The President rose slowly from his chair and walked closer to the screen.

"From what our scientists tell us Mr. President, this dark spot in space is solid. There are no stars or galaxies visible behind it. It's massive, and—" the general paused to take a drink of water—"it's growing."

"How long do we have?"

"Well sir, by our calculations, the object… or thing… in this image will reach our solar system within four to five years."

Several people in the President's administration gasped, but no one in the room dared to speak. The President of the United States reached out one finger and touched the screen as if he could feel the darkness. Without comment, he turned and left the room as a heated conversation broke out among the attendees.

He pulled a slender black rectangle from his pocket and flipped through the various faces on the screen. He stopped at the one labeled "Susan Pierce" and pushed the transmit key. The meeting could go on without him. He would be back. Right now, President Andrews had a very important call to make.

The End

www.ingramcontent.com/pod-product-compliance
Lightning Source LLC
Chambersburg PA
CBHW031111030726
47496CB00002BA/492